AND BY THE WAY

A BUTTERFLY NOVEL

Denise Deegan is the best-selling author of four novels and one book of non-fiction. She has been published in Ireland, the UK and Commonwealth, Germany, Holland and Korea. She is a regular contributor to the Irish media.

Denise lives in Dublin with her husband and two teenage children.

AND BY THE WAY . . .

DENISE DEEGAN

HACHETTE
BOOKS
IRELAND

First published in Ireland in 2011 by Hachette Books Ireland
An Hachette UK company

A CIP catalogue record for this title is available from the British Library

ISBN 978 1 4447 2119 5

Typeset in Sabon MT by Hachette Books Ireland

Printed and bound by CPI Mackays, Chatham ME5 8TD

Hachette Books Ireland policy is to use papers that are natural, renewable
and recyclable products and made from wood grown in sustainable forests.
The logging and manufacturing processes are expected to conform to the
environmental regulations of the country of origin.

Hachette Books Ireland
8 Castlecourt Centre
Castleknock
Dublin 15

Hachette UK Ltd
338 Euston Road
London NW1 3BH

www.hachette.ie

In memory of Rosemary
(and inflatable shamrocks)

1
THE ROCKSTAR

OK. So it's 3.40 p.m. All anyone's thinking of is going home. In ten minutes. Make that nine. At the top of the class, Ms Kelly (think sparrow) is rocking onto her tiptoes and off them again, waiting for an answer to the question she's just asked.

'What is a friend?'

We're sixteen years old. I think, by now, we know what a friend is. No one's going to answer a question that lame. I scan the class. Tired and bored sums up everyone. Including me. But then, a voice. It's Sarah, a friend of mine, who's so not into this touchy-feely stuff.

'A friend,' she says, looking meaningfully at Rachel beside her, 'is someone who returns texts.'

Uh-oh.

'Yes, Sarah. Very good,' says Tiptoes, cheerfully missing the point. 'Someone who returns text messages.' She looks around. 'Anyone else?'

Mark Delaney's hand goes up. The class stirs. Delaney fakes Attention Deficit Disorder so he doesn't have to work.

That he's actually paying attention is, like, a total novelty.

'A friend,' he says, 'doesn't lose it when you point out that her fake tan's patchy.' This is directed at Orla Tempany.

Who's already snapping back, 'A friend wouldn't say something like that in front of a whole class.'

And suddenly it no longer matters that we're minutes from freedom.

'A friend pays back what they borrow,' says Peter Sweetnam to Simon Kelleher.

'A friend doesn't leave you alone on the dance floor.' (Amy Gilmore.)

'All right. All right,' says Tiptoes, raising both palms towards us. 'Some very good examples of respecting each other and, yes, respect is a big part of friendship.' She places her hands gently together, like a nun. 'But I'm looking for something else, another essential element of friendship.'

She is Buzz Lightyear, who thought he was a superhero, but was just a toy. She thinks she gets us. She so doesn't. If she hadn't butted in, we might have got a decent debate going for a change. I check the clock. Four minutes. If everyone stays quiet, maybe she'll just let us go.

'A friend is someone who listens.' David McFadden says it simply, in his usual laid-back way. I look at him like he's a total loser, because if there's one person who bugs me, it's David McFadden. He just smiles and starts to close his books. Which is when I get it: the only reason he answered the question was to get the lesson over with.

It's worked.

'All right, people.' (I wish she wouldn't call us that.) 'Don't forget. The sailing course starts tomorrow. So, no showing up here at nine. It's down at the Motor Yacht Club.'

The class starts to empty. Rachel and Sarah make their way to my desk, as usual. They glide, rather than walk, movements fluid, posture perfect. Catwalk material. Rachel's a cross between Pocahontas (the hair) and Anne Hathaway (the face). Sarah's more Paris Hilton (but good-looking).

'I didn't actually get your text,' Rachel's saying. 'I told you that.'

'It sent OK.'

'Well, I didn't get it.'

'Let's get out of here,' I say, and start to walk.

They follow, still arguing.

'I was just making a point.' (Sarah.)

'Well, you didn't need to. I return most of your texts.'

'Most. Not all.'

'Some of them, Sarah, don't need an answer,' Rachel says.

A good 70 per cent, as far as I'm concerned. I'm surprised Sarah doesn't have repetitive strain injury. In fairness to Rachel, it's me who should be under attack here. I only reply to direct questions from Sarah – like, maybe, 30 per cent of her texts. Rachel's much more polite. She puts in the work. Though she's been slacking off lately. Which is probably why Sarah's being so sensitive. She thinks she'll run out of people to text.

'Anyway,' I say, adjusting the bag on my back, 'at least we're out of there.' I can't believe how much we looked forward to Transition Year. It sounded great in theory – a whole year to prepare us for life after school, in other words a complete doss. Instead of actual schoolwork, most of our time is taken up with projects, community service, adventure weekends, trips abroad, work experience. Or, at least, it's supposed to be. Two weeks in and all we've experienced is an overdose of touchy-feely.

We head out the school gates and down the hill. It's still not cold enough for coats, but I wrap mine tightly around me. For the last six months, I haven't been able to get warm – no matter what's been happening with the weather.

'Want to come back to my place?' Rachel asks.

'Can't,' I say. 'The Rockstar's back.'

'Oh, yeah?' Sarah perks up.

'How did the recording go?' Rachel gets on with her parents. If her dad was away recording an album, she'd be right up to speed on how it went.

'Fine,' I say to avoid questioning but, fact is, I don't know. On the rare occasions he calls, I answer his questions. That's it. I don't know why I'm looking forward to seeing him. I know I'll be disappointed. 'Let's go to the Jitter Mug,' I say, deciding that, actually, I'm not ready to go home just yet.

'Great,' says Sarah, who never wants to go home.

The Jitter Mug is this great coffee shop in Blackrock. It's big and airy with high ceilings and comfortable armchairs that you can lose yourself in. When school is out, we own the place. Ninety per cent of the customers are wearing our uniform. We get our usual order: three tropical smoothies. We find our usual spot, in the centre of the action, so that Sarah can keep up with the gossip.

'Isn't David McFadden seriously caliente?' she says, now, widening her eyes on 'seriously'.

'Caliente' is our code for 'hot'. We've been using it since the day we first met, the day we became friends. This was Day One at Strandbrook College. We'd randomly

}|{

sat together. Our first class was Spanish. In walked this amazing-looking teacher. Sarah started scribbling. Then she passed a note: 'Señor Martin is SERIOUSLY caliente.'

Señor Martin might have been caliente, he wasn't, however, amused. When he walked towards Rachel with his hand out for the note, Sarah snatched it from her and ate it. We were so shocked we laughed. And ended up in detention. A word of advice to teachers: if you don't want three people to become friends, don't send them to detention together on their first day.

Sarah, lifting the lid on her smoothie to check it out, continues on the subject of David McFadden: 'He surfs, you know.'

'Not a total shocker,' Rachel says, 'given that he's from California.'

'I could look at him all day,' Sarah says dreamily. 'He's like one of those sculptures you get in Rome. God, I'm so glad he'd to stay back a year.'

'I'm sure he wasn't,' I say. His mum died and he failed his Junior Cert exams.

'Mark's pretty caliente too,' Sarah says. 'I think that when two caliente guys hang out together it makes them extra caliente.'

Mark Delaney joined our class the same time as David McFadden, when his mum, a diplomat, returned from a posting in South Africa. And though they're totally different, he and David hit it off.

'David's cute,' Rachel says. 'But Mark. That whole ADD thing. Imagine tricking your parents like that. They probably spent money having him diagnosed. And the way he boasts about it, about looking up all the symptoms on the

Internet so he'd get it right. That's just sneaky.' She shakes
her head like he's not worth talking about.

'So,' Sarah says, leaning forward, 'want to know why I
brought up David McFadden?' Sarah is a walking gossip
column.

We wait. Something's coming.

'I'm pretty sure he fancies you, Alex.' She sits back, having delivered her news.

'I'm pretty sure I don't care.' I don't mean to snap but . . .
The thing is, I did like David McFadden when he first joined
our class. It wasn't just that he was caliente. He was different. Not in that he was American. American is not exotic in
our school. He was – I don't know. Let's just say, if I hadn't
known about his mother dying, I'd have guessed he'd been
through something. He's older than us by a year but seemed
much older, as if he knew about life and wasn't bothered by
the small stuff. And, still, he hung out with a total messer.
Which made him human. Likeable. But then, six months
ago, everything changed. I lost my mum to cancer. Everyone
fussed over me. Made their faces sad when they saw me. I
hated that, the spotlight that turns on you when you lose a
parent. I didn't want to be there. I didn't want anything. Just
Mum back. Sometimes, I'd look at McFadden and think,
You know. Because only someone who has lost someone
they loved can know the hollowness, the feeling that your
guts have been ripped out and there's nothing left inside. I'd
look at him and wonder if he ever wrapped his arms around
himself and folded over to try to squeeze the nothingness
away. I'd look at him. And he'd look away. David McFadden
avoided me. Completely. That's not the kind of thing you
forget. Then, two weeks ago, he came back to school after

}I{

the summer, smiling. Laughing and joking with Mark, as if life's one big joke. As if losing a mum is nothing. So, no, I don't care about David McFadden. I don't think there is anyone I care less about. Apart from The Rockstar.

We finish our smoothies. Or, at least, the others finish theirs. I haven't tasted anything in six months. So the motivation of all that sucking is kind of gone. Part of me wonders when I'm going to be normal again. Part of me doesn't want to be. Because that would mean moving on. From Mum. The person I was closest to in the world.

I like that I've furthest to go on the DART, Dublin's light rail system that runs along the coast. It means I'm alone when I come out of the station at Dalkey. This is a good thing. Because I'm met – by a driver. If The Rockstar had his way, I'd be collected directly from school, something he wanted after Mum died. I had to use all my powers of persuasion then. And I'll use them again as soon as I hit seventeen, the legal age for driving. I have my arguments ready: (1) a car equals independence, a key ingredient of maturity; (2) if I drive, I can't drink; (3) me driving will be a lot safer than taking lifts from friends, especially boys, who, as everyone knows, are lunatics on the road.

I won't need to convince him that we'll all have cars then. At Strandbrook, we are Kids Of. Kids of diplomats, media stars, musicians, artists, actors, oh, and wealthy people who aspire to all of that. I could give out about our school but at least no one stands out because of their parents. We know who they all are but it's like, so what?

I climb up into the four-wheel drive with the blackened-out windows.

}I{

'Hey,' I say to Mike our driver, who also doubles as The Rockstar's head of security. Mike's not the total worst. Doesn't drag me into conversations the way, say, a taxi driver might. He's friendly when I get in. And out. He just drives.

I take out my iPhone, watch a downloaded episode of *Friends*, and pretend that my life is normal.

Outside the gates of our house, a group of fans has gathered. Mike gives them a careful once-over. They look harmless to me. Italian, I'm guessing by their cool clothes and the way they stand around, like waiting's the best part of the whole experience. If I didn't know my father was home, I'd know now. His fans are like a tracking device. When he's away, so are they. The minute he's back, we have company.

We drive past, hidden by the darkened windows. The gates close immediately behind us.

Mike drops me at the door, then goes to park. I let myself in. There's no sign of Homer, my Golden Retriever (who's too pale to be golden and who doesn't retrieve). Instead, my father's stylist, Marsha, struts across the hall, in tight black leather trousers, disappearing into his office, talking loudly in that brassy New York accent of hers. Her heels have left pockmarks in the wooden floor that my mother chose because it was environmentally friendly. I hear The Rockstar say something from the office. His manager, Ed, laughs. From the kitchen, people talk over music. The Rockstar's back. And he is surrounded – reminding me how much lonelier I feel when he's home. Not for me a reunion in front of a live audience, so I retreat to my room.

Homer's lying on my bed, hiding too. His ears pop up, then he's bounding towards me. I drop my bag and crouch.

He nearly knocks me over. I hug him, putting my head next to his. He turns quickly and licks my face.

'So you met The Stylist.'

He whines. Which makes me laugh.

I lie on the bed, take out my phone and text Sarah. I make sure to sign off with the butterfly emote }|{ the three of us have been using since First Year. It's, like, a symbol of our friendship. Sometimes I forget it and Sarah gets genuinely upset. I hit 'Send'. I know that texting Sarah will set off an avalanche of messages about absolutely nothing. Sometimes there's a right time for nothing, like when your home has become a circus and the ringmaster's your father. It won't click with Sarah that I'm texting instead of enjoying an emotional reunion. Which is why I'm not messaging Rachel, who's so on the ball it's scary.

With Rachel, I have to keep my distance. When Mum died, I fell into a million pieces and into Rachel's arms. She listened. She held me. She was there. Unlike The Rockstar, who'd taken off as soon as Mum got sick, always finding something to do rather than be there for her, or me. I hated him for that. Still do. But, Rachel. Rachel was there. Then one day, when she was holding me, my heart started to pound, as I realised I couldn't go through losing someone I loved again. I pulled back from Rachel, then. And I've been pulling ever since.

Sarah's been easier to stay back from. Poor Sarah. When Mum died, she didn't know what to say. When she did speak, she usually put her foot in it. She couldn't know, but this was usually a relief. Careful's the worst thing you can be around someone who's dying inside. Say something stupid, something totally inappropriate and you might actually make them laugh. Inside. For 0.5 of a second.

So, no. I don't do close. With anyone. At any time. Or anywhere.

I had this therapist once who said I had a 'fear of attachment'. But I'm not afraid of attachment. I just don't want it. The therapist – God. I had to go to her after Mum died. The Rockstar's idea. Her name was Betsy. Betsy! Seriously. First time I went, she introduced herself as a psychoanalyst. If I had said anything (at all), it would have been (a) I'm not psycho and (b) I don't need analysis. But I knew she'd analyse that too. And anyway I'd decided not to cooperate. The only reason I was going was because The Rockstar wanted me to. On our way there, I realized why – so he wouldn't have to talk to me himself.

I sat on a couch. She sat opposite. In the front room of her house. It was yellow. There were hankies on the table between us. Like she expected me to cry. So I laughed. She looked at me for a long time. So I looked at the floor. Under the table were crumbs. Which I counted. I went to The Therapist five times (enough for The Rockstar to think I'd tried), and always the crumbs. I'd sit and count them. Every time. I'd imagine who'd left them. A son aged fifteen, who liked biscuits. Chocolate chip cookies. He wasn't the only one I imagined. Through the double doors to the right I dreamed up a dining room, filled with guests – people like Betsy, middle-aged and too intelligent. They'd be talking about art and vague writers from Eastern Europe. I wondered if she ever discussed people like me – her patients, clients, or whatever she called us. I decided she wouldn't have much to say about me, seeing as I never said anything about me. I was angry for her other patients, though, the ones who did cooperate. I wanted to tell her it was unprofessional to use the same room for business and life. I wanted to tell her to tidy her front garden, polish her door knocker and get a decent haircut. But I never said any of those things. I never said anything. It was only when I got out of going that I realised it had actually helped. For the whole hour I was there, I was so busy distracting myself from Betsy that I forgot to be sad about my mum.

Sarah isn't texting back. Must be out of credit. Or in the shower. I take out my laptop and send her an MSN. From downstairs, more laughter. I put my iPhone on speaker. Loud. I go into Games on my laptop. Solitaire seems a bit sad. Chess is a battle. And I feel like a fight. I put the computer aside and from under the bed take out my own, totally worn-out chess set. When I was a kid and we still went on tour with him, The Rockstar used to play me, to kill time. He'd let me have white so I could go first, but apart from that he never went easy on me. His favourite pieces were the knights because they were hard to see coming. I used to look up to him then. He could make people sing, dance, scream, clap, cry, light things and hold them to the sky. But afterwards, he'd always switch The Rockstar off and become Dad again, the person with the warm eyes and the hugs, the person who loved me. When we stopped touring with him, the chess stopped too. And when Mum died, he stopped being my dad. He just gave up. He's still The Rockstar. Means nothing to me, though.

I set up the pieces. I let him have white and lift one of his knights out onto the battlefield. Then I twist the board round and take my turn, play my game. Back and forth I go, plotting, counter-plotting. Killing. I've just taken his castle when there's a knock on the door. I throw the quilt over the board and grab my phone. I lie back on the bed and pretend to be texting. The door opens. I count to three before looking up. And, though I use my best bored expression, I'm hoping that things will be back to normal. That it will be my dad again. Not The Rockstar.

But his eyes are blank, empty of the dad I knew. Suddenly everything about him is so freaking annoying. I mean, does he have to look like a hobo? His hair is long and greasy, like it hasn't been washed in months. His clothes are dark and sloppy. Massive shades sit on top of his head like a trademark. His shoes. Oh, God – he's wearing wedges!

'Hey,' he says, like he's cool or something.

My, 'Hey' is flat. And I don't get up. Neither does Homer. My pal.

'Why didn't you tell me you were home?' he asks, like he cares.

'You were busy.' As usual.

'It was just Marsha and Ed.'

It's always someone, I think, but say, 'How *is* The Stylist?'

'Marsha's great.'

'Apart from her taste.' I give him a slow once-over. Doesn't he see it?

He laughs like I've cracked a joke.

'And by the way . . . No man should dye his hair.'

He stops laughing. A hand goes, automatically, to his head.

'You look retarded.'

'Actually retarded?' He pretends to look impressed.

'And the state of your shoes! You don't, like, have polio or something?'

His smile is forced. 'No one else is complaining.'

}|{

'Not to your face.'

He closes his eyes and pinches the bridge of his nose. When he looks at me again, it's to say, 'I've work to do.'

'Course you do.' And as I watch his back disappear, I feel like calling after him that I'm not stupid: I know when a person comes to say 'hi' because they should, not because they want to.

2
LEE HO

My house is like the UN. The chief gardener is, actually, Irish, but apart from that, it's representatives from around the world. The cook's French. The cleaner, Moldavian. The handyman, Polish. The Rockstar's personal trainer is Ukrainian. Mike's a Cockney. We didn't always have these people. We weren't always totally useless. The Rockstar hired most of them after Mum died. What he doesn't see is that, even if he hired an army, he still couldn't replace her. Because none of them would be her.

If anything summed up my life, right now, it would be breakfast. Imagine a chef pouring your cornflakes. I look at Barbara – the chef – and know she'd have liked me to have kippers, smoked salmon, a fry, even a croissant, just to keep her stimulated. But I lost my appetite six months ago. The Rockstar's not going to fire her for pouring cereal. My mum had this thing about breakfast being the most important meal. She'd make me eat slow-release carbohydrate (brown bread) and protein (egg or bacon). Every day. If I had her back, I wouldn't argue. And I'd taste every bit.

}|{

Oh, great. The Stylist (think Cher, pre-plastic surgery) has just walked into the kitchen. Which means she must be crashing here, like half the world. There's a pocket missing on her skintight denims. It's deliberate. Everything about her is. If I'd been consulted when he was hiring a stylist, I'd have told him to get a guy: Asian, totally camp and so passionate about clothes he'd die if he had to work at anything else. Not this ordinary person who's made a career out of knowing a few celebs. During The Cowboy Phase, I couldn't look at The Rockstar. Now she has him wearing shoes that look like they're from a medical supplier. The Stylist has been on the payroll, like, forever – or at least that's how it feels. Once, he offered me her services 'for a makeover or something'. It was a few days after I stopped going to The Therapist. It was no coincidence.

'No thanks,' I said to him. 'I like to look good.'

'What's your problem with Marsha?'

'Have you got an hour?' I asked, then added, 'She wears bullets in her belt, for God's sake.'

'They're not real.'

I'd worked that one out when wondering how she got through airport security.

'Hey!' she says now, like she's woken to blue skies.

The only blue in Ireland is how you feel about the weather. And the only reason I say 'Hey' back is that manners have been hammered into me and I can't help it. She sits up at the island beside me and asks Barbara for an egg (soft-boiled), and toast, (brown). I'm so close to telling her that Barbara's not her slave. And I don't even like Barbara – who's snooty. I get up. Bring my bowl to the sink.

}|{

'So. Is that what people wear to school in Ireland?' The Stylist looks like she's cracked a joke.

I look down at the wetsuit I've bought for the sailing course. I could have borrowed one from the sailing school but the thought of dragging on some damp, manky suit worn by a million other people nearly made me barf. And so, the wetsuit.

'Pretty much, yeah,' I say, and head for the door. Why does he even need a stylist? I could tell him what to wear *and* get it right.

'Have a good day,' she calls after me.

Doesn't she have a home to go to? Oh, yeah. It's in New York.

I get to the yacht club late and in no mood for bobbing up and down on the sea like a bottle. A small group of my class are hanging around outside, wearing sailing gear that's so grungy it has to be their own. In my brand-new gear I look like a retard. Not that I care.

'Where's everyone?' I ask David McFadden, who looks like he was born on a boat. His wetsuit's faded and worn at the knees. He's wearing surfing shorts over it. And on his hands some sort of fingerless gloves.

'Inside. Changing,' he says.

I'm about to go in to Sarah and Rachel when our PE teacher (nicknamed 'Very Peculiar', because it's his favourite expression) stops me.

'Here, there's enough nonsense going on in there. You're dressed. Give me your bag. I'll bring it in.'

Reluctantly, I hand it over. He disappears with it. I glance at the sea. It's grey and choppy. I think of my bed and wonder why I didn't stay in it. I fold my arms. Cold already.

'By the way, you're with me,' McFadden says.

I turn to him. 'Sorry?'

'We've all been paired off.'

'You're not serious. Can't we pick ourselves?' At least with Rachel or Sarah we wouldn't have to take the thing seriously.

'And I'm dying to sail with you too,' he says, but he's smiling, like he couldn't care less either way. He's different out of uniform, his spiky blonde hair ruffled by the wind like he's already been out at sea. He looks even more laid-back than usual – if that's possible.

The rest of the class start to spill from the club, some still struggling into life jackets: all looking like amateurs. I have a rethink. A little expertise might come in handy after all. With McFadden, I could sit back. Relax. Let him do the work.

He's climbing into some sort of nappy-type thingy and tying it round his waist. It has a hook on the front.

'What is that?'

'A harness.' He hands me one. 'Here. You'd better put one on. You'll need it.'

We're standing, knee deep in water, on a slipway, holding our boat, which, by the way, we've had to push into the sea ourselves on a rusty old trailer with wonky wheels. I look down through the freezing salt water, at my new runners. They didn't tell us we'd have to get our feet wet. I glance up and catch McFadden smirking.

'What?' I shout over the noise of flapping sails.

He shakes his head. Nothing, apparently.

'OK. I'll just get in,' I say.

'I thought you wanted me to helm.'

'What?'

'Steer.'

'Yeah, I do.'

'Then, you push off.'

What happened to women and children first? 'No way.'

He smiles, as though he's holding all the cards. 'Unless you want to helm.'

'No!'

'Right then, push off so I can steer.'

'How am I supposed to get in?'

'Jump.'

'When the boat's moving?'

'Yep.'

'You're joking, right?'

He's laughing. 'Wrong.'

I am such an eejit. Instead of shoving off and staying behind on land – which didn't occur to me until I was leaping into the freaking boat – I've rocked it so much, it's tilting right over. And I'm yelping.

'It's all right. It won't capsize.' He pulls the thing that directs the boat towards him. 'Yet.'

'Hilarious,' I say, turning away from him and looking ahead.

He gives me a minute, then says, 'Move up and pull in the jib sheet.'

I ignore him. Don't know what he's talking about anyway. He leans forward and grabs a rope with a knot at the end of it. He hands it to me.

'Pull it. Unless you want to listen to that sail flapping around all the time.'

It was beginning to bother me. Without acknowledging Master Mariner, I take it from him and pull.

'You can cleat it if you want.'

'English, please.' Such a show-off.

He leans forward again, takes the rope off me and whacks it through these two metal thingies. 'So you don't have to hold it all the time,' he explains. And, for a minute, he doesn't sound so bossy.

'Right,' I say, instead of thanks.

We sail out and I'm beginning to think, *this is easy*, when he says, 'Ready about.'

'What?'

'Weren't you listening at all back there?'

'No.' I thought I was going to be with a sailor.

'OK. When I say "lee ho" . . .'

"Lee ho", for God's sake.

'When I say "lee ho", let the rope go, duck under the boom . . .' he taps the wooden beam under the sail, 'and pull in the rope on the other side.'

'And this is supposed to be fun?' I mutter into the hideous grubby orange life jacket I had to borrow. Why I never thought to buy one . . .

He laughs again and I'm so close to dunking him.

We 'go about'. I survive. We do it again. And I do more than survive, because I'm so freaking annoyed by his overall smugness I'm not giving him the opportunity to boss me around. I do my end of things before he can tell me to. Soon we're way ahead of the other boats. In fact, I'm beginning to think we're going out a bit far. The tub has started to lean over towards the water on the opposite side from us.

'Hike out,' he says.

'Excuse me?'

'Clip on that yoke.' He touches the metal hook on my harness. It feels a bit intimate, so I glare at him but he's too busy bossing me around to notice. 'Stand up on the side of the boat and lean out.'

'You must be joking.'

We tilt over further.

'Do I look like I'm joking?'

'Oh my God. Can't you keep it flat?'

'You have to hike out.'

'Forget it.' I look back at all the others. 'No one else is doing it.'

The boat goes right up on its side now. 'Want to capsize?' he asks, looking like he's enjoying this.

'You're doing this.'

'We're going over,' he warns, and water starts to spill into the boat.

'Jesus!' I clip the hook onto a metal wire, climb backwards until my feet are against the edge of the boat. I squat there, afraid to go further. It's not my most poised moment. From behind, it probably looks like I'm taking a dunk over the side. Never again, I think. But the boat does flatten a lot. Which is kind of surprising, given that I'm a total squirt.

'It'd be easier if you straightened out,' he shouts.

'I'll take your word for it.'

'It's actually fun. Go on. Hike right out.' The boat heels again. Not wanting to look like a wuss, but especially not wanting to capsize, I close my eyes and straighten out. I don't fall into the sea. And I don't pull the boat with me. Actually, it's working. The boat's starting to skim over the water. It feels like we're flying. It feels amazing. Not that I'd tell him that.

'You can let go of the wire. You're hooked on.'

Why not, I think, and let go.

'Cool, isn't it?' he asks, cheerily.

I ignore him but close my eyes and pretend I'm Kate Winslet at the front of the *Titanic*. We're like this for a few minutes when a voice calls McFadden's name through a loudspeaker. I look behind us. It's the rescue boat.

'Dave! Where the hell are you off to?'

He waves casually. 'Just going about,' he shouts.

I look at the guy in the inflatable, then at McFadden. 'Do you know him?'

'Eh, yeah. You'd better get in. We're going about.'

This is unbelievable. Not only do we have to heave the boat back up the slip and return it to its spot on dry land, we have to take it apart. There's a freaking system to everything. McFadden is so anal. Like it matters if we don't take the knots out of the ropes. He has just given me one to undo when he asks, matter-of-factly: 'Why are you so stuck up?'

I laugh in shock. 'Excuse me?'

'So Ice Queen.'

I stare at him and drop the rope. He can so undo it himself. I'm about to leave when he takes my face in his hands and kisses me. I pull back immediately.

'What the hell?' I look quickly around us. We're hidden behind the huge flapping sail.

He just smiles and kisses me again. And now – someone, please tell me why – I'm kissing him back. I pull away, like I've kissed a toad. 'What are you doing?'

'Same thing you're doing,' he says, his smile lazy now.

}|{

And suddenly it's not a boy in my class any more, but this windswept, tanned and totally hot guy who wears beads around his neck and plaited leather on his wrist. My face is inches from his and getting closer when I stop. What am I doing? I look at him, totally cold.

'That was a one-off thing.'

I turn quickly and walk. My legs have never felt so wobbly.

3
Drowning in Clothes

My clearest memory of my mum . . . I'm thirteen and stand-ing in front of the mirror in my room. Close to suicidal. I'm starting secondary school in three days and the uniform that's arrived by post is enormous, despite us doing a fitting at the start of the summer. I look in the mirror and see a nerd, drowning in clothes. Behind me is my mother. Who's started to laugh. She can't seem to stop. Then I'm laughing too, though really I want to cry. I'm about to turn up for my first day at secondary school with 'Bullying Material' writ-ten all over me.

Then, Mum stops laughing. 'Right. Let's go.'
'Where?'
'To town. To change it. Clearly, they've made a mistake.'
That simple.

Sometimes I don't just miss my mum, I miss having a mum, someone to fall back on, to take the pressure off, to explain. Like why I can be a total bitch sometimes. And why I kissed a guy I don't even like. After he'd insulted me. Oh and why I can't stop thinking of him – or the kiss. At two in the morning, I make a decision. I'm being a tard. He was just amusing himself. It meant nothing. He's getting no more room inside my head. And from now on I'm going to avoid him. Completely.

Hard to avoid someone when they don't show up. Next day, he's not there. I'm paired with Sarah. Who knows (and cares) as much about boats as I do. We toss a coin to see who'll drive the thing. Sarah loses. We end up going round in circles – anticlockwise. Finally, we drift into the pier wall, where we take advantage of our stranded situation to have a rest.

'So,' she says. 'What were you doing with McFadden yesterday?'

I stomach jolts. 'What?'

'Hanging out the side of the boat like that.'

I breathe again. 'Oh, I was just out on the harness.'

'The what?'

I look at her. 'You know, the harness. For balancing the boat. Didn't you get one?'

'No. None of us did.'

I stare at her.

'We're not that advanced,' she says matter-of-factly.

Oh my God. I'll kill him. He made the whole thing up about having a harness. He was having me on, the whole time.

The rescue boat tows us away from the pier. I'm hoping they'll give up on us as hopeless cases and bring us back to shore. But no, they abandon us at sea, again. Sarah refuses to helm. That's when I get my turn to prove that sailing really is just bobbing up and down on the water like a bottle. Only more chaotic.

* * *

}I{

Next day, McFadden's back. I live up to the Ice Queen rep he gave me and blank him completely. He smiles like he finds me amusing. He's paired with Rachel.

'Poor you,' I say to her, looking at him.

He laughs and goes off to get their boat ready.

'Did I miss something?' she asks.

'You so didn't,' I say and walk off, over to Sarah, who is supposed to be rigging up our boat. She's standing looking at it like it's a spaceship. And, hey, I don't blame her.

We're last out on the water, which totally suits. After about twenty minutes, we hit the pier again, only this time I'm steering.

'See,' Sarah says. 'It is magnetic.'

I laugh. We settle down to wait for the rescue boat. But then I see McFadden heading our way. I have to get going. Look capable. In control. I jerk the steering thing (the tiller? the rudder? who cares?) back and forward, trying to get moving. The wind catches the sail and the boom cracks into my head.

'Jesus!'

'Want a hand?' he calls. Smiling. As usual.

I give him the finger. Which was not part of the plan. Ignore him, I remind myself.

He laughs, pulls in his sail and speeds by.

'Hey, Dave, where're you going?' Sarah calls after him. 'I thought you were helping?'

'Alex seems to have it under control,' he shouts.

She looks at me, astonished.

'I do.'

'Ready about?' I hear McFadden say to Rachel.

'Ready,' she says, like she's having a great time.

}|{

'He could have helped!' Sarah says.
'We don't need his help.'
'Why not?'
'Freaking show-off.'
'I'm sick of the rescue boat,' she moans.
'We don't need the rescue boat. Here, grab that oar.'

We spend the rest of the week sailing. Or trying to. Actually, in the case of Sarah and me, it's more like giving the impression that we're trying whenever an instructor looks our way. Most of my energy is going into avoiding McFadden. On land, if he goes one way, I go another. If he looks at me, I look away. I learn from The Rockstar and surround myself with people. On Friday, though, when we break for lunch, he manages to nab me. By coming up behind me.

'Nice wetsuit.' He says it like he's laughing at me.

'Pity about yours.'

Then he does actually laugh. He walks off, singing: 'Ice, Ice Baby.'

If I had a dead fish, I'd fire it at the back of his head. Instead, I go find Rachel and Sarah, who both rushed ahead to the loo. We hook up again. Get our packed lunches. And go outside to eat. We sit on the top level of the pier, huddled together against the cold, our legs dangling down. We're so tired, no one speaks. I look out at a sea I'd no problem with until this week.

'If you're not eating that, can we swap?' Sarah asks me.

I look down at the untouched lunch in my lap. Quiche and salad made by Barbara with her usual enthusiasm. I hand it over willingly. I get a chocolate-spread sandwich in return. It's so badly thrown together, I suspect Sarah made it herself.

}|{

I start to squish the slices of bread together between my thumb and finger, making circular dents all over it. It's kind of relaxing, feeling the bread cave in under pressure.

'What are you doing to my sandwich?' Sarah asks, disgusted.

'Not yours anymore.'

'Yeah, but I made that.'

'Jesus, Sarah, I wouldn't be proud.'

'Hey,' Rachel says suddenly, 'why don't you guys stay over tonight? We haven't done that in ages.'

'Great!' Sarah says immediately. I've never known her to turn down an invite.

There's no way I'm staying over. Late at night, conversations get deep. And deep is a place I don't go. Not anymore. I make a disappointed face.

'Eh, sorry, Rache. I can't actually stay over, but I can probably come for a few hours. That OK?'

'Sure,' Rachel says. But sounds disappointed.

I take out my phone and check with Mike to see if it's OK. I don't call The Rockstar. Don't want to disturb his busy schedule. Which is actually rubbish, given that Mike's going to have to disturb him anyway. I just want him to get the message.

I love Rachel's. It's how a home should be. No hired help, no stylists – just family. Rachel's father wears a shirt and tie. Not a clingy black designer T-shirt. No shades on the top of his head. No earring. No wedges. But what I love most about Rachel's is her mum. Yvonne is warm and funny, like my mum used to be. She cooks simple meals, like meat and two veg, like mine used to do. She doesn't spend hours on some French dish that's trying too hard to impress. Even though we're sixteen now she still reminds us to wash our hands. I love her.

Dinner is noisy, with Rachel's brothers, Harry and Jack, talking over each other and slagging Rachel at every opportunity. It's, like, how they get their kicks. Her comebacks are so quick, though, she keeps burning them. The only person not laughing is Sarah. Who is so busy eyeing up Jack she seems to have lost the power of hearing.

When everyone's finished, I stand up and start to collect the plates.

'What are you doing?' Rachel says, looking at me like I've lost it.

So I sit back down. When what I'd really like is to clear up, so I could hang around the kitchen with Yvonne. When Mum made me help after dinner, I'd think of all the things I could've been doing. I never once appreciated it was time with her. I never once thought that the conversations we had were important. Until we couldn't have them anymore.

'Thanks, Alex,' Yvonne says, 'but it's Jack's turn to clear up.'

'Listen,' Jack says, eyebrows up. 'If Alex wants to help, I wouldn't want to interfere . . .'

Yvonne gives him a look.

'OK. OK,' he says, hands up.

'Off you go, girls,' Yvonne says. 'Have fun.'

Fun, I think.

* * *

If you walked into Rachel's room you'd think she was a med student. Her shelves are full of medical encyclopaedias. Her walls are covered in posters of people's insides. She has one of those plastic model thingies with dummy organs you can take out and put back. She even has a skeleton. Pierre. He wears a cerise wig, a beret and a scarf. He has one hand behind his head, the other on his very obvious hip. Rachel doesn't just want to be a doctor, she wants to be a cardio-thoracic surgeon. Specifically. She also wants to be an actress. Which explains all the awards and trophies lining her shelves. She's been taking acting classes since she was four. If anyone could do both, it'd be Rache.

On her bright red Budda Bag, there's room for us all.

'So,' Sarah asks, 'Jack going out with anyone these days?'

Rachel shoves herself up on the beanbag. 'If you have even the slightest interest in Neanderthal Man, I suggest getting your head examined. And I'm serious about that.'

Suddenly, out of nowhere, when I should be laughing, it all comes down on me. Like a weight. Like a black cloud. Mum's gone. And she's not coming back. No matter how often this happens, it always floors me. One minute I'm OK, the next I'm drowning.

'I'm going to the loo,' I say, struggling to get up. Get out. Get air.

Their faces drop. They look at each other. Then back at me.

I don't know how they always know. But they do. I put a hand up. Smile. 'I'm fine.'

In the bathroom, I wash my face in cold water. I sit on the side of the bath. Take deep breaths. I try to think of something else, other than the fact that she won't be in the kitchen when I go home. I text Mike to tell him I'm ready to leave. Because the only place for me when I'm like this is bed.

Finally, I get up and go back. The bedroom door is still open. Inside, I hear them talking. Their voices are so low, I know it's about me. I stop. Listen. Not wanting to hear. But having to anyway.

'How long's this going to last?' Sarah asks.

'I don't know.'

'I wish she'd talk.'

A big sigh. Then, 'Me too.'

'I miss the old Alex,' Sarah says, forgetting to whisper. 'The one who used to beat me in pillow fights and smoothie races. Who threw parties and slagged the hell out of me.'

'I miss her too.'

'It's like we've lost her.'

'And it's just getting worse.'

'Can't we do anything?' Sarah asks.

'I don't know any more.' Rachel sounds so frustrated. 'I try to talk to her. I tell her we're there for her. She just pulls further away.'

They're silent and I'm about to walk in, when Rachel speaks again. 'Mum says the best thing to do is just be there for her. Let her come to us. When she's ready.'

Not going to happen, I think. Then I walk back in. They look so guilty that, if I hadn't overheard, I'd have known they were talking about me.

'Hey,' I say, forcing cheer into my voice. 'Mike just called. I have to go. Sorry.'

'Sure,' Rachel says. And gets up. 'I'll walk you down.'

* * *

Saturday afternoons are for my gran, my mum's mum. Every time I call, I have to open the curtains. I know that when I leave first thing she'll do is close them again. She says she's fine, but isn't. We sit together, surrounded by the clutter of a lifetime (Gran can't part with anything, even the most useless of presents – ugly vases, a foot massager she never uses, two coat stands). We sit together and we pretend. She sews. Needle going in, needle going out. I talk about school. It's all very positive. If she notices I'm really slapping on the old enthusiasm, she never says. I've always loved my gran, who'll never be old, because she's gutsy, always doing stuff for herself – and us. When I was a kid, every Friday night, she'd have me for a sleepover with my cousins. For an only child, it was heaven, a night of pillow fights, midnight feasts and talking late into the night. Sometimes we played tricks on her. No matter how late it was, she always laughed. Then my cousins moved down the country. And I grew up.

Gran still smiles, though not with her eyes. She sighs a lot and thinks I don't notice. We never talk about Mum – we'd just upset each other – but just being together is like a tribute to her in some weird way. She was Gran's only daughter. She was my only mum. Well, obviously.

Today, for, like, no reason at all, I start telling her about this really annoying guy in my class. Whose kiss I can't seem to forget. Not that I mention the kiss. Or the fact that he called me 'Ice Queen'. That might make her think I've emotional problems or something.

'I mean, he's obnoxious.'

She lifts her head and looks at me. I mean, really looks at me. For the first time in six months, I have her attention. Her full attention. It's kind of like a victory. So I get on a bit of a roll, telling her exactly what I mean by obnoxious. Him making me shove the boat off. Practically dumping me in the water. Taking me way too far out. And tricking me into putting on a harness and hanging out the side of the boat.

She's laughing. Genuinely laughing. 'I like the sound of him.'

'Oh no, you'd hate him. He is so full of himself.'

She's laughing again. 'Sounds like your grandfather.'

I'm horrified. 'Granddad was nothing like that.'

She goes all dreamy. 'Once he was. When we met.'

You never really think about your grandparents in love, do you? I mean, it must have been so long ago.

'I hope you're giving that young man a run for his money.'

'Don't worry. I don't put up with any crap.' Gran doesn't mind bad language.

'Good girl. Now, keep me posted on developments.' There's a sparkle in her eye, and suddenly I know what's got her so excited. She thinks this is another boy-meets-girl story. And I hate to burst her bubble, but I quickly reply, 'There won't be any developments.'

She gives me a look that says, 'I know better.'

She so doesn't.

'D'you know what?' she says, 'I think I feel like a walk.'

'Really?' It's a good sign. She always used to walk.

Sometimes I see my mum's face in mine. But never when I try. Sometimes I draw it in my sleep, clearer than I can remember it. At night, I go to bed with a sketch pad, pencil and the dog, hoping that in the morning I'll wake to a picture of her. If I don't, I've always got Homer.

She didn't hide it from me. Because she didn't have much time and wanted to use it, to get me ready . . . But you never do get ready. How can you? Maybe if we weren't so close it'd

}|{

be easier now. But I wouldn't swap that for anything. She was my best friend, though I didn't know that then.

I wanted to hold on to her for ever. Sometimes, though, I wanted it to be over. For her. So there'd be no more pain. But always I wanted a miracle. I prayed for one. Every minute of every hour of every day. Though I knew, maybe because she kept telling me, it wasn't going to happen.

Her last words to me: 'You're going to be so great.'

Great is the last thing I feel.

Monday, and everyone's moaning about being back in class. McFadden acts cool but I'm pretty sure he misses having someone to boss around. I carry on the Ice Queen routine. And it's going fine.

In the canteen, I sit with Sarah and Rachel as usual. He sits with Mark, also as usual. Only now Orla and Amy are joining them.

'We are seriously due a party,' Sarah says.

I look at her. My first thought is: *It's too soon.*

My eyes slip back to the other table. Does that guy ever get cold? I don't think I've ever seen him in his school jumper. Always just the shirt – hanging out, sleeves rolled up – and his tie looking like he's just been in a fight. He's doing all the talking. Amy is leaning across the table towards him, fiddling with her hair. Oh my God, she's totally flirting. Tipping her head back and laughing. Ha. Ha. And now she's lowering her chin and looking up at him with big eyes. Slag. I glance at McFadden. Crud! He's caught me. I look away.

'My parents are going away for the weekend,' Sarah's saying. 'For once in my life, I have a freer. And I'm going to make the most of it.'

I glance over again. He catches me again. This time he waves. Jesus. Now Amy's looking over to see who he's waving at.

'I'm going to do proper invitations. I'm going to get fairy lights. And booze, obviously.' Sarah frowns. 'If I've enough money.'

And there it is, my one hope. That she won't have enough money. And it won't go ahead.

For the rest of lunch – in fact, for the rest of the day – I avoid looking at McFadden. I can't believe how much willpower that takes. But I do it. And then, after trying so hard, it's all a waste because, in our last class, I get paired with him for sign language. When our names are called out together, I stand absolutely still. I close my eyes, and can't believe it. All around me I hear people starting to hook up. I don't move.

'Together again!' I open my eyes and he's in front of me. Beaming. I throw him a Bored-Ice-Queen look. 'Except this time I didn't set it up,' he says.

I squint and shake my head impatiently. 'What?!'

He shrugs. 'I set it up for us to sail together,' he says, matter-of-factly.

I stare at him. 'You did not.'

Mr Regan (too scary for a nickname) walks over. 'This is sign-language class. I'm not supposed to be hearing anything.'

'Sorry,' David says.

I'm thinking back to the course. He knew everyone: the guy with the loudspeaker, the instructor . . . Everyone. He could have arranged it. If he'd wanted to. But why would he want to?

}|{

'OK,' I whisper, and I know I've got him here, 'so tell me, why would anyone deliberately trap themselves in a boat with . . .' I put my fingers in quote marks, '"a stuck-up Ice Queen"?'

His smile couldn't physically be any wider without breaking his face.

'Shut up,' I say.

'Did I say something?'

'Just answer the question.'

'Maybe I thought you could use a friend.'

I laugh out loud. People turn in our direction.

'Well, thanks,' I whisper. 'But I have friends.'

'Not according to Ms Kelly's definition.'

'What would you know? I've great friends, thank you very much.'

He shrugs.

'You are so smug, d'you know that?' I want to hit him (understandable). And kiss him (not). 'I'm going to the loo.'

'I'm not the person you need to tell.'

'Oh my God. You're so obnoxious.'

I whip around to leave, ignoring Mr Regan and the need to announce my exit. At the last minute, I say one word: 'Toilet'. I mean, we're practically adults, do we really need permission? I march out, aware that the whole class is looking. Nobody behaves like that in Regan's class. But, surprisingly, he takes it.

Outside, I regain my inner poise. When I come back, I'm cool. McFadden signs away at me. And I don't know whether it's his bad technique or my inability to get this whole signing thing, but I haven't a clue what he's saying – if he is actually saying something, that is. I wouldn't trust anything he does, that guy. There's so much I want to say. Like, there's nothing wrong with my friends – the problem's with me. They'd be good listeners if I was a good talker. And how do you know anyway? Are you spying on me?

What I do say, when the bell finally goes, is, 'Thank God for that.'

As I'm leaving, I'm glad to hear the teacher call McFadden back. But it's nothing. He just wants him to set up the room for an assignment tomorrow.

I power out of the school. I mean, who does he think he is? Talking to me like that. Talking about Rachel and Sarah like that. They're my friends. And they're good friends. Actually, you know what, I can't let this go. I stop walking. Rachel and Sarah catch up. I hadn't noticed I'd left them behind.

'Damn. I forgot my mobile.'

'We'll go back with you,' Rachel says.

'No, it's OK. You go on.'

Rachel looks at me a little too long.

'You sure?' asks Sarah.

'Yeah, sure. See you tomorrow.' I smile innocently at Rachel.

'OK. Tomorrow,' she says, and they both turn to go.

Back in the classroom, Mark Delaney's helping McFadden drag all the desks into a circle. They look up when I come in. McFadden smiles. I start to walk to my desk like I've forgotten something.

'You go ahead,' I hear him tell Mark. 'I'll finish up.'

Mark looks from me to his friend, then shrugs. He flings his bag over his shoulder. 'See you later.'

}|{

I feel McFadden's eyes on me. And turn suddenly. 'Look, I don't know what all that was about, but my friends are the best, OK? And I don't want you going around slagging them.'

'Sure.'

'So you can just back off.'

'Fine.'

Is that it? No, it's not it, because I'm walking towards him now, so angry. Then I'm wondering why. I stop. Shake my head. 'There's no point talking to you.'

'You know, I'm not that bad,' he says, looking like he's having a great time, amusing himself.

'You so are.'

He folds his arms, pretends to be serious. 'What's your problem with me anyway? For the record.'

'OK. I'll tell you. For the record.' And I don't know where this is coming from. 'You're too happy.'

He laughs, raises his eyebrows. 'I'm too happy?'

'You just don't care. Your mother died. And everything's a big joke.'

His face changes, smile fading like a light going out. 'So that's it,' he says slowly.

'That's what?' I say, like he's the most annoying person in the world. Which, outside of The Rockstar, he is.

'Nothing.'

'Oh for God's sake.' I turn from him. But he's between me and the door. So escape is out. For a moment, there's silence, then his voice, gentler than I've ever heard it.

'It does get better.'

I swivel around, furious, not just with him, but the entire world. 'Yeah well, maybe I don't want it to get better.' It gets better, then I've forgotten her. Tears spring to my eyes, which makes me even angrier. I look away, so he doesn't see.

Then, somehow, I'm in his arms. Someone's holding me. Right now, I don't care who. He feels strong. I need strong.

'It's OK,' he whispers, over and over. He smooths back my hair, like my mother used to do. And just for the tiniest moment, it is OK.

Then it hits me, I'm standing in the middle of the classroom in David McFadden's arms. I pull back, swiping at my eyes.

'I'm fine. Perfect. Never better.' I back away, grab my bag. Make my voice hard. 'That never happened, OK?' Then, I run.

4
THERE GOES GRAVITY

I miss the DART and have to wait twenty-five minutes for the next train. I plug in my earphones, tune out of my life and into Eminem, the one person who makes sense, who can sum up life in four words: 'Oh, there goes gravity.' But I don't want to think about life or gravity or anything, actually. So I stare out at the sea, at the curling, white lips of breaking waves, at the clouds like continents, slowly separating. Only when I'm getting off the DART do I remember Mike. I should have texted to say I'd be late – a deal we made when I convinced everyone I didn't need collecting from school. I hurry through the station.

There he is, standing beside the car, muscular arms folded across equally muscular chest, neck straining to better see the crowd in front of me, his eyes scanning for a familiar face. Mine. I wave – because I don't want this to become a big deal.

His face relaxes when he sees me.

'Sorry,' I say, deliberately sounding out of breath. Like I tried. 'Missed the DART. Forgot to text.'

)|(

'I was only going to worry if you weren't on this one,' he says. But I sense relief, and it feels good that someone cares – until I remember that it's his job.

We get into the car.

'Can you take me to Dundrum?'

He looks in the rear-view mirror. It's like he knows me, like he knows I shop when I'm down.

'Just a little harmless retail therapy,' I say.

He checks the mirror again.

'I'm fine, seriously. Can we go?'

'I'll just let your father know, in case he's expecting you.'

I picture him, absorbed in his music or some fitness routine, or in conversation with his manger or stylist – and laugh to myself.

'I'll text him, then,' Mike says.

'Whatever.'

In the giant indoor shopping mall, I go straight to the hole-in-the-wall. The money situation is this: my mother can't say 'no' anymore; The Rockstar, when he's around, doesn't like to. So there's a bank account in my name. And a card that always works. It's like the magic porridge bowl that keeps filling up. I don't take advantage – unless I really need to. Right now, I need to. I go a bit mad in Tommy Hilfiger. And kind of madder in River Island. In Schuh, I buy a pair of Converse trainers, a pair of black pumps and some three-inch heels. Then it's back to the hole-in-the-wall for more ammo. I seriously stock up on Mac make-up, then perfume and jelly beans in House of Fraser. They squeeze me in for a St. Tropez tan at the beauty salon. I come out feeling much better. I even buy Mike an ice cream.

When I get home, I carry my bags through the hall. And stop. From the kitchen comes the hum of conversation. The Rockstar never eats alone. There are always, always others. And I always, always avoid them. Today, though, I recognise the voices and smile. The band are as close to family as I get. Like uncles, only friendlier. Growing up, they were always around. There's Bob, the bass guitarist, who still, sadly, wears a ponytail; Tony, the drummer, who's been shaving his hair tight ever since he started to lose it; and Streak, who wears a bandanna, probably to bed. They've been together longer than I've been alive. They've been through divorces, scandals, illness, death, life . . . They're as close as a group of guys can get. I walk towards the kitchen, but stop when I hear Streak's voice. It's all serious.

'No, Mike's right. This has gone on too long. Get a barring order.'

'Come on,' argues Bob. 'She's just some sad, lonely person who thinks this geezer here' – I hear a backslap – 'will solve her problems.'

'Think of the publicity,' says Tony. 'Do we really want that kind of attention? It'll just encourage others.'

I walk in. 'Hey,' I say, throwing my bags down.

They all go quiet. Four heads turn in my direction. Then they stand, like I'm royalty, which is the way they have been treating me since Mum died. Tony pulls out a chair. Streak extends his arms for a hug. Of the band, he says the least. And I like him the most.

'God, you're getting more like your mum every day,' Bob says.

Which shuts things up again. But I don't mind. Bob wouldn't be Bob if he didn't put his foot in it.

)|(

'Barbara,' my Dad says, 'set a place for Alex, *s'il vous plaît*.'

I sit furthest from the French speaker, next to Bob, to show there're no hard feelings.

'So what's all this about?' I ask.

'What?' asks Tony, innocently.

'Something about a barring order . . .'

'It's nothing,' The Rockstar says.

'Just one of your dad's fans getting overenthusiastic,' says Bob.

The Rockstar glares at him, as if to tell him to shut up.

That's what I don't get. Fans. OK, I can see why Kurt Cobain had fans. Or Brandon Flowers has fans. My father is forty-five years old. He dyes his hair.

'What's she like?'

'Just some poor woman who thinks I'm something I'm not.' The Rockstar sounds tired.

'So, how's school?' Streak asks.

'School is school.' As always. 'How's work? You guys starting something new?'

'Give us a break,' says Tony. 'We've just finished recording. You're as bad as Ed.'

'Sorry.'

I love when they're here. Especially when they're working on something, down in the basement. Sounds rising – laughter, experimental strumming, melodies being changed each time they're played, cursing, slagging – and finally the finished product. I mightn't be a fan of their music – OK, I'm absolutely not – but I appreciate the work that goes into it. I also appreciate that when they're here, it's more like home.

* * *

After dinner, I'm halfway up the stairs with all my bags when the front door opens and in bursts The Stylist in a bluster of autumn leaves. She slams the door shut with her bum and leans against it to catch her breath. Her hands are full of bags. Her arms are full of bags. Over her shoulders, more bags. She's outshopped even me. She trots across the hall. Doesn't she see what she's doing to the floor? I'd tell her to get slippers, if I thought they wouldn't have heels.

She checks her watch. 'Crud,' I hear her mumble.

'Missed dinner?' I ask, just to annoy her.

She looks up and bursts into a smile. 'Hey, Alex!' she says, like we're best friends. Then, she sees my bags. 'You've been shopping!' She totters to the end of the stairs where she raises and lowers her eyebrows. 'I'll show you mine if you show me yours.'

I can't say I'm not tempted to see what's inside of all those bags. Silently, I come back down. She perches on the bottom stair and gathers her bags around her feet. Then, she pats the stair beside her. There doesn't seem to be any other comfortable option. So I join her.

'Who's first?' she asks.

'You.'

'No, you,' she says, like a three-year-old.

I'm trying not to laugh here. 'OK.' I start to take out my things. First, my tartan leggings – 'Oh my God. They're so you.' Then, the top to go with them. 'Black is so your colour.' Now the pumps – 'Cute.' The three-inch heels. 'Oh, yes!' It's Meg Ryan in *When Harry Met Sally*. Lastly, the denim mini.

The Stylist holds up a hand. 'Wait! That would be amazing with this belt I got.' What is it with stylists and belts?

She rummages through her bags, sending skirts, shirts, tops and dresses flying. There are some serious fashion disasters – like the belt itself, when she finally roots it out. She holds it up to me. 'I'd wear it high,' she says. I'm about to say, 'forget it' when she beats me to it with, 'You've a great little figure.'

Still don't like her.

'Here.' She holds it out to me. 'You have it.'

She's giving me the belt she's just bought. She's just handing it over.

'It's OK,' I say awkwardly. 'But thanks, anyway.'

'Go on. I'll get another.'

'Actually, Marsha' – can't believe I called her by her name! – 'It's really not me.'

'Oh, OK,' she says brightly, reminding me of Sarah. 'Hey! Wait till you see these really hot shoes I got . . .' She reaches for the nearest bag. I'm not hopeful. Which is why I'm so surprised. Underneath wads of pink wrapping is the most amazing pair of sandals I've ever seen – about seven inches high, black patent, with a zip running up the centre and about ten skinny straps emerging from either side. My hands move towards them like magnets. She holds them out to me, looking at them lovingly, like they're her children.

'Don't you just love them?' she says with a sigh.

I nod, sighing too as I take hold of them.

She looks like she's missing them, so I hand them back. 'Where d'you get them?'

She squints, trying to remember. 'Some little store off Grafton . . . Let's see . . .' Suddenly, her face lights up. 'You know what? I'll take you!' Then she remembers who she's talking to. 'Sometime – if you like.'

I smile thanks. But start to collect my things. 'There's probably some food left,' I say.

5
PANDA SLIPPERS

Our first class next day is, wait for it, Road Safety. We're sixteen and we're still alive: couldn't someone put two and two together? It *is* a school. We're on the fascinating subject of motorway safety when I decide I can't take any more. I put my hand up. I'm not the first person that's ever used the loo as an excuse to relieve boredom rather than themselves. I walk the corridor, stop at the noticeboard. It's as exciting as Road Safety, so I wander on into the bathroom where I give my hands the slowest wash they've ever experienced. And finally, before they send out the cavalry, I make my way back.

I'm rounding the final corner when I see McFadden. What did he do – ask to go as well? He's heading straight for me, eyes holding mine. My stomach churns, my pulse quickens. I think of the kiss. And feel myself blush. I think of what he said about my friends. And want to slap him. I think of how I lost it in front of him. And want to run. I tell myself to get a grip. It's just McFadden. I don't even like McFadden. He reaches me and slows to a stop, shoving his hands into his pockets.

}|{

'I was thinking about your question,' he says.

I squint. 'What question?'

'You wanted to know how I can be happy.'

Oh God. That question. This is what I get for breaking down in front of him.

'You know what? I don't want to know. None of my business. So forget it, OK?'

He doesn't. 'My mom would want me to be.'

'I don't want to talk about this, OK?'

'Look. I've been through it, I can help – '

'Yeah? So where were you six months ago?' I snap before I can help myself.

His face softens. 'Where you are now. Not much good to anyone else.'

I choose to misunderstand. 'Thanks very much.'

He looks me in the eye. 'That's not what I meant. And you know it.'

'Whatever. Look. Thanks for the offer and everything but I don't need help, and I don't need a "real friend", if that's what you're offering.'

'I was offering advice.'

'Right, well, I don't want your advice.' I start walking. Because he's wrong. Being happy is not that simple. It's not like flicking a switch, whatever your mother would have wanted. It's more like climbing a mountain, where every step you take towards the happy peak is a step away from her. I can't do it. I won't.

Back in class, I try to block it out. Not easy, when the subject is what distance your car should be behind another. I'm so aware of the door opening and McFadden walking back in. I keep my eyes on the teacher. And the clock.

* * *

I've never been happier to get out of school. On the DART, Sarah goes on (and on) about the party. The party that is going ahead. Saturday night. I stare out the grimy window. The sky and sea are a matching murky grey. The only bright thing for miles is a single white yacht in the distance. I think of McFadden at the helm, yelling and generally being obnoxious. He was better that way.

'So, do you guys think you could make, like, a contribution or something? You know, towards booze and stuff.'

Rachel and I look at each other. My gut feeling is that it's her party. But then I think I've more money than I need and she doesn't have enough, so why not? But then I think if I hand her cash, Rachel will feel she has to, too. So I'm kind of stuck.

'OK,' says Rachel, 'I'll see what I can get.'

'Me too,' I say, relieved.

'Thanks, guys, you're the best,' she says, like a kid on Christmas morning. She hugs us both. Then it's her stop.

'Hope it lives up to her expectations,' Rachel says, as we watch her walk along the platform.

'Impossible.'

Today, I get off the DART with Rachel. We've a joint project – due tomorrow – that we should have been working on. If it was just me, I wouldn't bother. Nothing like that matters any more. But Rachel wants to submit something. And it wouldn't be fair to let her do it alone.

We walk in her front door to the smell of frying garlic. I follow her into the kitchen where we drop our bags.

'What's for dinner?' she asks Yvonne.

I remember that question. Must have asked it every day.

Yvonne looks up from the hob and smiles. 'Chicken casserole. And hello to you too.'

}|{

Rachel offers me a drink. I have one so that we can stay in
the kitchen a bit longer. We sit up at the island and watch
Yvonne cook. In one pan, she's frying garlic, onions and peppers. In another, chicken pieces covered in flour. And suddenly, I'm remembering the funeral. How, afterwards, I was just
standing there, with all these people coming up to me, taking my hand and squeezing it, saying things that meant nothing to me. My head was spinning, my legs weak. I'd forgotten to eat. And I was going to drop. Then Yvonne was there
suddenly, swooping me into her arms as if I was a child. I
don't know how long she held me for, but it wasn't long
enough. When she pulled back, she took my chin between
her thumb and index finger and brought her face up to mine.
'You need anything, you call me. Any time. For anything.' I
noticed then that she'd been crying.

Now, back in the kitchen, they're both looking at me.

'Sorry?' I say.

'Will you stay for dinner?' Yvonne asks gently.

I feel like saying, I'll stay for ever. 'That'd be great,
thanks.'

'Good.'

Upstairs, Rachel takes out her laptop.

'Should find most of what we need on the Web,' she says.

We sit side by side at her desk, watching the screen as the
computer boots up.

'So,' she says, turning to me. 'What's with you and Dave
McFadden?'

I nearly die on the spot.

'There's something going on. Isn't there?'

I force a laugh. 'No.'

She raises an eyebrow. 'You sure?'

}|{

My brain's kicking in. 'Are you serious? With that eejit?'

'In fairness, I wouldn't call him an eejit.'

'I would.'

'He was really nice to me on the boat. I got to know him a bit.'

'Lucky you. Here, gimme the mouse,' I say, ending the conversation.

Or so I thought. 'What's your problem with him, anyway?'

'Who said I'd a problem?' I click into a website. It's no good, so I click back out.

'You're kind of emotional about him, though.'

'I am not. God Almighty.'

'You see, there you go. All dramatic and stormy.'

'Oh for God's sake.'

'OK,' she says. 'You don't have to tell me.' She sounds hurt.

'There's nothing to tell.'

'If you say so,' she says. Definitely hurt.

'Look, Rache. If there was something to tell, you'd be the first, OK?'

'I doubt that.' She looks at me. 'Because you don't tell anybody anything, do you? You keep it all in.'

I say nothing.

'Look. I don't care about David McFadden. Doesn't bother me. But I do care about us. What's happening, Alex? You're pulling away from me. Not telling me stuff. We used to tell each other everything. What's going on? Don't you trust me anymore?'

I look at her and feel so sorry. 'Of course I do. It's not about trust, Rache. And it's not about you. I just don't do close. With anyone. Not anymore.'

}|{

She stares at me. 'What do you mean you don't do close? What about the people you're already close to?'

I want to tell her. I want to explain. You get close to someone, anything can happen. They can decide they don't like you anymore; they can move to another country; they can die. You stay back, at the edge, not caring, and you're safe. You're also cool. People want to be with you. Want to be like you. I used to do close. Then Mum died. And I died too. I can't go through that pain again. I just can't.

'Look, Rache, honestly, there's nothing going on. I swear.'

She looks at me like she's giving up. 'Let's just do the project.'

We work in silence. After about ten minutes, I get a text. I check the screen. It's from Gran. And when I read it, I almost drop the phone. 'How's McFadden?'

'Let me guess,' Rachel says. 'Sarah?'

'Eh, no.' I place the phone upside down on the desk and shove it away.

She turns back to the computer. But not before I see her face.

'It was just my gran,' I say.

'Whatever.'

And I don't know why, but all of a sudden David McFadden's ruining my life.

＊ ＊ ＊

As soon as I'm home, I make a call.

'Gran, never text me about guys, OK? Someone could be around.'

'I thought you were supposed to be keeping me posted.'

'And I told you there was nothing to keep you posted on.'

}I{

Why did I ever teach her to text?

'You can't just tell me about this really interesting boy and then not mention him again. Come on now, spill.'

Spill?! I feel like reminding her she's seventy-two. 'Nothing to spill.'

'Really? So why get into a flap about my text?'

'I'm not. I'm just saying.'

'Go on, remind me how annoying he is.'

I remember how the subject of McFadden made her perk up. 'OK. He's extremely annoying.'

'On a scale of one to ten.'

'Two hundred and fifty.'

'What was the last thing he did that was extremely annoying?' She's getting enthusiastic.

I sound tired when I say, 'Gran, it's not just one thing. It's everything. He's a total know-all. I don't know why we're even talking about him.'

'OK,' she says, reasonably, 'we won't.'

'Good,' I say. But the weird thing is, I do. I do want to talk about him. Which makes absolutely no sense whatsoever.

Friday morning, The Rockstar joins me for breakfast. Which never happens.

'Hey,' he says, sitting up on the stool beside me.

I look at him suspiciously. Then go back to my cornflakes. Barbara hovers, hoping for a challenging order – a mix of exotic, out-of-season fruits; an omelette with a special type of mushroom; a kipper done medium rare . . . He asks for a mug of coffee. Black. Some day soon, she'll hand in her notice.

'How're things?' he asks me.

'The usual.'

He smiles awkwardly. 'Good.'

I feel like saying, actually, no, not good. But I don't.

'Just wanted to let you know I'm going to New York tomorrow.'

I can't believe it. 'When'll you be back?'

'Maybe next Friday?'

'No. You can't! It's Mum's birthday on Sunday!' We make a serious big deal of birthdays in this house. This is the first one Mum won't be here for.

He grimaces. 'We have to meet this guy who does album covers. He's impossible to get. It's the only time he's free. I kind of have to go.'

No you don't, I think, *you want to go*. But Ice Queen's back. ''Course you do.' I stand, grab my bag and heave it onto my shoulder. Homer, who's lying at my feet, gets up and stretches. He trots by my side out into the hall.

The Rockstar follows. 'Alex, wait, maybe I could make some calls . . .'

'Don't put yourself out.' As if. I reach the front door where I normally squat down to say bye to Homer. Today, I keep going.

'Look. I'll cancel. I'm sure I can . . .'

I stop. Swivel round. 'Don't bother,' I say. 'On second thoughts, it'd be better if you weren't here.' Mum's life revolved around his, fitted into his. And he can't even be here to remember her, can't even be here for me. It's going to be so hard, Sunday. He could at least pretend to care.

Mike drops me to the DART. But I don't get on. I wait till I think he's gone, then leave the station. I start to walk, as the emptiness expands inside me. I haven't lost one parent,

I've lost both. I walk fast, not caring in which direction. I walk for hours. In the rain.

I don't plan to end up in school. But somehow I do.

I sign in late. Make my way to the classroom. At the front of the room, there's some novelist talking about her latest book. She has everyone's attention, including our English teacher's, who just gives me a brief look when I walk in. I sit at the back and try to listen. But my head is filled with all the things I want to say to The Rockstar but never do. Then everything's a blur. I lean my chin on my hand and let my hair fall over my face. So no one can see me cry.

At break, Sarah starts going on about the party. Again. Her teeth look whiter because of her St Tropez tan. Tomorrow she's getting her hair done. I wrap my arms around myself and squeeze. I catch Rachel looking at me. She says nothing, though. I remember yesterday, at her house, and am sorry. But I'm not going to change. I can't.

'Alex!' says Sarah.

I wake up.

'What are you're wearing?'

I look down at my uniform.

'Tomorrow night,' she prompts.

'Oh, right.' A moment passes. 'I don't know.' Another moment. 'Actually, Sarah, I'm not sure I'll be able to go.'

Her eyes widen. 'You have to. I need you there.'

'I think I'm coming down with something.' Like depression.

'Come. Please. You could stay in bed all day Sunday.'

Don't worry, I think.

'Freaking hell, Sarah,' Rachel says. 'Leave her alone. There'll be other parties.'

'Not like this one.' Sarah pouts. 'I mean, how often do my parents go away? Seriously, it could be years before I can do this again.'

'I'll see, OK? I'll do my best.'

In the end, I do go. Anything's better than hanging around the house when he's there, getting ready to leave. To hell with him, I'm going out. And I'm going to have a bloody good time. Whatever happens, I won't be thinking of him.

'You OK?' Mike asks when I climb into the car.

'Yeah, I'm OK. Why wouldn't I be OK? We're going to pick up Rachel first.'

'Sure,' he says. 'But maybe you should change out of your slippers first?'

I look down. How could I have missed them? Two giant pandas on my feet! I hurry back inside and swap them for my new black three-inch heels. My pace back to the car is slower.

'Preferred the slippers,' Mike says, smiling.

'Just drive, Mike.'

He laughs.

And suddenly, I wonder if he's right, if I should stay in the slippers. And stay home.

6
AIR

All the lights are on in Sarah's house. The front door's wide open. From the road, we can hear the music. Lady Gaga. So Sarah. We climb from the car and thank Mike.

'So, what, twelve?' he asks, through the lowered window.

'Yeah, fine.' I'm pretty sure I'll want to be out of here by then. We head up the path, taking it easy in our heels.

'I wonder who'll be here,' Rachel says.

'Everyone.' I look up at a figure lounging at the front door. 'Including Louis.'

Rachel groans. Sarah's older brother is a complete slimeball. The way he looks at us (and I'm not just talking about tonight) would give you the creeps. We're used to guys staring when we go out. It's kind of appreciative, you know? But this is too much. If I could pull my skirt down three inches, I would. I'd also get my slippers.

We reach the porch.

'Good evening, ladies,' he says, like some kind of gentleman. 'I must say, you're looking ravishing tonight.' His T-shirt says 'Durex, Connecting People'.

⅜⅋

We look straight ahead as we pass. 'Can it, Louis,' I say.
'Anything for you, Alex,' he says.

'Especially if it's a condom,' Rachel whispers to me.

I look at her deadpan face and burst out laughing. And
suddenly it's like nothing's happened between us and we're
OK again.

Luckily, Louis stays where he is. We find Sarah in the
kitchen, making some kind of punch thing. She's got glitter
on her skin and it sparkles when she moves. She totally
brightens when she sees us.

'Hey, you guys,' she says, and hugs us like she hasn't seen
us in years. 'It's so good to see you.' She looks weepy with
emotion and I wonder if she's had a few already.

There's booze everywhere. And plenty of people to drink
it. Sarah's invited pretty much everyone from school. The
plan is, they'll bring friends, people we don't know, especially boys we don't know. Sarah's stated very clearly she wants
to have sex before she dies. She'd better hurry up, then,
because you never know . . . I look around, already kind of
bored and vaguely wanting to leave. But then Sarah hands
me a vodka and orange like I'm definitely going to drink it.

And tonight, I definitely am.

McFadden's by the kitchen door, looking like a dude, talking to a group of people: some I know, some I don't. I catch
him glancing over. I look away. More people join our group.
There's Amy. And Orla. And now Simon. I look at Sarah but
she doesn't seem to notice him at all. Simon and Sarah have
a history. Well, sort of. He asked her out just before the summer and she turned him down, saying she couldn't go out
with anyone while I was 'in mourning'. Which was sweet.

}|{

But also just as well. Simon isn't exactly boyfriend material.
He has no real friends, just drifts from group to group, moving on when he gets bored. Which usually takes about a
week. Can't imagine he'd last much longer in a relationship.
Someone like Sarah would be devastated. I watch to see if he
talks to her. But he seems more interested in Amy.

And then, beside me, there's Louis again.

'Hey, beautiful.'

I give him a 'drop-dead-jerk' look.

He doesn't. 'OK. I'll start again,' he says. He clears his
throat. 'Hey, gorgeous.'

'Louis, you're wasting your time.'

'Trust me Alex, talking to you is never a waste of time.'

'I think I'm going to barf.'

He laughs. 'And I think I'll stick around.'

'Suit yourself.'

'Always do.' He looks cheeky and confident, and maybe
slightly interesting with his dark hair and even darker eyes.

I don't say anything. Let him talk to me, if he's so keen to.
I look around as if I'm bored.

'See anyone interesting?' he asks.

'You mean, more interesting than you?'

'Impossible.'

I like giving him grief. And, weirdly, he seems to like taking
it. So it's back and forth like this for I don't know how long.
But it must be a while, because I'm beginning to feel the room
spin a little. And I know I need to stop drinking. I'm standing with my back to the wall, which is just as well. Louis's
leaning across me, arm out, hand against the wall. We've
become a satellite to the main group. When did that happen?

'So, you want to get out of here?' he asks.

}{{

It's taking a while for that to register.

'Get some air,' he says.

Oh, right, air. I could do with some of that. He takes my hand and drags me from the wall. God, I'm floppy. Then his arm's around me, steadying me. It feels good to have someone there, someone strong, minding me. Or is he? Hang on. Why's he walking me towards the stairs?

'You said air.'

'We can open the window in my room.' His smile is dreamy.

I'm not so sure about this.

'Hey, Alex!' The voice is loud and cheery and I kind of wake up a bit. I turn. It's McFadden. Weird thing is, it's good to see him, like a real friend showing up just when you need one.

'Get lost,' Louis says to him.

McFadden squares his shoulders. And looks pretty hot. Everyone's tall to me, but I hadn't realised just how tall he is. He looks down at me and smiles.

'So. How's it going?'

Suddenly Louis's arm, draped over my shoulder, is annoying and clingy. I lift it off. Give it back to him. He looks seriously pissed. At me. Then I see it. I see what was going to happen and I almost puke. I walk to McFadden but it's more a stumble. How much did I drink? I lost track.

'Want to get some air?' he asks.

I look at him. And I know he means air.

The lights are on in the garden and it looks beautiful, like a magic fairy-tale place. McFadden links my arm. I think of old couples in places like Florida. I feel so much warmth for him suddenly, this guy who plays hockey, not rugby, who sails and wears beads, and who doesn't care until it matters. He sits me down on a bench. And then is beside me. Not too close. Not touching.

'You OK?' he asks.

'Fine.'

He smiles. 'As usual.'

'As usual.' I smile too.

'Kind of stuffy in there,' he says, as if maybe I don't know what almost happened.

'Thank you,' I say, so he knows I do.

He shakes his head. 'I don't think he'd have done anything.'

'Don't defend him. Louis is a slimeball. Don't know how I forgot.'

'Want a glass of water?'

'No thanks. Just need some air.'

We're quiet for a while. Then suddenly I'm asking, and I've no idea why, 'When your mother died, how was your father?'

'What d'you mean?'

'I mean, did he cry? Did he break down? Did he get visibly upset?'

He opens his mouth to speak.

'Or did he just not give a shit?' And then I'm crying. 'Oh God, not again.'

And his arm is around me and he's holding me to him, and it feels so right to be held by him, and only him. This time I'm not pushing him away. This time, I'm keeping him right here with me.

* * *

I don't know when, exactly, Rachel appears. She squats down beside me.

'You OK?' she asks, gently.

Rachel, I think, *where were you? Friends are supposed to look out for each other. You knew he was a creep. You saw me with him . . .*

'Yeah. I'm OK. Thanks,' I say, coldly.

'Good.' She sounds relieved.

She stands up and looks at McFadden. She smiles. 'Thanks,' she says, as if I'm not there. Then she's gone.

'What was all that about? Why'd she thank you?'

'Rachel was worried about you. She asked me to see if you were OK.'

Hang on. He helped me only because Rachel asked him to? He didn't do it himself? He wouldn't even have noticed. He wouldn't have come. I imagine her going up to him for help and feel so ashamed. I stand up.

'I'm fine now. Thanks. You don't have to mind me any more.'

He laughs. 'You make me sound like a babysitter.'

'Isn't that what you are? Look, thanks, and everything. I'm sure Rachel really appreciates . . .'

He stands and puts a hand out to me. 'Come here.' There's something in the way he says it, a kind of confidence, like he knows what he's doing, or something.

I give him my hand. And we sit back down.

'Alex.' God, I love the way he says my name. 'I'm here because I want to be, OK? If Rachel hadn't asked me to, I'd have been out there myself. I knew what was going on. I was just hoping that maybe I wouldn't have to do the knight-in-shining-armour thing. But there you go.'

)|(

I'm still taking that in.

'I want to be your friend,' he says.

I look at him, eyes wide.

'I want to be more than your friend.' And he's leaning towards me, and I know I could run, I could get out of here right now, right this minute. But I'm going nowhere. I close my eyes. And when we come together, I'm wondering why it took so long.

It gets cold. He takes off his hoodie and gives it to me. Even helps put it on. Which should be seriously sad – but isn't somehow. He runs his fingers through my hair, fixing it.

'We should probably make a move,' he says.

There is this whole embarrassing thing about getting home. David offers to bring me. But Mike's been waiting outside since midnight. Like I'm Cinder-bloody-ella. And I have to tell him that.

'Ok . . .' he says, as if trying to work out where that leaves us.

'I can give you a lift?' I say.

'Eh, it's OK, thanks.' After a moment, 'The driver. Is he outside?'

'Yeah.'

'I'll walk you to the car, then.'

I feel flat, not wanting to leave him. But I take off my shoes and get up. The ground is cold but it's better than having the heels on. He puts an arm around my shoulder. I lean into him. Not wanting this to end.

We get to the car. Mike gets out.

'Everything OK?' he asks David, eyeing him in a way that could definitely be taken as threatening.

David straightens. 'Everything's fine. Alex wants to go

home.' He's looking at Mike the same way, like he doesn't trust him either.

'Alright, Alex?' Mike asks.

'Thanks to David, I am,' I say.

Mike looks at him again, reassessing. 'Can I drop you somewhere, mate?'

'No. Thanks. I'm fine.' He looks at me. 'I'll call you.'

'You don't have my number!'

'I'll find it.' He smiles and touches my arm. Then he's gone. Back to Sarah's house. Back to the party.

7
WHAT BIG EYES YOU'VE GOT

I wake on my mother's birthday. Without her. My sketch pad is empty. But I have Homer. And something else. I have last night, slowly unfolding in my mind. I lie back and close my eyes (which is just as well because my head is killing me). I picture his face. Remember his kiss. Then I have the weirdest feeling. Like Mum wants this for me. Like she's here in the room, wanting this. For six long months, I've felt nothing from her. Nothing. Though I've tried. So hard. But now I feel her, happy, and wanting me to be too. But do I want to be? Do I really want this? If there is a 'this'. What if there isn't? What if he was just being kind? What if it's Rachel he really likes? He helped me for her, after all. She's beautiful and sweet and uncomplicated, not messedup like me. Or angry. I think of him walking back to the party. Who did he talk to then? Someone safe, someone sweet, someone who wouldn't throw his words back in his face? Someone who laughs easily. He won't call. He'll wake up and think of Rachel. And I won't know for sure till tomorrow whether he couldn't get my number or whether he just got sense.

Tomorrow. Oh God. I will never, ever, drink again.

But he does call. When I hear his voice, my heart soars. And then plummets. What if he's just ringing to back out? He'd be like that – polite.

'How're you feeling?' he asks.

'Rough.' Whoa, I'm hoarse.

'Did you just bark?'

I laugh. And sound like Tina Turner. Or possibly even Ike.

'So. You doing anything today?'

'No,' pops out too quickly. Like I'm desperate or something.

'Want to meet up?'

Then I remember. And even I can hear my voice drop. 'It's my Mum's birthday.'

'Oh. Right. Sorry. I'll call back another . . .'

Suddenly, I don't want him gone. 'No! Let's go out. Now. Today.'

'You sure?' He sounds like he doesn't want to intrude.

'Positive.' She'd want me to. I know she would. And I can't be on my own. Not today.

There's a brief silence. Then, 'Will I pick you up?'

'You've a car?'

'A banger I've just started sharing with my sister.'

'Cool!'

'Wait till you see it . . .'

'Hey, listen, you've got wheels . . .'

'So, what time?'

I check my watch. Then the mirror. OMG to both. It's two in the afternoon. And I look like a Goth.

'Gimme an hour.'

* * *

This is my life: I have to tell a bodyguard, not a parent, that I'm going out. The Rockstar has disappeared like he doesn't care (which he doesn't), leaving Mike behind to keep an eye on me. It's like he wants me looked after. But he just doesn't want to do it himself.

'Bring your phone,' Mike says. But he's cool about it. I can tell.

'OK. Thanks.'

He squints at the security camera. 'Is he driving an orange Beetle?'

'I don't know.' I peer at the screen. And see his face through the windscreen. He looks like he's singing. 'That's him,' I say. And realise I'm smiling.

I'm at the front door when he pulls up. I'm running down the steps. He's striding towards them. Now taking the steps two at a time to meet me. He smiles before he kisses me. I close my eyes and shut out the voices in my head telling me I'm playing with fire, telling me I'm going to get burnt. I can handle this, I argue to myself. I know what I'm doing. I can pull back at any time.

'You ready?' he asks.

And that's exactly what I should be wondering. Am I?

He opens the car door for me, and, when I get in, my head throbs and my stomach heaves, reminding me of last night.

'Where to?' he asks, when he's at the wheel.

I don't know. Where do you go with a person you hated till yesterday and now like too much?

'Surprise me,' I say, because it's (marginally) better than 'Duh.'

He starts the engine and pulls away. I sneak a look. He's so incredibly hot and so incredibly decent, I find myself

}|{

asking, did I really hate him or was I just trying to avoid this? We drive through the gates. Two fans peer in. David waves. We go over a bump. And my stomach heaves.

'You feeling as rough as me?' I ask.

He looks at me and smirks. 'Doubt it.'

I hit him.

'You know, this is supposed to be awkward,' he says, like I'm not playing my part.

'What?'

'First date,' he says. 'Awkward. Always.'

I feel my face fall. 'God. Don't call it that.'

'What should I call it?' he asks cheerfully, eyes still on the road.

'Do we have to call it anything?'

He looks at me questioningly, then, after a second, says, 'Nope.'

We're driving out the N11, the Wicklow mountains ahead of us. It feels good to be getting away from Dublin. Away from everything. My phone rings, and I ignore it.

'Aren't you going to get that?'

'Probably just Sarah.' I check. 'Oh no!'

He looks at me.

'It's my gran. I'm meant to be there. Like, now.' I hit the green button. 'Hi, Gran.'

'Where are you?' she asks.

'On my way,' I say, making a face at him to say sorry. 'See you in a minute.' I want to ask if she's OK, but it's not a question she likes. So I hang up. Look at David. 'I'm so sorry. I can't not go. Not today.'

'No problem. Where does she live?'

'Killiney. You don't mind dropping me, do you? I can get Mike to pick me up.'

}|{

'Sure.'

'I'm really sorry.' So sorry in fact, I go out on a limb: 'We can do this another time?'

'Sure.'

After ten minutes' silent driving, we pull up outside Gran's house. We look at each other. And I don't want him to go.

'Don't suppose you want to come in?' I ask, knowing he won't.

He looks at me and shrugs. 'Why not?'

And I know my smile is way too wide.

Gran opens the door, wearing black. She looks especially tired. Her eyes are red-rimmed.

'Hey, Gran,' I say. 'This is David, a friend from school.'

She looks at me, then at the stranger. 'David what?' she asks, with too much interest.

'McFadden,' he says, stretching out his hand.

And suddenly, it's like Granny-What-Big-Eyes-You've-Got. And those eyes dart to me. 'McFadden?'

I warn her with a look. Don't. Say. One. Word.

She doesn't. But . . . she's straightened right up. Her eyes are focused, sharp. And she's smiling. Genuinely smiling.

'Well, David McFadden,' she says, 'you are very welcome.' She steps back to let us in, giving me a significant look as I pass. Then, she's like I haven't seen her in ages, springing around like a bunny. Snapping the curtains open. Kicking the foot massager behind the couch. Offering tea and coffee.

Then, thinking she's very bold, she says, 'Sure, a bit of Baileys wouldn't do you any harm, would it?'

'It would actually, Gran,' I say, thinking of the vodka.

'I'll have a coffee,' David says.

After that, it's like I don't exist. She quizzes him on everything – where he got the accent, what his father does, what he's doing in Ireland.

'Gran!' I say, every so often. But she ignores me.

He laughs each time.

It might be embarrassing, but I find out more about him in one hour than I've known after a year in class. He's from San Diego. His father's in aeronautics. He has a brother (younger) and a sister (older). When we get to his mother, Gran remembers I'm in the room. She turns to me, with a long, meaningful look. 'This is good,' it says. 'He understands.'

After an hour, she shoos us out the door. 'I've taken up enough of your time,' she says, as if we're dying to be alone. Which, speaking for myself, is true. But she likes him. Which is good. He cheered her up on a day she needed to be distracted. And he's distracting me. He is very distracting in general. I look at him as she says her last goodbyes, and want to reach out and touch him. But the person who does the reaching out is my gran. She leans forward and kisses him on the cheek.

My mouth drops open. It drops further when she says, 'I can't imagine how anyone would find you annoying.' Then she looks straight at me. And I want to disappear.

Walking to the car, he wears a huge grin. 'So, you spoke to your gran about me?'

Christ.

'I'm flattered.'

'Don't be. It was all insults.'

He laughs. We get into the car. 'I'm still flattered.'

'So, back to Wicklow?' I ask, hoping to move it on.

'I was thinking . . . We could visit your mom. If you like.'

'You mean where she's buried?' I'm horrified.

He shrugs.

'I'm not dragging you to a graveyard. I'm not dragging myself to a graveyard.'

'OK.'

'They're the saddest, most depressing places in the world. I don't want to even think of my mum in a graveyard. If I want to be near her, I go to the beach or Killiney Hill. She loved Killiney Hill.'

He starts the engine. 'Want to go?'

I want to, but . . . 'What kind of . . .' – I try to think of a better word but can't – 'date would that be?'

He smiles. 'I thought it wasn't a date.'

'You know what I mean.'

We stop off to pick up Homer, who needs a walk and loves the Hill. He sits on the floor in the back with his head between the seats, not wanting to miss anything. When we get to the Hill, he bolts from the car, heading for the trees. He slows to a stop and has a good sniff around while we catch up. It's dark under the pines. Homer comes up to us, then turns and runs ahead, like a scout leading the way. Pine needles cushion our step. We hardly make a sound. The ground starts to climb. Exposed tree roots cross our path. David takes my hand. Homer keeps running back to us, crouching low and springing up.

'What's he doing?' David asks.

'He wants you to throw him a stick.'

David looks around, finds one and throws it far. Homer

dashes off. He returns with the stick and comes up to David with it. David reaches out, saying, 'Good boy', but just as he's about to take it, Homer swerves to the left and runs off. David looks at me.

'You have to chase him for it.'

'I thought he was a Retriever.'

'Who doesn't retrieve.'

'Didn't you get him trained?'

'I trained him myself. Trust me. Catching him is much more fun.'

Especially for spectators. David runs at the dog, confident that he'll get the stick this time. Homer ducks out of the way and trots along, ears pricked up, like some proud beast, taking it easy. David springs again. With a tiny movement of his head, Homer dodges him. He decides to give David a break, moving the stick so that a really long bit is sticking out of the side of his mouth.

'Tell me he didn't do that on purpose.'

'He did.'

'Christ,' he says with grudging respect. He dashes after the dog again in a sudden burst. 'A little help!' he calls to me.

We chase Homer till we're out of breath, collapsing onto the ground and lying there until our breathing returns to normal. Homer goes to sniff around again. I look up through the branches at a sky that seems so far away. Then I remember Mum. We're here on Killiney Hill for her. But for the last ten minutes I haven't thought of her once. Every day I carry her with me. But today, on her birthday, I forgot.

'You OK?' David asks. And I turn my head. He's propped up on one elbow, looking down on me.

'Yeah.' My voice is hoarse.

}{{

'Your mom?'

I nod. Force a smile. 'For a minute, I forgot.'

He lies back down, like he's giving me time to remember. I close my eyes and try to picture her face. But it's not coming.

For a long time, we lie in silence.

'What she was like, your mom?'

He's the first person who's wanted to talk about her – apart from the shrink, who was getting paid. I look at him and smile. I sit up. Then he does too. We sit with our arms around our knees.

'She was fun. She could make me laugh at anything. Especially myself. She'd this way of making worries disappear. All I had to do was tell her. And poof! They'd be gone. She got me, you know?' And just for a few moments, she's alive again. Not this distant shadow of someone I sometimes feel I dreamt up. 'She was normal,' I say, like it's the most wonderful thing. And, when you're surrounded by a rockstar's life, it is. 'She baked. Made me do chores. Set limits. You never think you'll miss those things.' I smile, to hide the fact that I feel like crying. 'If I ever got starstruck by someone who called to see The Rockstar, she'd remind me that everyone has an ass to wipe.'

He smiles and nods like he'd have liked her. Then he ruins everything, by asking why I keep calling my father 'The Rockstar'.

I hear my voice go cold. 'That's what he is. A rockstar, not a father. He doesn't care about anything except music. Not me. Not my mum. When she got sick, he disappeared, down to the basement or off on his trips. He was in New York when she died, acting like she'd already gone, like he wasn't going to waste any more time on her.' My voice wobbles, because it's so hard to admit to that. 'When he came back, it was like she never existed . . . But I don't want to talk about him.'

'I'm sorry,' he says.

'What do you miss most about your mum?' I want to know if we're the same. And I want so badly for us to be, because maybe then I won't feel like such a freak.

He stares into space and for a while doesn't speak. Then he looks at me.

'Just her being there. Every day. When I come down in the morning. When I come in from school. Just the normal, ordinary stuff.'

'Sometimes I can't believe I'll never hug her again,' I say and, even to me, I sound lost.

Then I'm in his arms, feeling his strength, smelling the smell that is uniquely and wonderfully David.

'You're so great.' His words float in the air, reminding me of Mum's last words to me: 'You're going to be so great.' I look up at him in surprise. And for the first time I start to believe in possibility.

8
SIBERIA

Monday morning and I'm in bits. How do you walk into a classroom, knowing that the guy you like will be there, but not knowing what the story is exactly? When he said, 'See you tomorrow', did he mean see me, as in, we're seeing each other, or just that he'd see me in school? I look in the mirror for the fortieth time. I want to look good, but not like I'm trying. I've straightened my hair. Put on make-up. Taken it off again. Now I walk out of the room and close the door before I can get near the make-up again. This is ridiculous.

I can't eat breakfast, so just have juice.

On the DART, I bump into Orla Tempany.

'You OK?' she asks. 'You look really pale.'

Crud, I think. I should have worn the make-up.

'Some party, at Sarah's!' She starts listing who ended up with who. I'm silently freaking, waiting for her to get to me. When she doesn't, I finally calm down. By then, we're getting off the train.

Arriving at school, I'm glad to have Orla by my side, chatting away. I do not want to walk in on my own. But I don't

}|{

even get that far. He's coming towards us, right now, along the corridor with Mark Delaney. Oh God. I try to act cool.

'Hey,' they both say, together, in their usual laid-back way, like nothing's changed.

My heart sinks. So that's how it is.

We pass each other.

I look back.

And then, as if in slow motion, David turns around and gives me the biggest smile.

My heart flips.

In class, I catch him looking at me. Which, I realise, wouldn't be possible if I wasn't looking at him too. I try not to. But no matter what class we're in, I always know where he is. I know what way he's sitting, standing, lounging. I know how his arm's resting on the table. I know when he looks out the window. His sneezes are louder than anyone else's. His coughs too. Is he getting a cold? I tell myself to stop being so lame. We spent an afternoon together. Once. It wasn't even a proper date. Which is just as well, because I don't date. I don't get involved. With anyone. Ever. But then my eyes meet his, again. And I melt.

At break, I'm stuck. If I go over to him, people (like Rachel) will wonder why. If I don't, what'll he think? I get my things together slowly, so I don't have to decide.

'Come on,' Sarah says, arriving beside me. 'Let's go.'

'Right.' I look towards David's desk.

He's gone. I tell myself it doesn't matter but somehow it does.

In the canteen, Rachel, Sarah and I queue up. I let my eyes wander around, totally casually, as if the last thing I'm doing is looking for anyone. When I see him, I keep my eyes

}|{

moving but take it all in. He's sitting with Mark Delaney, Simon Kelleher and a bunch of other guys. It looks like he's telling some kind of story. They're all leaning in, listening. Then he stops and they burst out laughing. Mark glances over at me. I look away. Oh my God! That was about me. Why else would he have looked over? That was about the weirdest first date in history, going to see a granny, walking a crazy dog. My face burns. My stomach tightens. I glance back. David's eyes meet mine. But this time, instead of a smile, he simply raises his chin. I turn away, sick.

When we get our food, I find the bench farthest from him.

'Here?' Sarah says. 'Are you kidding? This is social Siberia.' She holds her tray tight, like she's no intention of lowering it onto a table this far from the action.

'If you want to sit somewhere else,' I say, 'do.'

Sarah glances at Rachel. Who shrugs. They both sit down in silence. Sarah shakes her head like she doesn't believe it. It doesn't last long. She's back to the conversation she started in the queue. 'So, the party . . .'

What else? After, like, a blizzard of MSN messages last night and two conversations already today, you'd think she'd have exhausted the subject. She hasn't. The only thing I'm grateful for is that she missed the whole thing with Louis. Too busy trying to line up sex before she dies. Which mustn't have happened – or we'd have heard. I look up. Amy has just sat down opposite me – suspicious, given how far from the action we are. For a moment, she listens in, then cuts across Sarah.

'Speaking of the party . . .' Amy leans towards me conspiratorially. 'Was that you with David McFadden in the garden?' It sounds like an accusation in Cluedo.

Sarah drops her fork, and stares at me. 'What!?'

I struggle to find an answer but Rachel beats me to it.

'Alex was upset about her mum. David's been there. He knows what it's like. And was helping her through it. Right, Alex?'

They all look at me.

'Right,' I say, and start to breathe again.

'You looked kind of cosy, though,' insists Amy.

'Oh, get lost, Amy,' I say. I stand up, knowing I can't be here any more. 'You know what? I feel crap. I'm going home.' I walk off.

Behind me, I hear Sarah say, 'Nice one, Amy. That was real subtle.'

Hours later, I'm lying on my bed, still in uniform, covered in dog hair (and dog), trying not to think of my mum, my dad or David McFadden. There's a knock on my door, and when The Stylist pokes her head around, I feel like throwing something. I mean, why's she even here? Shouldn't she be in New York with The Rockstar? Hasn't she got any other clients? Or ever heard of a hotel? I'm serious: can't she just get lost?

'Really hot guy, downstairs,' she says. 'Asking for you.'

'Don't know any hot guys.'

'David Mc . . . something?'

'Hot, my ass.'

'Looks kind of cute to me.'

'Right, well, do me a favour and tell him to get lost.'

She comes into the room. 'He wants to know if you're OK. Said you left school early.' She looks concerned. 'Are you OK?'

‧⺇‧

'Yeah.'

'Good.' She smiles, then raises her eyebrows. 'He did come all this way.'

'So what are you, my mother?'

'No,' she says, calmly, 'I'm not your mom. Neither am I your messenger. So, maybe you should tell him yourself.' She produces a no-hard-feelings smile and closes the door.

I flop back on the bed and mutter the word 'bitch'. But know who's really being the bitch here. Another knock. And I'm really going to throw something this time.

The door opens.

'Hey,' he says.

I sit up. 'Who said you could come up here?'

He walks so casually into my room. 'Marsha,' he says, like they've known each other for ever.

'Marsha doesn't even live here.'

'So, what's up? Hey, Homer.'

Homer's tail starts to slap against the bed. He gets up and goes to him. Traitor.

'Look,' I say, getting up from the bed and standing with my arms folded. 'I don't know what you're doing here. But the weekend was a mistake. It's not going to happen again.'

He squats down to Homer, and pets him.

'You're getting hairs everywhere,' I say crossly.

He looks at my hair-covered uniform and raises an eyebrow. 'So. What did I do to bug you?'

'Who said you bugged me?'

He ignores that. 'Let me guess. I didn't come over to you at break. That it?'

I say nothing. Just shrug.

He stands. 'So, it never occurred to you that there might

have been a reason?' And he sounds impatient now. 'Look, Alex.' I still love the way he says my name. 'We never talked about how we were going to play it at school. Clearly, we should have. Anyway, for the record, I'm happy for everyone to know about us. I just didn't know how you felt. So I played it cool when I thought anyone was looking.'

'Oh.' I feel a fool. But there's still the canteen. 'What were you laughing at lunchtime?'

He looks confused.

'What were you telling Mark and Simon and the others?'

'I don't know.' He frowns, thinking. Then his face clears. 'I'd a hockey match yesterday before I met up with you. Probably that.'

'Must have been some match.'

'You wouldn't believe it.' He tells me about the umpire who didn't know the rules, the goalie with Tourette's syndrome, the fouling and the 'supporters' who took the word to extremes. It's actually really funny. So funny that he couldn't be making it up. I can't help it, I laugh.

He sits on the bed. A minute ago, I'd have told him to get off. Now, I sit beside him.

'So,' he says. 'What's wrong?'

'Nothing. I'm fine. I'm sorry. I guess I was a little angry at the world.'

'At me.'

And because I don't want to discuss it, I grab a pillow and hit him. He gets one and hits me back. In seconds we're pounding each other. Laughing. Homer's jumping up on us and barking. But then it all goes quiet. He looks at me for the longest moment and I think we're going to kiss. But I'm wrong.

'You have to trust me. OK?'

I nod. 'OK.'

'I'm not a bad guy.'

Those eyes. 'I know. I'm sorry.'

And then we are kissing, our mouths melting together, his lips so soft. But then he's taking my hands and pulling me up from the bed.

'Come on. Let's go.'

What? 'Where?'

'Hockey match for nine-year-olds.'

'Seriously?'

'I've got to pick up my brother.'

I smile. 'Oooh. I'm meeting the family already?'

'Do I have to remind you? Your gran kissed me on Saturday.'

'Oh God,' I say, closing my eyes. 'Don't remind me.'

I'm standing on the sideline trying to stay quiet, when really I want to shout, 'Hey, the wing's open', or 'Shoot!' or 'What are you doing?' I'd forgotten how great hockey is. Watching these little guys flying around makes me want to pick up my stick again and run onto the pitch. I used to captain the Firsts – before my world exploded. Now, David's brother Bobby, a skinny blond kid, moves like lightning, slipping past three defenders. Facing his fourth, he passes at the last second to a teammate who shoots for a goal and gets it. Beside me, David lets out a roar. The final whistle blows and Bobby's team go wild – for about two seconds, then they're running off the pitch, victory forgotten. If that was us, we'd be hanging around soaking up the victory, then heading for coffee, hanging out, having a

}I{

laugh. God, life was so simple before Mum died. Bobby's walking towards us now, pulling a bright green gumshield from his mouth.

'Did you get me a drink?' are his first words to David.

'Hi, Bob,' David says, widening his eyes at him. 'This is Alex.'

'Hey,' I say.

Bobby glances in my direction, then looks back at David. 'The drink?'

David raises an eyebrow. 'Good to see you, David. Thanks for picking me up, David. I know you'll get the drink on the way home, David. Because that's the kind of great guy you are, David.'

'You're a great guy, David.' Bobby smirks. 'Now can we get the drink?'

I'm still trying to decide if I like this little guy, when David takes my hand. We start towards the car.

Bobby squints up at me. 'Are you his girlfriend?'

Whoa, I think. Slow down, buddy.

'Alex has a name, Bob.'

'Yeah, but is she your girlfriend?'

'So, good game?' David asks, ignoring that line of questioning.

Bobby swings his stick. 'I was lege, wasn't I?'

'You were legend.'

Nearing the car, Bobby bursts into a run. He stops by the front passenger door, holding the handle.

'Alex was sitting there,' David says.

I'm about to tell him it's OK, when Bobby says, 'But I always sit in the front.'

I look at David. 'I don't mind. Honestly.'

}|{

I sit admiring the back of David's head, while he gets a blow-by-blow account of the match from Bobby. We stop for that all-important drink. As Bobby runs into the shop, David turns around to me.

'Sorry about that.'

'He's just excited about the game, I guess.'

'I mean about him sitting in front. He's kind of sensitive about stuff like that, you know – routine.'

'Sure,' I say, not quite understanding.

Their house is only about two miles from mine. I've passed it loads of times and never really noticed it. It's on a road of similar houses. Redbrick. And old. Inside, it's cold, and David turns on the heat. Then he bribes Bobby to go play on his Xbox 360. Bobby doesn't look thrilled but money's money, I guess, because he wanders off, and minutes later I hear a TV. I follow David into the kitchen.

'Want a drink?' he asks, ignoring the mess and heading for the fridge.

'No, thanks.'

He pours himself some juice.

'So, who looks after Bobby when your dad's at work?' I ask.

'Some days me, some days Romy.'

'No childminder?'

He laughs. 'It was like Mrs Doubtfire here for a while. He went through four in a month.'

'Wow.'

'You've got to understand something about Bob,' and I know he's about to defend him, which I think is cute. 'He's the youngest by eight years. When he was born, Romy and I

were at school. He spent most of his time with our mom.
Then our parents split up. Mom got sick. Before we knew it,
she was gone. We had to move back in with our dad . . .
who'd a new girlfriend. Bob's life has been a bit crazy. Which
is why he can be a bit . . . difficult. And why he needs routine.'

I can't believe all they've been through. 'What's it like
having to live with your dad's girlfriend?'

'Jackie? Oh, no, she's gone. I think we scared her away.'
He half laughs.

'Oh my God. I hope your dad didn't blame you or anything?'

He shakes his head. 'Nah. He was more upset about Mom.
I don't think he realised how much he still loved her until she
was gone. Which didn't help the girlfriend situation.'

'That's so sad.'

He shrugs, finishes his juice, leaves the glass by the sink
and walks towards me. 'Want to go upstairs?' He says it
casually but I'm suddenly nervous. What exactly does that
mean?

I act cool. 'Sure.'

I follow him up to his room. It's like walking into the
ocean. The walls are covered in posters of the sea. There's
one of a killer whale leaping out of the water, but mostly
they're of waves, great giant curling waves. Surfers cut
through some, blazing a trail of white. But my favourite is
the silhouette of a guy in a wetsuit sitting on his board, his
back to the camera, looking at the sunset. It could be David.

I smile at him. 'So, you like the sea.'

'I like the sea.'

The room has a pinball machine, a basketball hoop and a
snooker table. It also has a bed − a fact that makes me

embarrassed or something. I plonk myself down on his gaming chair. My iPhone slips from my pocket, onto the floor. He picks it up, sits on the edge of his bed and starts to check out my playlist.

'Eminem?' He looks surprised.

'What's wrong with Eminem?'

'Nothing. He's just not mainstream.'

'What makes you think I listen to mainstream stuff?'

'Everyone does. That's the point.'

'I'm not everyone.'

'I noticed.' His eyes hold mine, and my heart speeds up, then he turns his attention back to the iPhone. 'Who's Nina Simone?'

'If you don't know who Nina Simone is, I'm not telling you.'

'Can I've a listen?'

'Knock yourself out.' I get up and mess around with his pinball machine for a few minutes. Then I wander over to his desk. OK, so he's not a tidy freak. I pick things up, have a look, put them down. The usual stuff. Except for, oh my God, what's this? Mr Zog's Sex Wax – The Best for Your Stick!? I pick it up, turn around. Slowly I lift the 'Sex Wax'. And an eyebrow.

He smiles. 'For all the hot babes I have up here to my love nest.' He pulls out the earphones. 'It's for my board.'

'Your board?'

'Surfboard.'

'I should have known.' There's an edge to my voice, like surfing's a bad habit. It's like I'm afraid he's too cool for me or something. Or maybe I just don't want him to think he is. I don't know.

}|{

'I'm only getting back into it,' he says, quietly.

I feel mean. Don't know what to say. So I say nothing. Just act my usual tough self and go over to the pinball machine. He plugs the earphones back in.

After a while, he comes over and hands me back my iPhone. I'm relieved he's smiling.

'You've got kind of weird taste. No offence.'

'None taken, jerk.' OK, it's a standard joke. I still like it.

'So, is this what happens when you grow up in a musical house? You go all eclectic?'

OK, now that gets to me. 'What I listen to has nothing to do with him.'

He looks doubtful.

'Right. I'll prove it. First time I heard Nina Simone was watching *The Thomas Crown Affair*. There's this great song of hers, "Sinnerman", that's on during the art-gallery heist. I checked her out on YouTube and loved her stuff, especially "Ain't Got No".'

'The one I just listened to?'

I nod. 'A lot of the music I like comes from movies. The theme tunes from *Blood Diamond*, *Black Hawk Down*, *Inside Man*. The *Shrek* movies always have great soundtracks.'

'So you're a movie buff?'

I straighten up. 'You name it, I've watched it. Go on, try me. Ask me anything. About any movie. Don't be shy.'

'Okaaay,' he says, thinking.

I fold my arms, hold my chin high.

'All right, then,' he says, 'what movie was the Door Test in?'

I'm impressed. But don't let on. 'I was expecting a bit of a challenge here.'

}|{

'You didn't answer the question.'

'*A Bronx Tale*.' Great movie and not an obvious choice.

'OK. Who got an Oscar for *My Cousin Vinny*?'

'Marisa Tomei.' She deserved it.

'Who named all his fishing boats *Jenny*?'

'Don't tell me you like *Forrest Gump*?' I say it like I hated the movie. I've watched it eight times.

'Don't tell me you don't.'

I laugh. So, he's a softie who's not afraid to show it. If there was such a thing as a movie test, to judge a person by the movies they like, he'd have flown it. I feel silly now that I was nervous.

'OK, so you're a movie buff. And a music buff.'

'I'm not a music buff.'

'I might believe you if your iPhone was full of pop charts. Oh, and by the way, most people I know who watch a movie just watch the movie.'

I shake my head.

But he just lifts his eyebrows like he knows better.

We hang out for most of the afternoon, shooting hoops, playing snooker and watching random, hilarious stuff on YouTube. When he drops me home, we sit in the car for a while, neither of us in a hurry to go.

'So, what d'you want to do about school?' he asks.

My stomach twists. Today, we were just two people, hanging out. You tell everyone, you change it, you make it a 'relationship', you make it 'boyfriend and girlfriend'. You make it heavy. 'Can we just leave it? They'll just make a big deal out of it.'

He shrugs. 'Sure.'

I hope he doesn't mind. 'It'll be fun,' I say, 'pretending we don't see each other.'

}|{

'Might be tricky, though.' He leans across and kisses me. I know what he means.

Later, when I'm home, Rachel texts.

'You OK?'

My first thought is, why wouldn't I be? Then I remember. How I felt when I thought David McFadden was laughing at me.

'Yup. Ta. Back tomorrow,' I text back.

9
I KNOW

The Rockstar's back from New York and in the kitchen when I come down for breakfast. His hair doesn't seem so bad today. The shades aren't totally ridiculous. Couldn't tell you what's on his feet. And, for some reason, I don't want to argue.

'Hey,' I say. Just that. No smart remarks.

'Hey,' he says, like he's expecting one.

'How was the trip?'

He looks surprised by the question. I'm a bit surprised myself. 'Good. Good. It was good.'

I'm so close to saying, 'Great, great, that's great', but I kill the sarcasm, for once.

'I got you something,' he says, almost shyly, taking a package from a stool under the counter. He hands it to me, his expression hopeful that I'll like it, anxious that I won't. I think that maybe, just this once, I won't pass it on to Sarah. I open the pack to reveal clothes. Hoodies. T-shirts. Jeans. All Abercrombie. I lift each out for closer inspection. Everything's the right size. And exactly what I'd pick for myself. It's like he was inspired. Suddenly, I smell a stylist. He called her. He must have. And, for once, she got it right.

'Thank you. They're great.'

'It's good to see you in such good form.'

I think of David and smile. 'Sun's shining.'

He glances out the window. It might be shining but it's doing so from behind a thick bank of grey. His eyes form a question.

'Gotta go,' I say, getting up.

'Wait! There's something I want to tell you, in case it comes up in the media or on the Net. I've got a barring order against that fan. It's not a big deal. Just wanted you to know.'

'Why d'you need a barring order?'

'She was just getting silly.'

'What d'you mean?'

'She wanted to marry me.'

I burst out laughing. 'Really? That's it?'

'She was contacting me a lot. Mike thought it would be a good idea, you know, to put an end to it.'

'Who is she?'

'I don't know much about her. Apparently, I called her up on stage once.' He shrugs like he's no memory of it.

'And you've never actually met her?'

'No. It's daft. Completely daft. Anyway, I just wanted to let you know. In case it comes up.'

It will. Anything that affects him publicly always comes back on me. I just never know how, until it happens.

When Rachel gets on the DART, it's weird but it feels especially great to see her, like she's some long-lost friend that's just returned from years of exile. Or something.

}|{

'Well, you're obviously better,' she says.

'What?'

'You look great. You're even smiling.'

'Rachel. I do smile occasionally. I'm not an Emo.'

She says nothing. And now I'm wondering, *I do smile, don't I?*

'What was it, a twenty-four-hour thing?'

OK, now I get it. 'I think I was just kind of overtired or something.'

'Amy can be a real pain,' she says.

'Thanks for rescuing me.'

She shrugs like it's no biggie. We fall silent. I know she wants to ask about David. She knows I won't want to talk about it. So we sit in silence. Stuck. I really want to tell her. But that would make it something. And I don't want it to be something. I just want it to be. Rachel looks out the window. I look down at my bag, fiddle with the tiny blue skateboard hanging from it. Then I think of something she will want to talk about.

'So, you auditioning for the play?' (We're putting on *Macbeth*.)

She looks hurt. 'Only someone who doesn't know me would ask me that.' Rachel's been acting since she was four. It's, like, in her blood. Of course she's auditioning. She looks at me. 'We're becoming strangers and you're making it happen,' she says, so earnestly I can't look at her. 'OK, fine,' she says, then. 'Ignore me. Don't do close. Just don't expect me to either.' She looks out the window.

I feel sick. I never meant to upset anyone, especially not Rachel. I just thought I could pull back, protect myself. I look at the side of her face and can't believe we're here, like this. We could always tell each other anything. With no fear. We were so close. We'd think the same thoughts at the same time. Say the same things at the same time. Laugh out loud spontaneously. At the same time. I sigh deeply. Then I see Sarah coming towards us and feel like groaning.

She looks at the two of us.

'Jesus,' she says. 'Who died?' Then she goes bright red. 'Oh my God, I'm so sorry, Alex. I can't believe I said that. What's wrong with me? Jesus. Seriously, Alex. I am so sorry.'

'Forget it,' I say. And the good thing about Sarah is I know she will.

At school, it's not so hard to avoid David because all I can think of is Rachel.

In the afternoon, the auditioning kicks off. Rachel goes up for the part of Lady Macbeth. David decides to try out for Macduff. Sarah doesn't want to go up against Rachel, or play a guy, so she's not auditioning. Me? The Rockstar is a big enough star for the both of us. The big surprise is Mark Delaney, who wants the part of Macbeth. And nothing but Macbeth.

Orla Tempany is up on stage, auditioning for a man's part: Macduff. The rest of us are standing around in groups, vaguely looking on. Except for Rachel, who's totally into what's happening on stage.

'She's good,' she says, sounding surprised.

My surprise is more immediate. Mark and David are coming our way. I try not to react, to be cool. I'm wondering what's up.

But it's Mark who talks, not David.

'So, Rachel . . .'

She turns from the stage like she was miles away.

'D'you think we'd make a good couple?' he asks, kind of flirty.

She squints. 'What?!'

'You're up for Lady Macbeth. I'm up for Macbeth.'

She looks relieved. 'So are a lot of other people, Mark. No offence.'

'They haven't a hope,' he says. And I presume he's joking.

Rachel looks at him. 'That part's going to involve a serious amount of work, Mark.'

'So?'

'So it's not like you have to do this.'

'Wow. You really don't think much of me, do you?'

We all look at him suddenly. But then he laughs and walks off.

David's goodbye is a glance.

'Oh my God, he so fancies you,' Sarah says. I look at her in panic. But she's looking at Rachel. 'Mark Delaney is totally into you.' I start to breathe again.

'No offence, Sarah,' Rachel says. 'But according to you, everyone fancies everyone.'

'Well, everyone fancies someone, that's for sure.' Sarah says. Sometimes I just want to hug her.

'He won't get the part,' Rachel says, like she's reassuring herself. 'This is a serious production. And Mark Delaney is a total messer.'

But, later, when Mark takes to the stage and does his thing, she's silent. Totally silent. Because. He. Is. Amazing. And it is absolutely unbelievable that Mr So-Laid-Back-He's-Comatose can be so passionate, so alive, so convincing, so, actually, hot. He's like a different guy.

Rachel's staring. 'I think I might have underestimated him.'

'Told you he was seriously caliente,' Sarah says.

'I'm not talking about caliente. He's just seriously talented.'

And I think we've just found the way to Rachel's heart.

After a day of not being able to talk to him, look at him, be with him, I really need to hear from him. Going home on the DART, I'm hoping he'll ring. In the car with Mike, I'm hoping. I check that my iPhone is in my pocket, switched on, volume up. Then I keep my hand on it so I can feel it vibrate. I could ring him. Oh, God. What am I doing? I like this person too much.

The text comes at 4.30 p.m. 'Wnt 2 walk Homer?'

Yay! I call him back. Suggest Killiney Beach, which I can walk Homer to and he can reach by DART (no car today).

The beach is deserted, apart from the occasional dog walker. Homer yanks on the lead, straining to get to the sea. He crouches low, forcing his way forward. I tell him to sit. I scan the beach for David. I'm so dying to see him that I begin to panic. I thought I could control this, but what if I can't? I should stop right now, turn around, go home. But I don't stop. I don't turn around. I don't go home. I tell myself it'll be OK. I'll handle it. Pull back if things get heavy. I can do this. Homer is seriously pulling now, so I take off his lead. He shoots off, bounding over a band of grey pebbles, heading for the sea. I go after him. That's when I see David, sitting where the sand slopes gently to the water, looking out towards the horizon. He looks like the guy in the poster watching at the sunset. The dog makes straight for him.

'Homer!' I call.

}|{

He ignores me. But David turns. And sees the incoming missile. He manages to get to his feet but the dog's almost on him now and he prepares for impact. But Homer races past and dashes into the surf. David laughs. Seconds later, I reach him. His smile is intimate, like he knows everything about me. Which he doesn't. He couldn't. He pulls me into a hug, then kisses me.

'I've wanted to do that all day,' he says.

I want to give in, admit the same but I pull back. 'Want to see a trick?' I take a tennis ball from my pocket and throw it out past Homer.

'Wonderful,' David says, without looking. He slips his hands around my waist and pulls me to him. 'But I'm not dating Homer.' His lips are cold and salty from the sea air, and, when he kisses me again, I don't want it to end. It's just a kiss, I tell myself. Total strangers do it all the time in night clubs. Means nothing.

Then he's lifting me up. Laughing, I have to wrap my legs around his waist to stay there. We are eye-to-eye now.

'That's better,' he says. Then he's kissing me again.

Then a soaking wet dog is jumping up on us.

'Jesus!' David says and sets me down. Homer drops the ball at David's feet, then shakes water all over him. 'Jesus,' he says again. And we're laughing. 'I thought he didn't retrieve.'

'Only in water. It's either that or no more ball.'

He shakes his head like the dog's a genius. Which he is. David fires the ball way out, farther than Homer's ever been. His ears prick up and he's off. We sit on the sand, watching him. I feel like I could say anything. Which makes me keep it safe.

'I'm thinking of going back to hockey.'

He looks at me. 'You should. You're a seriously good player.'

I bump him with a shoulder. 'How would you know?'

His eyes hold mine. 'You don't think I just started noticing you now.' He leans towards me and I'm trying to work out how to get out of a kiss I want more than anything when, with perfect timing, two great wet paws land on my shoulder. A cold, wet and salty muzzle slobbers on my neck. I jump up.

'Homer! Get off!'

David stands, takes my hand and we start to walk along the beach, kicking the ball ahead of us to keep Homer busy.

'So,' he says, after a few minutes. 'Mark thinks we're doing the right thing.'

'What?'

'Not telling people.'

I stop, and look at him. 'Hang on. You told Mark?'

'Course I did.'

'I thought we weren't telling people.'

'We weren't telling the class. Mark's my friend. Didn't you tell Rachel?'

Guilty, I look away.

'What about Sarah?'

'Are you kidding? That'd be like making an official announcement. She wouldn't mean to let it out, but the information would win in the end.'

He laughs. 'But you trust Rachel, right?'

'Of course I trust her.'

'Then why not tell her?'

I look at him. And can't admit how weird I am.

His face changes. His hand falls away. 'I get it,' he says, voice flat.

'What?'

'It's because of me, isn't it?'

'What?'

'I'm not good enough.'

'What are you talking about?'

'For a rockstar's daughter.'

'Oh my God, I can't believe you said that. I can't believe that you, of all people, brought him into this. What's your problem? You know I hate him.'

'You haven't told anyone about us. There must be a reason.'

'There is! I just want it to be the two of us, hanging out, taking it easy. No big deal.'

'So why do you pull back from me?'

'What?'

'Sometimes you seem really into me. Then sometimes you pull back.'

'That's ridiculous!'

'It's like you like me, but don't really want to.'

'That's not true,' I say, but in a way it is exactly true. 'Is it a crime to not want to rush things?'

He's looking at me carefully. 'So you don't have a problem with me?'

'Oh my God. If I'd a problem with you, would I be here?'

'I don't know. You tell me.'

I squint at him. 'Are you just looking for compliments or something?'

His face relaxes. 'Well, if you want to give me a few . . .' And he's back. The real David.

}|{

I hit him.

'So we're OK?' he says.

'We are definitely OK.'

'Phew,' he says. 'Just had to get that out of the way. Sorry.'

'You should be.' I take his hand and lift it so that his arm is around my shoulder. I snuggle up to him so that he knows the problem's mine, not his. And if I hated The Rockstar before, it's nothing to how I feel now.

10
SERIOUSLY CALIENTE

The auditions run all the next day. And I'm not
Shakespeare's biggest fan but they are killing his work. And
my patience. Apart from the really, really bad performances
(some of which, admittedly, are hilarious), it's so boring I'm
close to suicidal. We're just hanging around the hall watching everyone make fools of themselves. OK, not everyone.
Simon Kelleher is a total surprise.

At three o'clock, our (absolutely undramatic) drama
teacher stands up on the stage and starts to call out the
names for the main parts. The role of Macbeth goes to
Mark Delaney. He punches the air. David pats him on the
back, and people around them congratulate him. Simon
Kelleher is Macduff. He looks stunned. David looks a bit
disappointed. But he gets the part of Duncan and seems
happy enough with that. He sneaks a look at me. And I give
him the biggest smile. Finally, Lady Macbeth – Rachel.
Though it's no surprise, Sarah and I whoop and clap. Sarah
throws her arms around a beaming Rachel.

'I knew you'd do it. Jitter Mug, after school, to celebrate.'

And I know that if money wasn't a problem, she'd also be saying, 'drinks are on me'. Sarah's like that.

I go to hug Rachel. But she stands back, her smile fading. 'It's OK,' she says, so cold. 'You don't have to hug me.'

I just stand there. Shocked.

'What is up between you two?' Sarah looks baffled. But then she's distracted. Mark, David and Simon are passing by.

'Hey guys, well done!' she calls after them.

They stop and turn. It's like something out of a movie. Sarah's caliente theory was right. Even Simon looks caliente next to the others.

'We're going to the Jitter Mug, after, to celebrate, if you're on?' she says.

Rachel and I exchange a glance. Rachel rolls her eyes. It would never occur to Sarah that Rachel mightn't want this.

'What say you, Lady Macbeth?' Mark asks Rachel.

Rachel smiles calmly. 'I say, congratulations! You really deserved the part.' It's like an apology for doubting him.

'So, the Jitter Mug?' Simon asks.

'The Jitter Mug,' Mark confirms.

David looks at me, and I know he's trying not to smile. We're going to be together without even trying.

In the Jitter Mug, I share a couch with Rachel and David. Sarah, Mark and Simon take the tub chairs.

'So, well done, you guys,' Sarah says, raising her smoothie in a sort of 'cheers'.

We clink plastic containers.

'I still can't believe I got Macduff,' Simon says.

I think of David who was up for that part. Even though

}|{

he got Duncan, he must be disappointed. In support, I press my leg against his. He presses his back. Then we're pressing together and it's becoming something else. I have to force myself not to look at him.

'Isn't Rachel the best?' Sarah says, looking especially at Mark.

'She's certainly got my vote,' Mark says.

Rachel looks uncomfortable.

'She's been taking acting classes since she was, like, four or something,' Sarah says. 'Haven't you, Rache?'

'Eh, yeah.' She blushes.

'She's even auditioned for actual television roles. Haven't you Rache?'

'Auditioned, Sarah. Have you actually ever seen me on TV?'

Sarah widens her eyes at Rachel, as if to say 'What are you doing?'

I am so conscious of David beside me. Of our legs touching. I want to reach out, take his hand and leave with him.

'The great thing is,' Mark's saying. 'I get to murder David in, like, the seventh scene or something.'

'So that's why you auditioned for the part,' David says.

Mark gives him a look.

'And I get to kill Macbeth,' Simon says, like it's some kind of victory.

'God. I'm sorry now I didn't audition,' Sarah says. 'It just seems so . . . exciting. All that murder.'

'They're still auditioning for parts,' Mark suggests.

'Nah,' Sarah says, 'too late now.'

* * *

)I(

Going home on the DART, Sarah is not happy.

'What is wrong with you two? You just blew a perfect opportunity. Those guys are seriously caliente.'

'Mark's a messer,' Rachel says gloomily.

'A caliente messer,' Sarah says.

Rachel sighs. 'Don't you get it, Sarah? He's messing. With me.'

'So mess back. Jeez!' Sarah says. Then she turns on me. 'And you. You didn't open your mouth.' She looks worried. 'I think he might have gone off you, Alex. He didn't look at you once.'

My iPhone sounds. A text. From David: 'Flirt.'

I realize I'm smiling and make myself stop. And even though I'm itching to reply, I don't until I'm alone.

'What?' I text back later.

'Cudn't keep legs to self.'

'Speak 4 self, perv.'

Next day, Ms Hall, the drama teacher, is late, so we're just hanging around the hall. Rachel, Sarah and me are at the back, sitting on a bench. Simon Kelleher comes up to us. And looks at me.

'So, your father's afraid of women?'

'What?' And here it is, the fallout.

'Don't tell me you haven't heard. He's taken a barring order out against one of his fans. It's all over the Internet.'

Heads turn. Could he have said it any louder?

'So?' I say like I'm bored.

'So. She's, like, a woman? What's she going to do, marry him?'

'That's so sexist,' is all I can think of saying.

}|{

'Simon,' Sarah interrupts. 'If Alex's dad has taken out a barring order, it must be serious. She's probably a stalker.' Her eyes widen at the thought. 'You don't joke with stalkers, Simon. Madonna had a stalker. It's very serious.'

I want to be somewhere else.

'Yeah, well,' Simon continues, 'if someone was sending me nude shots of themselves, I wouldn't exactly stop them.' He's looking very satisfied with himself.

I roll my eyes. And walk out. In the corridor, I stop. Nude photos. No one said anything about nude photos. At the risk of getting detention, I make my way to my locker and take out my phone. Mike doesn't take long to answer.

'What's with this stalker?' I use the word deliberately.

A moment's silence. 'OK. The first thing to know is that we're just being careful.'

So, he's not denying that she's a stalker, then. 'Who is she?'

Another pause. 'Her name is Sarah Cameron. She's South African. In her thirties. Your father had her up on stage back in the nineties.'

'The nineties? She's been stalking him since the nineties?'

'No, no. She only got in touch lately.'

'I don't get it.'

He takes a deep breath. 'She seems to be a religious . . .' he pauses, '. . . enthusiast. She says that when she, and I quote, "met" your dad, he was married and she respected that. She only got in touch after your mum died.'

'Psycho.'

'Look, Alex, there's no reason to worry . . .'

'I'm not worried, I just don't get why someone religious would send nude photos of herself.'

'You know about that?'

}|{

'Apparently it's all over the Internet.'

'Alex, this is not unusual. Fans sometimes get obsessed. But they're totally harmless. They just don't see that their behaviour has gone over the top until something wakes them up. Something like a barring order.'

'OK. I get that. But why does he need a barring order if she's in South Africa?'

'Recently, she moved to Ireland.'

'Because of him?'

'We don't know that. But it's why we acted. Just to be on the safe side.' His voice is reassuring. 'Look, Alex, I'm sure she's just a lonely woman who got a bit carried away. The barring order will put an end to this.'

And I wonder what it is about celebrity, that even an ancient guy of forty-five with dyed hair and wedges can attract such adoration. I also wonder when his life is going to stop affecting mine.

Ms Hall is there when I get back. She doesn't see me come in, too busy allocating the last of the roles. I go to the end of the hall with the other non-enthusiasts. I take out my jotter, sit on a table and start to doodle. A noose – for over Simon's head.

A sudden clap.

'Right,' Ms Hall says. 'The rest of you.' Why her eyes zoom in on me I don't know, but they do, before I've a chance to look away. 'Alex!'

Damn.

'Any thoughts on what you'd like to do?' She's walking towards me.

I snap the jotter shut. 'Eh. Something backstage.'

〕l〔

'What about sound?' she asks as if it's the obvious choice. And I am so sick of having a rockstar for a father.

'Why would I want sound?'

Her eyes widen and the room goes quiet. Which is when I realise I may have said that a bit loud. I may, in fact, have shouted it out. I close my eyes and shake my head. 'Sorry, I just meant I'd like something other than sound . . . Thanks.'

'What's wrong with sound?' she asks, her face grim, her mouth drawn tight.

'Nothing. I'm just better at other things.'

'Like?' she asks, like I'm being difficult.

I can't think. She's standing in my face, arms folded, looking like Mrs Tweedy from *Chicken Run*. Her hair is ordinary brown, cut in no obvious style; her jacket, skirt and shoes more last century than last season. And she's supposed to be a drama teacher?

'Well?' she asks, tapping a foot. Her shoes are almost as bad as The Rockstar's.

And then I have it. 'Costumes! I'll do costumes.'

The look she gives me. Like I'm making the biggest mistake ever. 'Fine. If that's what you want.' Already, she's striding away. And swooping on Amy.

I glance at David. Roll my eyes at myself.

He winks.

Then Sarah's hurrying over, looking all dramatic.

'I'm fine,' I say, to cut her off.

'Oh. OK. Good.' She sounds deflated.

'Let's go find Rachel,' I say. I scan the hall. She's standing at the far end, looking over, but not coming. And then I remember the way it is between us now.

* * *

One reason it's so easy with David is that he never pushes it, never expects us to go out on, like, official dates or anything. He never suggests we go to a movie, to parties or discos. He knows that having 'fun' means feeling guilty after. So, later, we just walk Killiney Hill with Homer. It's starting to rain but the drops aren't getting through the trees yet.

'You're quiet,' he says.

I look up. And realise we've been walking for ages. 'Sorry. Just thinking.'

'About what happened in drama?'

Actually, I was thinking about Rachel but now that he mentions drama, I shake my head. 'Such an idiot.'

'She hasn't a clue.'

'I meant myself. I can't believe I lost it like that.'

'You didn't lose it. You got a bit angry. She deserved it.'

'I just wish people would stop bringing him up. He's got his own life. It's not mine.'

He stops walking. 'OK. First of all, Ms Hall is not "people". Ms Hall is just Ms Hall.'

And Simon Kelleher is just Simon Kelleher, I think, and start to feel better.

He puts an arm around me and we start walking again.

'Does Mark like Rachel?' I ask, looking up at him.

He stops walking. Smiles widely. 'Does Rachel like Mark?'

'I don't know.'

'Then I don't know.'

'You do know. You're just not telling me.'

'It's classified information.'

'Oh my God. He does. Doesn't he?'

'Don't tell her.'

}I{

Then I remember where we are, Rache and I. 'It's OK, I won't.'

He looks at me. 'Is everything OK between you?'

I make a face and sigh. 'Not really,' I say.

And I'm relieved he lets me leave it at that.

Later, I take out my laptop and google The Rockstar's name and the word 'stalker'. I scan the results.

'Typical!' I say aloud, thinking of Simon Kelleher.

It's not 'all over the Internet'. Just a few bloggers hyping it up. Anything in the actual media is just a mention, nothing I don't already know. The downside of that is that there aren't any photos of her. Maybe they do that with stalkers, keep the news to a minimum, so they don't encourage it. Could the press sometimes actually have a conscience?

11
THE MACBETHS

No one else would notice. Only me. Mostly, it's the things Rachel doesn't say, the times she doesn't step in – to distract Sarah from a difficult topic, to deflect Amy, to ask if I'm OK. But it's not that I miss. It's her just looking me in the eye and saying what she wants to say.

On Thursday, in the canteen, I surprise everyone, including myself.

'Hey, why don't we go see a movie tomorrow and you guys can stay over?'

'Great!' Sarah says, automatically.

Rachel looks into her lunch. 'Sorry,' she says. 'I've something on.'

'What?' Sarah asks straight out.

Rachel starts to blush. She hesitates. 'A family thing.'

My stomach tightens and I blush too. Because there is no family thing.

Sarah looks at me. 'I'm still OK,' she says cheerfully.

'Oh, right, great.'

* * *

When I get home, the place is full of people. Which means The Rockstar's home. Not that it is a home any more. The kitchen is all noise now. Noise and strangers. And exotic food I don't want. I go upstairs with Homer, the next best thing to Mum. From under the bed, I take out my photo album and go straight to my absolutely favourite shot of me and Mum, taken in a phone booth only a year ago, just before she was diagnosed. It's the last record of us when things were normal. Looking at it, I remember how alike we were, same colour hair (browny-blonde), same shaped face (kind of pixie-like), same shaped eyes (big and round) but different colour (her green, me blue). I wonder where she is now, if she can see me, hear my thoughts. Or if she's gone for ever. My throat burns, and I start to cry. I put the photo back and close the album. I hold it to my chest. Finally, I reach over to put it under the bed. Something falls out. An envelope. I haven't had much post in my life, so I know who sent me this. I leave the album on the floor and lie back up on the bed. I take the letter from the envelope.

It's written on A4 foolscap paper. It has no address at the top, but I know where it was written. Irish College. Rachel spent three weeks there, two summers ago, trying to improve on the language we're all forced to learn. It doesn't start with 'Dear Alex'. It just dives straight in:

> *Get me out of here! OMG, why do we have to study this freaking 'language'? It's, like, from the Ark. So's Irish College. Our teacher's Damien from* The Omen. *Our* bean an tí *(lady of the house, in case you don't know) is like the witch in 'Hansel and Gretel' – except instead of making us fat, she's starving us to death. I can't believe this place cost 1,000 euro. If*

I didn't think my mum would kill me, I'd speak English just to get kicked out. Oh God, it's so good to speak English – even if it means I have to write a letter. No offence.

Write back. Or else.

Seriously miss you.

I HATE IRISH!

Rache.

P.S. Send chewing gum. Preferably cherry flavour.

I fold it away, knowing she'd never write that now.

Friday night, we're at the cinema. Sarah's glued to the latest romantic comedy while I wonder how I got myself into this i.e. Sarah coming home with me for an entire night. Maybe I could drug her. The movie is a four out of ten and not worth talking about as we leave the cinema. Outside, Mike's waiting. I climb in the back and slide across to make room for Sarah. But when I look, she's not behind me. A door slams up front, and there she is, reaching for her safety belt. A confused-looking Mike glances back at me. I shrug, then stretch to close the back door. We take off. As we drive, Sarah keeps glancing at him.

'Is that a new haircut?' she asks finally. There's something about the way she says it – like she wants to run her fingers through it or something.

'Eh, yeah,' Mike says, keeping his eyes on the road.

'Suits you,' she chirps.

Inside, I groan.

'So, what part of London you from?' she asks.

In the rear-view mirror Mike's eyes widen, as if to say, 'help'.

I try not to laugh.

'Tower Hamlets,' he says.

Means nothing to me. And I'm pretty sure it means nothing to Sarah.

'And how d'you get into security?'

I have to turn my sudden burst of laughter into a coughing fit. Mike hands me a bottle of water.

'I answered an ad,' he says.

Anyone else would take the hint. Not Sarah. The questions keep coming. The weird thing is, they're so ordinary but she delivers them like Marilyn Monroe singing 'Happy Birthday, Mr President'. What is she doing? Even if she had a hope, which she so doesn't, Mike would lose his job. If he was that stupid. Which he's not. I don't suppose it'd make any difference if I told her he's got to be in his thirties? Eeew!

At last, we turn into our driveway. Mike looks relieved. I know I am.

Sarah's 'Bye!' to Mike is delivered like a line from *Romeo and Juliet* – that one, 'parting is such sweet sorrow'. And I wish Rachel was here, rolling her eyes.

If I told Sarah, 'My house is your house', she'd take me up on it – for real. Apart from the fact that her mum isn't here (they don't get on), there's a cook, and a stylist. And Mike. There's entertainment too: gym, swimming pool, tennis court and hot tub.

'Where's Homer?' Sarah asks when we get inside.

'Probably upstairs, hiding from The Stylist.'

'God, I love this house. Where is she?'

'Could be anywhere,' I say, depressed. I mean, why's the New Yorker still hanging around anyway?

Sarah's eyes open wide. 'D'you think she'd give us a makeover?'

'She kinda works for my dad.'

Sarah looks disappointed. But only for a moment. 'I know! Let's play on the Wii.' She gives me the wide-eyed look she does so well. 'The cow race one, that's so fun.'

After the Wii, she wants to check out the hot tub. I haven't been in it for so long. On my own, it'd feel kind of weird. And lonely. We sit submerged, heads and shoulders above water, looking up at the stars, steam rising all round us. Sarah's cheeks are rosy from the heat.

'So,' she says, sipping her Coke. 'Rachel and Mark Delaney.'

'The Macbeths!'

She sits up. 'Oh my God! That's a great name for them if she says yes.'

I squint. 'Yes to what?'

She puts down her drink. 'Mark asked Rachel out.'

'What? Oh my God! When?'

'Yesterday. Didn't she tell you?'

I feel my face fall.

Sarah looks guilty, like maybe she shouldn't have said anything. She sinks under the water a bit. 'He just asked her. She didn't say yes or anything.'

She told Sarah. But not me. I'm surprised how much that hurts.

'She doesn't even know if she likes him.'

And I'd so love to be hearing this from Rachel. For her to

}|{

be sitting here with us, telling us how she's feeling, and what she's going to do. I've so many questions. And she's not here. Which is totally my fault.

'Alex. Don't worry about it. She probably forgot to tell you.'

'Can we talk about something else?'

Costumes for Macbeth is not what I had in mind and shows how desperate Sarah is to come up with something fast. But I don't think it would matter what subject she picked: all I can think of is how it feels to be left out in the cold and how many times I must have done this to Rachel.

Sarah passes out at midnight. And snores. Not loud, like a man, but whistly and regular. It's like Chinese water torture. I make it through the night without suffocating her, but only just. In the morning, she asks if Mike could drop her home, then right in front of me rings her mum and tells her she won't need a lift after all.

'Can I borrow your hair straightener?' she asks, cheerily.

I think about all the ways you could use a GHD to murder someone.

She spends an hour in front of the mirror, updating me on the latest gossip on Perez. I know she's loving this. While she 'tries out' my lip gloss, my mind flashes back to Rachel. And my stomach tightens.

When Sarah's finally leaving for home, I go with her. Mike might be ancient, but he still needs protection. Walking to the car, I give a sudden spurt of speed and beat her to the front seat. I feel like Bobby, David's little brother. I also feel like laughing.

Mike's smiling when I get in. But he says nothing, just starts the engine.

'Wow, that hot tub's amazing,' comes from the back.

I look out the window.

'Ever tried it, Mike?'

His 'no' comes out as a cough.

I don't know anything about soccer apart from the fact that Mike's a Man United fan. I ask him how they're doing. He comes alive. His answer is a long, boring ramble with no pauses for breath or thought. But it gets us to Sarah's without further interruption – which was, of course, the point.

'Sorry about that,' I say when she's gone. 'I don't know what's got into her.'

He looks at me. 'That girl's trouble.'

'Actually, she's kind of harmless.'

He says nothing, but doesn't look convinced.

'Mike, can you drop me to Gran's?'

'Sure.'

Gran opens the door with a smile. Then loses it.

'Where's McFadden?' She stretches her neck out and checks the porch, as though I'm hiding him.

'David has a hockey match.'

'Oh, it's David now, is it?' she says, eyebrows raised, like I've just told her we've got engaged.

I shake my head and follow her in. She makes tea. Then it's the Spanish Inquisition. Is he a good hockey player? (Dunno.) What's he like at school? (OK, I guess.) Is he still annoying? (No answer.) And finally, 'How many times have you seen him this week?'

'Every day,' I say, to get her excited. Then, 'We're in school together, Gran.'

'Smarty Pants.'

}|{

But actually, apart from last night, we have met up practically every day after school too.

'Does he hold the door for you?' she asks, like it's a crucial question.

'Gran! Nobody holds doors any more.'

'But does he?'

I give in. 'OK. Actually, he does.' He's kind of caring like that.

'I knew it!' She's so happy with herself, she forgets to ask any more questions, and we're quiet for a while. My mind flashes back to Rachel. How many times in the last six months have I blocked her out? And she still stuck by me. Until now.

'You're not listening,' Gran says, crossly.

I look at her. 'I am.'

'Then what did I say?'

I draw a blank.

She folds her arms. 'I said, "That boy's a keeper."'

'Oh. Right.'

'You don't know what you've got there,' she says, crossly.

'I haven't got anything.' But when I see her face, I add, 'I do like him, OK Gran?' And that's typical of her – getting me to admit stuff like that.

She smiles. 'Here, give your old gran a hug. We might get through this yet.'

It's the first time she's admitted that there's something to get through.

* * *

David's coming off the hockey pitch, stick across his shoulders, hands draped over it. He's talking with two guys I don't know from his club. He sees me, and his face lights up, making me feel lucky. He leaves his mates and comes to me. He takes the gumshield from his mouth and kisses me. It's the hottest thing I've ever experienced, him all testosterone-y and victorious.

'Hey,' he says, smiling.

'Hey.'

He puts an arm around my shoulders and pulls me close. We start walking to the car. 'So. What's up?'

'Guess you heard about Mark and Rachel?'

He looks surprised. 'Why so glum?'

'I'm not. Just wish I wasn't the last to know.'

'Sorry. He swore me to secrecy.'

'Not you. Rachel. She never told me. I had to find out from Sarah.'

He looks at me. 'I don't get you two. You don't tell each other anything.'

We reach the car. He throws the stick in the back.

Then, I make a decision. I take a deep breath.

'It's not Rachel's fault. It's mine.' I tell him what happened between us. He listens in silence. Until I try to explain, 'I just don't do close.'

He looks at me. I mean, really looks at me. 'Then what are we doing?'

The question hangs in the air.

'We're not close? Is that what you're saying?' I look away, my heart pounding. 'Alex?'

My palms are sweaty. My mouth dry. I don't want to think about this.

'I feel close to you,' he says, so easily. 'Don't you feel close to me?'

}|{

I feel like I'm being backed into a corner, forced to admit something I don't want to admit, especially to myself. I can't do it. I just can't. I fumble for the handle. Then I'm out. It's cooler. More air. I'll be OK. But then I hear his door open. And I'm panicking again. I turn away, my back to the car. But he comes around and stands in front of me.

'Come on, Alex. If we can't be honest with each other, what's the point?'

'Stop, David. Please. I can't do this.' His face falls. 'I need to go home now,' I say and my voice sounds so flat.

There's a long silence.

He takes a deep breath and blows it out again. 'OK,' he says, finally, like he's giving up.

In the car, we don't talk, and when I get out, all I can say is, 'Bye.'

'Bye,' he says, like it's our last.

I rush inside and upstairs. I hear Homer bounding up behind me, probably thinking this is a game. In my room, I stop. Homer comes up to me but then he slows to a stop. His ears flatten and his head drops. He knows something's wrong.

'Why did he have to push me?' I ask him, wrapping my arms around myself. 'Why couldn't we just have stayed the way we were?'

Homer sits right up against my leg and pulls himself close with his paw. It's the way he hugs. I look into his honest brown eyes and see that the problem is not David's.

'What's wrong with me? What am I so afraid of? Getting close?' Homer snuffles his nose into my hand. And finally I admit the truth. 'I am close.' It wouldn't hurt like this if I wasn't. I'm close to David. And I'm close to Rachel. Which

}|{

means I could lose them at any moment. That is the scariest thought in the world. I sink to the floor with my back to the bed, throw my arms around Homer and cry into his fur. Because it's too late. There's no way out. Running now only hurts. If only I could just not care, or, better, hate, like I hate The Rockstar. I'd be safe then. Oh God. Is that what I'm doing, hating The Rockstar on purpose? No, that's crazy. I hate him for what he did. But I can't hate Rachel, and I can't hate David. Somewhere along the way, I've let them get under my skin and creep into my heart. I'm not protecting myself by pushing them away. I'm just losing them faster. Then a terrible thought hits: *maybe it's too late – maybe I've already lost them.*

I've only one option. I know what it is. But not if I'll be able to do it.

I look at the phone. Then walk in the opposite direction.

I go wash my face.

Come back.

Look at the phone again. It's gone nowhere.

I pick it up, put it down. Talk to myself out loud: 'Do it, Alex. Just do it.'

I dial the number and cancel. I dial it again and force myself to let it ring.

'Hey,' he says.

'I'm sorry, David. I was afraid.'

'No. I'm sorry. I shouldn't have pushed you.' His voice is warm and relieved and Davidy.

And this helps me say, 'I'm just afraid of losing . . .' But, even now, I can't say 'you'.

'I'll pick you up in five.'

I get to the door before he can ring the bell. Outside, we

hug. He's first to pull back. He looks into my eyes like what he's about to say is very important. 'You're not going to lose anyone, OK?'

I drop my head and mumble, 'I never thought I'd lose my mum.'

He takes my hand. 'Let's get out of here.'

This time, when he holds the car door open, I think of Gran, the Door Test, and what she said about him being a 'keeper'. We don't drive far, just up the road to a quiet spot where people stop to view the sea. David cuts the engine.

'Come here,' he says, gently.

'Where?'

He pats his lap.

Despite everything, I laugh. 'I won't fit.'

He slides his seat back. Raises his eyebrows.

Smiling, I climb over. I sit with my legs across his. He kisses my cheek. Then kisses it again. And again. I turn my mouth to his. His hands are in my hair and mine in his.

'I'm not going anywhere,' he whispers, over and over.

12
CALL ME STUPID

It's like he's asked me to jump from a plane without a parachute. And I've taken his hand and leapt. No more holding back. No more pulling away. I never thought it would be a relief to let go, to let myself feel what I want to feel.

But it is.

On Sunday, for the first time, we spend a whole day together. Last time I went around the zoo this slowly was when I was two years old and insisted on pushing my buggy myself – all the way round. Today, we keep stopping. To look at the animals, but mostly to look at each other, to smile, touch, kiss. I never really got why people snogged in public. I used to think it was corny, kind of show-offy. Now I understand. Sometimes you just can't keep your hands off a person. It's the middle of October. And cold. But for the first time in seven months, I feel warm. Like there's blood in my veins. Like I'm alive.

A small elderly couple walk toward us, linking arms.

'Oh my God,' I whisper, 'They're so cute. That's how I want to be when I'm old. Still going to the zoo. Still holding

}|{

hands –' I don't say, '– with you.' Because that would be like saying, 'Let's get married.' But I would like it to be him. I can't imagine it being anyone else. I try to picture what he'd be like. I think of Benjamin Button. Then I think, *stop thinking.* He pulls me closer and turns me round, and then we're kissing. And I'm thinking again. Why get old? Why not freeze this moment, right here and stay like this forever?

'Ooh, lovers,' a kid calls at us.

We look at him, then at each other and burst out laughing. It just seems like such an old-fashioned thing to say.

We spend ages at the sea lions. I have to drag David away. He reminds me of my dad (when he used to be my dad), who had a thing about the orang-utans. He'd have spent all day at their enclosure if we'd let him. They knew how to live, he said, how to play, how to just hang out, have fun, be a family. He could do with being locked in with the orang-utans for a few days now. But I'm not going to think about him. And ruin a perfect day.

David buys me a miniature pink kangaroo. I buy too many sweets. We take photos of practically every animal. And of each other.

When he drops me home, neither of us want it to be over, so we take Homer out to the beach. I fire a frisbee at David. Homer leaps to catch it, all four paws leaving the sand. But, as they say in *Chicken Run*, he doesn't have thrust, and can't reach. At the same time, David throws himself at it, his hoodie lifting to reveal a smooth, tight stomach. I want to climb in there and snuggle. He catches the frisbee, hits the sand and slides. He gives me a piggyback, trying to outrun Homer. We write our names in the sand, then, tired, fire a ball into the sea and sit on the sand in easy silence. I gather

}|{

a bunch of pebbles and let them fall through my fingers. I do it again, noticing the colours – not just grey but white, yellow, black, olive green and a browny purple colour I don't know the name of. I pick my favourites and set them out on the back of my hand.

He smiles. 'What're you doing?'

'Making a little universe.'

He roots in the sand. Then, he's placing a tiny white pebble, at the edge of my universe. I don't have to think, just take his planet and move it to the centre. We look at each other for a long time, then we're kissing. He takes me in his arms and holds me. Imagine how lame it would be to tell a person they make you warm. But he does. He makes me warm. He gives me energy too. I want to do things. I take his hand and drag him up.

'Want to race?'

'Want to get beaten?'

I take off without waiting for him.

He runs after me, catches me and wrestles me to the ground. There's sand everywhere. In my hair. On my eyelashes. In my mouth. But I'm laughing, shoving him over and climbing on top of him, pinning him down and kissing sand into his mouth.

I get home, walking an inch off the ground. I sail into the kitchen to tell Mum about this really great guy. But she's not there. Of course she's not. And I can't believe that all this time can pass and I can still forget that I'll never be able to tell her anything again. I stand in the empty kitchen, sadness spreading through me like a pool of water. I want her to be here for this. I want her to share what I've found. I want her, full stop.

* * *

}|{

Monday morning, Rachel gets on the DART. I want to hug her. Tell her everything. Say sorry. But the carriage is crammed with commuters and I don't want to be their entertainment. So I wait. Outside of 'Hey', neither of us speaks. She looks out the window. I answer a text from David. He sends another. I send one back. I realise I'm smiling and force myself not to. Finally, we reach our stop. On the platform, we get caught up in a stampede of commuters hurrying to get somewhere they probably don't even want to be. I wait till we're out of the station.

'Rache?' I say, stopping. People hurry past. She turns.

'Remember when you thought there was something going on between me and David McFadden?'

Her face comes alive.

'Well, there wasn't.'

It dies again.

'But now . . .' I raise my eyebrows because I know with Rachel that's all I have to do.

'Now what?' she asks, like she wants me to say it.

'Now . . . we're kind of together.'

She breaks into a smile. 'I knew it!' Then she's serious. 'Thanks for telling me.'

'Should have told you before now. I'm sorry, Rache. I just wasn't ready.'

She shakes her head, as if to say, doesn't matter. 'He's such a nice guy. A seriously nice guy. You deserve this.' But her eyes are teary.

And I'm worried that we're not OK after all. 'Rachel what's wrong? What is it?'

She shakes her head. 'I'm just happy for you.'

'Really? That's it?'

She nods. 'Call me stupid.'

'Stupid.'

We laugh.

Then I'm serious again. 'Rache? When I said I don't do close . . . That was me trying not to be close to you – in case anything happened you and I couldn't cope. But I am close to you, how could I not be? You've been the best friend, Rache.' Now I'm getting teary.

'Don't. Don't get upset.'

'I am so sorry, though.'

'Alex. You lost your mum. You're allowed act weird.'

I pretend to be annoyed. 'So I was acting weird, was I?'

She laughs. Then is suddenly serious. 'Mark Delaney asked me out.'

I look down. 'I know.'

'I'd have told you if I thought you'd wanted to know.'

I look up again. 'Weird thing is, I did want to know.' I smile at her. 'I've changed Rache. The old me is back.'

'Good.' She bumps me with a shoulder. Then she picks up her bag and walks over to the wall beside the path and throws it down again. She sits down. I join her. 'So,' she says. 'What d'you think of him? Honestly.' She's looking at me as if my opinion is crucial.

And I don't want to let her down. 'OK. I'm kind of changing. He used to bug me a bit . . .' I say this only because she knows, '. . . but now I'm starting to think he's funny. Seriously funny.' It's true. He's not half as annoying. But then, nothing seems to be any more.

She makes a face. 'The whole thing with the ADD, though. Scamming people.'

'Oh my God! If you went out with him, we could all go

)|(

out together!' I say, but then I wonder if I'd really want that. If I'm ready for it.

'Alex. I don't know if I even want to go out with him.'

I'd so like her to have what I have, though. 'You like him, though, don't you?'

'OK. He's kind of cute. But I don't know. I'm afraid he's just fooling around. He never takes anything seriously.'

'I could ask David?'

She looks panicked. 'No! Don't say anything. He could go back to Mark.'

'He wouldn't.'

'I know, but just don't say anything. Please. OK?'

'OK.' It'll be hard not to, though.

'So. What should I do?'

'Let me think.' I wave back to someone from school who's passing us. 'OK. Well, why not go out with him once and see how it goes?'

She makes a face. 'I don't know.'

'Or. You could play hard to get, just to see how serious he is. You know Mark. He'll give up if he's not.'

'It's an idea.'

'What're you talking about? It's a great idea.'

'OK, it's a great idea.' She smiles.

And it feels so good to be talking like this, joking like this, telling each other stuff again.

'Hey, guys!' We turn. It's Sarah, hurrying up to us, ahead of another bunch of commuters. 'Is this a private party or can anyone join in?'

Rachel and I pick up our bags, and we all fall into step together. Sarah launches into a moan about perverts on public transport. I look over at Rachel. She looks back at me. We share a smile. And that's all it takes for me to know. We're OK again.

When we get to class, I see David and can't believe how close I got to losing him.

'You go ahead,' I say to Rachel and Sarah.

I can feel their eyes on me as I walk right up to him.

'Hey,' I say, smiling.

'Hey, yourself.' He's smiling too.

I squint. 'Can you bend down for a sec?'

He stoops, putting his ear to my mouth, assuming I want to tell him something. But I don't want to tell him something. I want to show him. I take his face in my hands and turn his mouth to mine. In front of the entire class, I kiss him.

'That's how close I feel to you,' I whisper in his ear.

There's a whoop. 'Go, McFadden!' from Mark Delaney.

People start to call out.

'Get a room!'

'Save it for Biology.'

David's looking at me like there's no one else in the room. He puts his arms round me and kisses me back – a long, lingering, slow kiss that makes my toes curl.

'Oh, come on,' someone says.

I'm smiling all the way back to my desk. Where Sarah is waiting for me. On full gossip alert.

'Oh my God! You and David McFadden! Since, like, when? Just now?'

I look over at Rachel who's smiling at me and shaking her head like I'm mad.

And I am a bit. But who cares?

}I{

Tiptoes walks in. The class ignores her as the scandal spreads.

She claps her hands. 'OK! OK, people. We've work to do here.'

Like I said. Buzz Lightyear. Work, I mean, what a carrot.

Next class is *Macbeth* rehearsals. I sit on my table at the back of the hall, pretending to doodle but really watching Mark Delaney. I can't believe I didn't see it before. He keeps looking at Rachel. I mean, all the time. They're only quick glances, like he's just checking she's still there, but he's totally aware of her.

David sits next to me.

'He's totally into her,' I whisper.

'Has been for ages.'

I look at him, amazed.

'They'd be good together,' he says.

I look back at Mark and frown. 'What about the ADD thing?'

'What d'you mean?'

'What kind of person does that? It's scamming people.'

'Just his pushy parents.'

'What?'

'Mark's a bright guy. He just wants to go at his own pace. When he has to study, he will. He wants to do medicine. He knows he'll have to put in the work next year.'

'He wants to do medicine?' Mark, whose only ambition is finding the easy route? But then I think of the play. He worked so hard to get that part. 'Oh my God! He wanted Macbeth to get close to Rache, didn't he?'

David raises his eyebrows then mimes pulling a zip across his mouth.

}|{

'He tried so hard for it. For her. That's so romantic.'

I must look a bit overexcited, because he says, 'You better not tell her, though.'

'Do you know how hard that'll be?'

'Alex. I couldn't tell you he was going to ask her out. Of course I know.'

I hit him. 'That was so mean.'

He leans right into me. 'So,' he says, 'is she into him?'

I mime pulling a zip across my mouth.

He pulls a face. 'So mean,' he says, trying to sound like me. But sounding like a squirrel instead.

At break, David comes over to sit with the three of us. Mark's with him. Simon too. (I don't know whether Mark grabbed him for moral support or whether Simon just invited himself along.) But here we are. After what happened this morning, it feels right – and great – that David's beside me. Mark acts like Rachel's not there. She looks everywhere but at him. Sarah's eyes flit from me to David, and from Mark to Rachel. I've never seen her so animated.

'Brave move, this morning,' Simon says to me.

'Not sure I'd have done it,' Mark says.

'I don't know,' Sarah says to him. 'Sometimes it's better to get things out in the open.' She eyes him meaningfully.

He coughs like he's just choked on something.

But already she's moved on, leaning across the table to David and me. 'So, when did you two lovebirds get together?'

I know that if I don't answer she'll never let up. 'At your party,' I say, hoping that's the end of it.

She sits back suddenly. 'That was three weeks ago.' She turns to Rachel. 'Did you know about this?'

Rachel glances at me, then back at Sarah. 'Not till this morning.'

Sarah looks at me. 'We're your friends.'

Mark and David exchange an uncomfortable glance. And I know they want to be somewhere else.

'Sarah, let's talk about this another time,' Rachel tries.

'If it wasn't for me, they wouldn't even have got together.' Her eyes appeal to everyone at the table.

'I gotta go,' Mark says, grabbing his tray and standing.

'Me too,' says David. He winks at me. 'See you later.'

Simon just stands.

Then they're gone.

I turn to Sarah. 'Look, I'm sorry for not saying anything but I wasn't sure where it was going myself.'

'You looked pretty sure in class.'

Oh God. 'That was a spur-of-the-moment thing. A vote of confidence in David. Or something. If I'd known it was going to happen, I'd have told you. I swear.'

She looks at Rachel, then back at me. 'You don't trust us to keep a secret. That's it, isn't it?'

'No.'

Then she looks really shocked, like something's just struck her. 'So that time in the Jitter Mug when I was trying to set you two up, you were already going out with each other?'

'Not going out. More like seeing.'

'Like there's a difference?'

'Sarah. I didn't want this, OK? I guess I just couldn't help it.' She looks at me like she just doesn't get it. 'I'm new to this, OK? I don't know what I'm doing half the time. It's complicated.'

'You're going out with a guy. How complicated can it be?'

I feel like laughing. If only she knew. 'Sarah, I'm sorry, OK? There's never been any great plan. I've just been blundering along.'

'It just that we're friends. We're supposed to tell each other everything.'

'I get that, and I'm sorry. It won't happen again. I swear.'

'People forget their friends when they start going out with someone. It happens all the time.' And suddenly it's like she's this kid that needs comforting.

'I won't forget my friends. I promise.'

She looks at me as if she wants to believe me.

'So, are we OK?' I ask.

'Yeah, we're OK.' She smiles. And that's what I love about her: the way she can just bounce back like that, put stuff behind her, in, like, a second. 'So,' she says, leaning towards me again, 'are you totally mad about him?'

I smile. 'A bit.'

'You can't be a bit mad. You either are or you aren't.'

I look at Rachel. 'OK, then I am.' Even the thought of him makes my heart flip.

'I don't blame you,' she says. 'He is seriously caliente.' She sighs. 'You're so lucky.'

And that's when I realise: things have changed. I am lucky.

13
POPPADOMS

On Friday, Rachel wants us to stay over. I know it's to make up for not coming to mine that time. She says nothing, though. Neither do I. I just go. We watch *Mean Girls*. Give each other manicures. And talk.

'So, what've you done about the costumes for *Macbeth*?' Rachel asks me, then goes back to blowing on her nails.

I look up from watching Sarah work on mine. 'Plenty of time.'

'Not really, when you think of all the costumes there are.'

'There are costume shops aren't there? *Macbeth*'s, like, a standard play. I'll just go in and order a load of *Macbeth* gear.'

'How about you, Sarah? How's sound going?' Rachel asks.

That's when I realise how quiet Sarah's been. She hasn't said anything in ages.

'Crap,' she says now. Which is so not like her. Sarah's always up.

'What's wrong with it?' Rachel asks, surprised.

'Everything. I wish I hadn't picked it.'

'Why did you?' I ask.

She shrugs.

I look at her, not believing that something like sound is getting her so down.

'Are you OK?' I ask.

She looks at us for a long moment, like she's trying to decide something. Then she takes a deep breath.

'Look, this isn't, like, a big deal or anything. It's not even worth talking about. But you should probably just know. Because you're my friends and that. It's not, like, a disaster or anything.' All I can think is, *what is it*? 'My parents are splitting up.'

'Oh God,' Rachel says. 'Sarah!' She goes straight to her and wraps her in a hug.

Sarah pulls back. 'It's no biggie. People split up all the time.'

'But these are your parents,' Rachel says.

'It's their problem, right?'

'I can't believe you're so cool about it,' Rachel says. 'Aren't you upset?'

'The only thing I'm upset about is that it's my dad moving out, not my mum.' When she sees Rachel's face she adds, 'It's OK. It was a joke.'

The thing is, I know exactly how Sarah feels. At least she had the courage to say it. I've never told anyone that sometimes I wish it was my dad who died.

'I didn't know your parents were having problems,' Rachel says.

'Neither did I.' Sarah laughs.

I hear the pain in that laugh and think, *maybe enough questions*.

But Rachel doesn't know what it's like to lose someone. 'What happened?' she asks.

Sarah looks away when she says, 'Mum found out he was having an affair and made him choose. Us or her. He chose her.'

'Oh, Sarah,' Rachel says again. Rachel would die if anything happened with her parents.

Sarah clears her throat and turns back, chin high. Determined. 'But it's their problem, right?'

'Right,' we both say, with maybe a little too much conviction.

And then, so Sarah can breathe again, I move the conversation back to *Macbeth*. For the rest of the night though, she says very little. Every so often, I glance at her to see how she's doing. She seems miles away. Lost in her thoughts. Around midnight, the house starts to get cold. Rachel and I insist that Sarah take the bed. We slip into sleeping bags on the floor. And maybe it's the comfort of the bed or maybe she just doesn't want to be awake, but soon Sarah's breathing changes and she's no longer with us.

'Sarah?' I whisper.

Nothing.

My tummy rumbles loudly. And we laugh.

'You hungry?' Rachel asks.

'Starving.' Which is a totally new experience.

Still in our sleeping bags, we shuffle out of the room. On the landing, Rachel develops a kind of penguin walk, stuffing one foot into each corner of her sleeping bag, then stepping forward, one corner at a time. It'd be a good technique for sack races, I think, adopting it. At the top of the stairs, we face a new challenge. Rachel tackles it headon, sitting on the top step and slinking down on her bum.

I follow.

'Race you to the kitchen,' she says when we reach the bottom.

We try not to laugh or fall over. But we do both. In reverse order. In the kitchen, we microwave poppadoms and make hot chocolate. Then we remember Sarah.

'I can't believe her dad did that,' Rachel says. 'I always thought he was really nice.'

'You thought mine was nice too.'

She grimaces. 'Am I totally stupid about men?'

'Totally,' I smile. 'Which reminds me. How're rehearsals going with Mark Delaney?' I raise and lower my eyebrows.

She breaks into a smile.

'That good?'

She shakes her head. 'He's just funny . . .'

'What?'

'Nothing.'

'Come on, you're leaving something out.'

She rolls her eyes at him. 'He keeps calling me his Lady Macbeth.' She's smiling again. 'He says I'm a bad influence.' She waves her hand dismissively. 'Total flirt.'

Not so fast, Rachel Dunne. 'You like him. Don't you?'

'I like the flirting. Does that mean I like him?' She makes a non-committal face.

'I asked David about the ADD thing.'

Her eyes widen.

'Don't worry, I didn't say anything.' I tell her about Mark wanting to do medicine.

Her whole face lights up. 'Really?'

I imagine the two of them, operating side by side on some

}|{

patient with major heart problems, frowns of concentration above their surgical masks.

'OK,' I say. 'Here's what I think. Scrap Plan A. Go straight to Plan B. One date. See how it goes.'

She makes a face. 'I kind of like Plan A, though. He tries harder. And he's funny when he tries.'

'He'll still try if you go out with him.'

She looks doubtful.

I shrug. 'OK. Stick to Plan A. You know what you're doing.'

'No, I don't.'

'That makes two of us.'

We laugh, and, for at least another hour, we sit chatting at the counter, swinging our legs inside the sleeping bags. Two mermaids having a snack. At 1.00 a.m., we go back up. Rachel falls asleep first. I lie on my back, looking up through her Velux window at the stars. I feel different. Relieved to be able to admit that I care for Rachel and she cares for me (but not in a gay way), and that I'm mad about David and he likes me. I don't feel alone any more. Or freaky. And nothing bad has happened. The world hasn't fallen apart. Yet. I look up at Sarah and hope she'll be OK. In the morning, we bring breakfast upstairs and lounge around in our pyjamas.

'I was thinking,' Sarah says, wrinkling her nose. 'I don't know about Mark.'

Suddenly, she has Rachel's full attention.

'I think you could do better,' Sarah adds.

'I haven't said yes.'

'Yeah, well, I wouldn't. If I were you.'

'Why not?'

'He's just a messer. You can't trust a word he says.'

Rachel looks at me. And suddenly I have to defend him.

'He took the Macbeth part to be near you, Rachel. He learned all those lines for you. He's mad about you. He's been mad about you for ages.'

Her face lights up. 'Really?'

'You're not supposed to know, OK? Or I'm dead.'

She's beaming. 'David really told you that?'

'He really told me that.'

'Wow.' Rachel looks like I've given her a present.

'He's not a messer. Not when he knows what he wants.'

'I'd still be careful,' Sarah says, defiantly, giving me a 'you're-not-always-right' look. And I wonder if this has anything to do with her father leaving. If maybe she thinks all guys are creeps now.

When I get home, I throw my bag down and go looking for Homer, wondering why he hasn't come to meet me. I find him in the kitchen. And instead of coming to say hi, he takes off in the opposite direction, head down, tail between his legs. I follow, curious. That's when I see that he has some-thing in his mouth.

'What is it? What've you got?'

He lies down, big brown eyes looking up at me, like one of those martyred saints in pictures.

I put out my hand. 'Give.'

He drops an oversized pair of shades.

'Homer!'

On the black Prada sunglasses that The Stylist loves so much there are thick tracks where his teeth have scudded across the lenses, leaving ridges in places.

}|{

'Oh my God!' I frown at him. 'Bold dog.'

Maybe they're not so bad when they're on, I think. I hold them out in front of me and look through them, hoping the scratches won't interfere with my vision.

They're wrecked.

Normally, Homer's not a chewer. He's never gone for the furniture. Or carpets. Or curtains. The odd sock, maybe. Nothing serious. I don't know what's got into him. Doesn't he like her either? Then I remind myself – he's a dog.

I take a deep breath.

Better tell her.

She's not in any of the main rooms. Not my father's office. Nor the sitting room. No answer from the bedroom she's staying in. I'm about to give up when, from the third-floor landing, I see her outside, sitting on a low, cobbled wall in the garden, facing out to sea. I've never seen her so still. I've never seen her still, full stop. Better get it over with. Downstairs and out into the garden I go, Prada in hand, trying to work out how to tell her it's mangled Prada. I come up behind her.

'Marsha?' I say tentatively.

Her hands go immediately to her face. Then she turns and smiles. The tip of her nose is red, her eyes puffy.

'Oh, God. I'm sorry,' I say, backing away. 'I didn't mean to –' It doesn't seem right for her to cry. She's always so, I dunno, sunny.

She smiles. 'Meet the new divorcee.' She lifts a padded yellow envelope from the wall. 'Just got the papers. It's official.'

I'm totally stunned. I didn't even know she was married. 'Oh God. I'm so sorry.' Or is that not what you say?

'Nothing to be sorry about. He was just the love of my

life.' She laughs. And wells up. Before I know what I'm doing, I'm putting my arms around her. I. Am. Hugging. The Stylist.

'Here's a hint,' she says, when she pulls back. 'When you love a guy, don't spend your time on the other side of the world to him.'

I nod. 'OK.'

'You grow apart,' she says, blowing her nose. 'I didn't think we could. But we did.'

A week ago, I'd have thought, *your fault for letting him into your life*. Now I really feel for her.

'Maybe it's not too late,' I say.

She waves the envelope. 'He's found someone else – who has no interest in fashion, who never travels beyond the supermarket, who spends her time making him happy.'

'She sounds boring.'

'He wants boring.'

We're silent for a while. And if it wasn't for David, I might think all men were creeps too. Then I remember the shades. And feel guilty. Homer is my dog. 'Is there anything I can do?' I ask. But the minute I say it, I feel dumb. What can I do?

She smiles. 'Your dad's been great, letting me hide out here.'

OK, so now I get it.

She takes a compact from her bag and checks out her face. She closes her eyes and shakes her head.

'Complete mess.'

'No, you're not!' I lie. 'You're lovely.'

She looks at me. 'Actually, Alex. There is something you could do. You could get my shades? I think I left them in the kitchen.'

}|{

I bite my lip. The one thing. The one thing. I take my hand from behind my back. Make a face. 'That's what I came to tell you . . .'

When she bursts out laughing and says, 'Good old Homer,' I can't help thinking, *maybe she's not so bad.*

After lunch, I go see Gran. Without David. Because there's something I want her to know.

'We're going out, Gran,' I announce, when she asks after her 'favourite American'. I can't stop smiling. I want to tell everyone.

'Oh, I've known that for a long time, love,' she says.

'Really?'

'But it's good to hear you admit it.' She smiles. 'So I can give you a hug.'

She hugs me and I'm smiling again.

'We have to celebrate,' she says, suddenly. 'Let me bring you both to lunch.'

The good thing about that is that Gran will have to leave the house, something she doesn't do much any more. The bad thing is the questions.

'On one condition,' I say. 'Go easy on the questions. Last time he was here, it was like the Gestapo.'

She smiles. 'Alright. I'll go easy.'

When Mike drops me home, I change into my togs and wet-suit. I did remind David it was almost winter. Then he reminded me that people swim in the Irish Sea all year round. And a lot of them are over seventy.

He picks me up, looking like a beach bum, reminding me of the sailing course and the chemistry that was between us even then. And when he kisses me, I remember our first kiss.

I feel like a hippy, driving along in a clapped-out VW Beetle with two bodyboards thrown in the back. The one thing David can't do is sing. But he sings anyway. Totally out of tune and with no clue of the lyrics. Laughing at him only encourages him. He drives and sings with one hand on the steering wheel, the other resting on my leg, like it's the most natural place in the world for it to be. And it is.

I tell him about Sarah's parents.

'Bummer,' he says.

'She acts like it's no big deal. But it has to be, right?' He's been through it.

He looks at me. 'He hasn't just walked out on her mom, he's walked out on her. At least, that's how she'll feel.'

Like I feel, then. 'I don't suppose there's anything I can do?'

'Listen. If she talks.'

'She won't.' Because in that way Sarah's like me.

We get to the beach and carry the boards to the sea. I test the water with one toe. And tell him I'm not going in. When he comes towards me, I know what he's planning. And I run. But he catches me, lifts me up and carries me back to the water's edge. Then he wades in, and, when he's waist-deep, despite my screams, he drops me.

It's freezing.

I scream. Call him an asshole. And worse. I scramble up quickly, planning a quick exit.

He blocks me. 'You're wet now. So stay in.'

'No way.'

'Yes way.' He grabs me again, and I think he's going to fling me back when he lifts me up instead and kisses me. I forget the cold. I forget the sea and melt into him, wrapping my legs around him. He sinks down so I'm fully immersed. And I don't care.

'Come on,' he says finally, 'Let's get the boards.'

We catch the waves, paddle like mad and glide to shore. Then we're running out again and boarding in. It's amazing. I've never felt so alive. So happy. And then suddenly it's clear. I'm here on Killiney Beach, one of Mum's favourite places, and I can laugh. And it's OK. It doesn't mean I've forgotten her. Or love her any less. It is possible to be happy and not forget. To not feel guilty. I look at David and remember what he said. She'd want me to be happy. It makes so much sense now. She wanted me to be happy when she was alive. Why would it be any different now?

When I get home, I want to burst into The Rockstar's office and tell him. I want him to know that he may have abandoned me but I've someone else. Someone who has brought me back to life. Despite him. But I don't burst in. I don't tell him. Because he doesn't deserve to know.

Next day, Gran brings us to lunch in a seafood restaurant in Dun Laoghaire. It's big and bright and the waitress is friendly.

'You're looking well,' Gran tells me.

And I know she's not lying. Last night, in the mirror, I hardly recognised myself. Must be the sea air.

'You're happy,' she says to me, then looks meaningfully at David.

I don't argue. I am happy.

'So,' Gran says to him. 'What was she like? In the beginning. Was she impossible?'

I'm appalled.

He looks at me and smiles. 'Impossible.'

I hit him.

She laughs.

He's looking at Gran again. 'Gave me a seriously hard time.'

'Excuse me. Hel-lo? I'm, like, here.'

Gran laughs again. She's loving this. She looks at me proudly, like she's glad I was tough.

'And how did you get together, in the end?' she asks him, knowing she won't get the answer from me.

He looks at me. 'I guess I eventually wore her down.'

I'm relieved he didn't bring up the party. Or Louis. But then I know he wouldn't.

'She's worth it, though, isn't she?' Gran asks.

Then he's looking at me again. 'Seriously worth it.'

And suddenly it's like no one else is in the room.

14
THE GREAT SEDUCTRESS

Monday morning, David and I walk into class.

'Here comes the bride,' sings Orla Tempany.

I force myself to keep walking, to not react. But I'm thinking, *Oh my God.*

'Daa, dum, de dum,' sings Simon Kelleher. As imaginative as ever.

David squeezes my hand. We smile like we don't care, like it's all hilarious. Then I have to leave him and make what seems like an expedition down and across the class. I ignore all the eyes, all the comments, all the grins. I sit down and look across at David. He turns and smiles.

It'll blow over, I think.

Then Amy Gilmore twists around in her seat. 'So, why the big secret?'

'What?'

'I asked you straight out about David. You acted like you didn't know what I was talking about. You might as well have lied, Alex.' She turns back around as if I'm some sort of criminal.

}|{

For the rest of the morning, I keep my head down. At break, David waits for me. We go to the canteen with Rachel, Sarah and Mark.

'That kiss was definitely a bad idea,' Mark says.

'Can we talk about something else, please?' I say.

But Sarah's looking at Mark. 'So don't you make the same mistake.'

He squints. 'What?'

'Come on, Mark. Don't act dumb. News is, you and Rachel are next.'

'What?' he says again. He's gone totally white.

Suddenly, Rachel's standing, looking at Sarah. 'Hasn't anyone ever told you not to believe the news?' She grabs her tray and walks.

Mark looks like he's been slapped.

I stare at Sarah as if to say, what the hell did you do that for? Then I go after Rachel.

I find her marching around the hockey pitches. I have to run to catch up.

'You OK?' I ask.

She slows to a stop, then turns to me, looking totally frustrated. 'Why did she say that?'

I make a face. 'You know Sarah. Can't keep anything in.'

'I know, but now I've gone and insulted him.'

'No you haven't.'

'I practically said no to him in public.'

'Rachel, all you said was not to believe the news.'

'Which means, more or less, "no." And now he knows I told you guys. He probably thinks I've been gloating.' She puts a hand to her forehead. 'Oh God! Just when I was going to say yes.'

}|{

I brighten right up at that. 'You were?'

'It didn't seem fair to hold off, after what you told me about *Macbeth* and everything.'

'That's great, Rache.'

'If I thought he'd ever talk to me again.'

'Of course he will.'

She looks at me hopefully. 'D'you think he'll get that I was just embarrassed?'

'Sure,' I say. Though, from my limited experience, guys don't 'get' a lot of stuff.

'Oh God,' she groans. 'Now I have to go in and rehearse with him.'

I'm surprised. I really didn't think Rachel said that much. But Mark has totally backed off. At rehearsals, apart from when they've lines together, you'd think he didn't know she existed. If it's any comfort to Rachel, and I know it's not, he does look pretty miserable. Rachel looks like she wants to be somewhere else. As for Sarah? The only thing she looks sorry for is having to stay back to work on 'acoustics'.

'Did you see him?' Rachel whispers, as soon as we hook up. 'Totally cold.'

We watch him leave – one of the first out the door. David, with him, looks back to see if I'm coming. I wave him on.

'Go on,' Rachel says.

'No, sure I'll see him later.'

'Go on. I'm fine.'

I widen my eyes at her. 'Rachel. I'm not going.'

She half smiles. 'Thanks.'

We walk to our lockers. Rachel looks miserable.

'D'you think he's gone off me?'

'No.'

'Then what was all that about?'

'I don't know. Maybe he's just recovering his pride?'

'You think?'

'Sure.' I'm not, though.

'What'll I do?'

'Rachel, don't worry. He'll probably be fine tomorrow.'

'No. He won't.' We get our bags from our lockers and head out. Outside, wind blows rain into our faces, so we reverse back under the shelter. I get my cap from my bag and pull it down. We brace ourselves and walk out. 'Oh, God. Why didn't I just say yes when he asked me out? How am I going to face him tomorrow?'

'Just be yourself,' I guess.

'What about lunch?'

I think about that. She's right. The canteen might be tricky. 'We won't sit with them. I'll talk to David.'

'But what about you two?'

'Rachel, we see plenty of each other. Seriously, don't worry about it.'

'I'm sorry, Alex.' She sounds so down.

'It's Sarah who should be sorry. I know she has her problems. But still.'

It's David's turn to mind Bobby, so we just hang out in his room. It's like our refuge, the one place we can go without anyone bothering us. We lie, facing each other, talking. I gaze into his eyes and wonder if it's normal to want to climb inside a person and live under their skin. I've never loved anyone's ears before. Or anyone's eyelashes. They're not things I normally notice unless there's something wrong with them. David's ears are perfect, tucked neatly into his head. His eyelashes are long, dark and curled. Which is, like, amazing, given he's so blonde. I run a finger along them.

He laughs. 'What are you doing?'

'Just checking they're real.'

He rolls on top of me. 'Everything about me's real.'

And I don't know if it's chemistry or biology or physics, but when two people who're mad about each other lie down together, it's impossible not to kiss, impossible not to touch. Mouth on mouth, skin on skin, mouth on skin, it gets faster and faster, hotter and hotter. It takes on its own speed, and if you don't step in, it will leave you behind, like a boat heading for the rapids. And that's a problem.

I roll him over so I'm on top. I sit on his stomach. Pin his arms down. Like I'm messing. Playing.

But he gets it. 'You OK?'

I bite my lips together. Nod. My heart is pumping. I look at him. Guilty. 'I'm not ready.'

He looks at me for a long time. Then smiles. 'Who says I am?'

I know he's just saying that but am so grateful.

He lifts me off him. 'Let's go get a drink.'

'Sorry.'

'Come on.' He springs from the bed, then takes my hand and drags me up.

In the kitchen, he goes to the fridge. I watch his back and imagine the body under the T-shirt. I tell myself to stop.

'Is Mark OK?' I ask.

He turns from the fridge, serious. 'Do we really want to do this?'

'What?'

'I tell you about Mark, you go back to Rachel. Pretty soon, information's going round in circles.'

'I just want to know if he's OK. He seemed a bit upset.'

He pours two glasses of juice. Then hands me one. 'He just took it as a no. Which I guess it was.'

'No! It wasn't!' I rush, putting down the juice. 'She was just embarrassed that Sarah brought it up in front of everyone.'

'Right,' he says, like that's the end of it.

'So, what now?' I ask.

He looks at me. 'I guess that's up to Rachel.'

'What d'you mean?'

'Well, if she's interested, she should try telling him.'

It sounds so simple. I feel stupid for not thinking of it. 'You're right!'

He shakes his head. And laughs. 'Come here.' He takes me in his arms and kisses me. I kiss him right back. The genius.

Mike drops me home. I don't know if he's told The Rockstar that I'm seeing someone (assuming he's worked it out himself). If he has, nothing's been said. I walk past his office. It's 9.00 p.m. The door's slightly open and the light's on. And there he is, as unimaginative as porridge, working.

I go up to my room and call Rachel. I tell her what David said.

'So just say yes,' I sum up.

'Just go up to him and say yes?'

'Yes.'

'Oh God.'

'I don't think you've a choice here, Rache.'

There's a pause. 'OK. When'll I do it?'
Yay! 'The sooner the better . . . Tomorrow.'
'God.'
'Maybe after school, if you can get him alone.'
There's a longer pause now. 'Can you distract Sarah?'
'Leave it to me.'

I hang up, hungry again. It feels like I haven't eaten in months. Which, actually, is pretty much the case. I go downstairs and ask Barbara for a smoothie. To cheer her up, I make it complicated. Strawberry and banana with kiwis and grapes. Hopefully, it'll taste OK. She breaks into this really amazing smile I never knew she was capable of. And because she seems happy and because I've nothing else to do, I sit at the counter and watch her work. She does everything with such care, like she takes pride in her work. I think about the only work I'm supposed to be doing right now – *Macbeth* costumes. And feel guilty. Rehearsals are flying ahead. And I haven't done anything. Any day now I'll be asked for my thoughts. I don't even have thoughts! I should, at least, do a Google search. I force myself upstairs for my laptop and carry it back to the kitchen, feeling a little better for taking some action. I slide it onto the counter just as Barbara delivers the smoothie in a tall, elegant glass she's been hiding somewhere for just this sort of thing. I take a sip.

Oh my God. 'Yum!'

Her expression goes all soft. And I think she might be starting to like me. I google 'Macbeth' and 'costumes'. Up pop the sites. Mostly drama companies showing off costumes they produced rather than actual online shops. At least they give me some idea of what people wore back then.

'Oooh, I think I'll have one of those,' says a voice behind me. It's The Stylist. She seems so different now. Not this annoying, sunny person, but someone who's sunny despite everything or at least is trying to be. And it seems mean to go on calling her The Stylist.

'What's up?' she asks, taking a peek at the computer.

'I have to do the costumes for the school play.'

'Hey! That should be fun.'

I imagine Lady Macbeth in tight leather trousers and wonder if I'm making a mistake when I say, 'You can help – if you like.'

'Really?' She says it like I'm doing her the favour.

She starts to examine the images of Lady Macbeth posted by some theatre company.

'What were you thinking?' she asks.

'I wasn't really. Just starting.'

'OK.' She moves her stool closer. 'Let's think about Lady Macbeth. Who is she? What does she want? What drives her?'

Since Mum got sick, my concentration hasn't exactly been the best. But I got this much: 'She wants the throne for her husband, Macbeth.'

'Ah, but to get it, he has to kill his beloved cousin, right?'

She knows *Macbeth*?

'So what kind of person is she?'

'Ruthless?' I try, starting to get into it.

'Exactly. A power-hungry, ruthless bitch.'

I laugh. It's like she's talking about a real person. Her ex's girlfriend?

'So,' she says, 'how does Lady M. persuade her husband to become a murderer?'

I'm trying to remember.

Marsha doesn't wait. 'She uses her womanly ways. She comes on to him.'

Doesn't sound familiar. 'I don't think that's in the play.'

'Maybe not in words. But it's there. It's meant. You got a copy of the play?'

'Somewhere.'

'Well, what're we waiting for?' And you've got to admire her, the way she can just zone all her energy in on this and forget the other Big Thing.

I find my copy of the play at the bottom of my bag. It's a bit ragged, but pretty much intact. Marsha flicks through the pages and skims the lines with a finger.

'Here we go. Act 1, Scene 5. First time they're together. She's all over him, telling him how great he is.' She reads the lines. 'Can't you see her?' she says, 'totally coming on to him?'

When she reads it like that, I can.

'It all ties in,' she says. 'Here look, later, when he's backing out, she tells him he's not a man. She builds him up. Knocks him down. Complete cow.'

I get it. Absolutely. But what about Rachel having to come on to Mark Delaney? 'Doesn't the director decide that kind of stuff?'

'Well, yeah, technically.' She looks at me. 'Who's playing Lady Macbeth?'

'My friend, Rachel.'

'Well, then. All we do is dress her like a tramp –' I almost choke here ' – and have her seduce him. Trust me, the director will love it.'

But I'm not thinking about the director. I'm thinking

about Mark. I try to bring Marsha back to reality. 'So, clothes-wise, what did you have in mind?'

'OK,' she says, like she's already got it sorted. 'I was thinking, something corseted. Low cut. Low belt, like that one there.' She points to the screen. 'You know, coming down in a V over her crotch.'

I burst out laughing.

'And wide sleeves.'

I don't think anyone will notice the sleeves.

She starts sketching like she's on fast forward. In minutes, she has three different costumes. 'Wow. This feels great,' she says. 'I haven't designed in such a long time.'

'You're an actual designer?'

'What did you think I was?' she asks, curiously.

I go a bit red at this.

'Design is my background. It's what I do. Or at least it was before I got sucked into this whole stylist business.'

'You sound like you don't like it.'

'It's OK.' She starts to sketch again. 'Like a lot of things, the problem is the people. When celebrities get their hands on you, they suck you dry. They want you all to themselves and they want all of you. All the time. Not your dad,' she rushes, 'but the others, they think they own you.' Then she looks up like she's decided something. 'Tell you what, I'll help make Rachel's costumes if you help me source the fabrics and accessories. If you want, I'll even help put together the other costumes.'

'Really? Have you got time?'

'Honey, I've nothing but time.'

'The school's budget. I don't think it's huge.'

'Trust me, Alex, they're doing me a favour here. If they

cover the costs, I'm happy.

'OK. Great.' But I'm starting to worry about Rachel again. What if she doesn't want to play a 'tramp'?

'We should have Rachel over for a fitting, soon as we can,' she says.

One way to find out what she wants or doesn't want.

I lie in bed, thinking of David. Thinking of his eyes, his body. When I'm with him in his room, I want to do it. It's so hard not to. But I'm not like Sarah. Sex was never on my list of things to do. You have sex, you change. Grow up. Move away from your parents. And I don't know why that feels so important now, given that they're both gone. But it does. My mum would want me to wait. I know that. And it seems so important. But wait for how long? And why exactly, if it feels so right? There are so many things I want to ask her, so many things I need to know. But if she was still alive and life was still normal, would I ask? This is between David and me. Yeah, so why haven't we spoken about it?

Maybe you don't.

Maybe you just let it happen.

Or keep stopping it.

Maybe I'm ready. I just don't know it.

Oh, God. I wish I knew.

At lunch next day, Rachel and I walk by David's table. Sarah follows. As soon as we set our trays down at the far side of the canteen, she asks, 'What's going on? Why aren't we sitting with David and Mark?'

There goes my theory about her going off guys. 'You can, if you like,' I say.

'What happened? Did you two have a fight?'

Suddenly I'm so mad. 'Sarah, if we'd had a fight I wouldn't be telling everyone about it.'

'So you did have a fight?'

'No. We didn't have a fight. If you must know, you embarrassed everyone yesterday. All your talk of relationships has put people under pressure.'

She laughs. 'God, you're so touchy. I was just clearing the air. People should be honest about stuff. Guys should be honest.' She sighs, looking over at the others. 'It's no fun without them.'

I shake my head. Has she any idea what she's done? 'Off you go then.'

'I might just do that,' she says, looking at me like I've challenged her. She gets up, takes her tray and goes over.

When she gets there, David turns around to look at me, a question on his face.

I shrug.

To cheer her up, I tell Rachel about Marsha's offer.

'Really? I'd love that.'

After lunch, as I'm leaving the canteen, David comes up to me.

'Hey!' I say.

He's not smiling. 'Can I talk to you for a sec?'

There's something up. 'Sure.'

We find a windowsill to lean against, in a quiet part of the corridor.

'Sarah just announced why Mark tried out for *Macbeth*.'

I close my eyes. 'Oh no.'

'I can't believe you told her. Now everyone knows. Mark feels like a total loser.'

}|{

'I didn't tell her. Or at least, I didn't mean to. Sarah was talking Mark down to Rachel. I just wanted Rachel to know how far he'd gone for her.'

'Maybe you should've waited till Sarah wasn't there.'

'I'm sorry. I didn't think.'

He takes a deep breath. 'Don't worry about it.'

'She likes him, David. I mean, really likes him. She was going to talk to him today after school.'

'I'd rethink that. He's about to kill someone. Probably me.'

I grimace. 'I'm sorry.'

'Forget it. Come on, we'd better get back.'

We start to walk slowly in the direction of the classroom. Suddenly, I don't want this to be the end for them.

'D'you think you should tell him she likes him?'

'No.'

'Why not?'

'Because this is getting like Chinese Whispers.'

'But he should know, though, shouldn't he?'

No answer.

'If you do tell him, will you let me know what he says?'

He laughs. 'Alex. Stop. Seriously. This has to end somewhere. If I talk to him, and I'm not saying I will, then after that, it's between him and Rachel. We butt out. Completely.'

And even though I want them to have what we have, so badly, I also know he's right.

Rachel stands before Marsha, no clue what she has planned for her. She still looks depressed.

Tape in hand and moving like lightning, Marsha measures her up.

}I{

'You are a total babe,' she gushes. And though it's over the top, it's just what Rachel needs to hear. 'Now! Here's what I was thinking.' She wedges the tape into a back pocket and reaches for her sketches. She reveals them like she's unveiling a plaque. 'Lady Macbeth, the great seductress.'

Rachel looks at me.

I shrug.

She looks back at Marsha.

Who explains her theory.

Rachel's face lights up. 'I totally get that. It would so bring Lady Macbeth's character to life.' She looks at Marsha like she's seeing her for the first time. 'You're a genius.'

'Let's start by working with what we have.' Marsha starts to experiment with Rachel's hair, lifting it all up, then letting it fall. She lifts a section and pulls the rest forward. Every few seconds she tilts her head to the side, examining the look. She's so into it, so alive, you'd never think that her husband just divorced her. Or that she's even old enough to be married in the first place. She almost looks like one of us.

When they finish up, they hug goodbye. Seriously.

'Oh my God, Alex. She's so sweet,' Rachel says in the car when Mike's dropping her back. 'The way you were going on about her . . .'

I grimace. 'I think I might have got that kind of wrong.'

'I can't believe she's giving up all her time to do this –'

'She likes it.'

'She must like you too, or she wouldn't bother.'

'She's just distracting herself.'

'It's more than that. She likes you.'

And I must be desperate, because this makes me feel good.

* * *

I can't wait till tomorrow to see David so, after dinner, I ask him over. It's not like The Rockstar will notice.

But, just my luck, he's coming out of his office as we're walking down the hall.

'Oh, hello,' he says, then looks at me for an intro.

'This is David, a friend from school. We've a project.'

He sticks out his hand. 'How're you doing?' he says, making his accent more Dublin, like he's some regular guy or something. He does it all the time.

David shakes his hand.

'So, what's the project on?' Like he's interested.

'Stuff,' I say. 'Look. We gotta go.'

He looks relieved. 'OK. Well, make yourself at home, David. Plenty of grub around. Movies downstairs.'

'Thanks,' David says.

The Rockstar retreats back to the office, forgetting whatever he came out for.

'Better get stuck into that project,' David says. But he's smiling.

I shrug. 'No point him knowing my life if he doesn't care.' I head for the stairs.

David looks back at the office. 'You sure he won't mind a guy in your room?'

'He is oblivious.'

15
A LITTLE HELP

I expect Mark to change. To show an interest in Rachel again. To ask her out. But that shows how much I know. He acts like he doesn't see her. For days. By Friday, I've had it with not interfering.

'David?' We're making out on his bed.

'Hmmm?' His face is in my neck.

'Did you talk to Mark about Rachel?'

His head pops up. 'Is that what you're thinking, right now?'

'It just kind of flashed into my head there, for a quick second.'

'D'you think it might flash out again?'

I smile and shake my head.

He rolls off me, lies on his side, propped up on an elbow. 'I thought we were going to leave this between the two of them.'

I sit up. 'And we will. I just want to know if you told him Rachel liked him, that's all. Because he's acting like you didn't.'

'No.'

}|{

'No, you didn't tell him?'

'No, I'm not telling you.'

'Why not?' He's so frustrating.

'Because if I tell you I talked to him, which I'm not saying I did, you'd assume something that wouldn't be right.'

I try and work that out. 'So you did tell him. And he's still interested?' I'm squinting.

He bursts out laughing.

'What?'

'You never give up, do you?'

I smile. 'No.'

'Right, well, I'm saying nothing from now on. I'm sealing my lips.' He mimes zipping them shut.

'But I'm right, amn't I?'

He makes a muffled sound like he's trying to talk and can't.

I make a face.

He shrugs, as if it's hopeless trying. Then he's grabbing my feet and pulling me down in the bed, from sitting to lying. His mouth lands on mine, and as distraction techniques go, it's pretty successful. We kiss and caress, and kiss and caress, faster and faster, hungrier and hungrier. And it takes off again, our bodies moving together in a rhythm I don't want to stop. I press myself to him. But he's pushing me away, suddenly.

'OK,' he says. 'Time out.' He jumps from the bed. Runs his hands through his hair. Turns away from me and walks to the window.

'It's OK. I want to. I really do. Come on.' And I genuinely want him to come back.

He turns. 'No. You don't,' he says firmly.

}|{

'I do. Seriously.'

'Downstairs. Now.' He drags me from the bed.

'Oh God.'

'Come on.' At last, he smiles.

Going downstairs I begin to wake up, to realise just how close we came. I would have done it if he hadn't stopped. But I know I can't rely on him for ever. I should carry a condom, just in case. But if I do, will that just mean we won't stop next time?

Next day, Rachel's acting like she's never heard of Mark Delaney. I watch them in rehearsals, avoiding each other. I wish there was something I could do. He likes her. She likes him. It's simple. Or at least it should be. And that's what inspires me.

After rehearsals, I go up to her.

'I thought you were supposed to be playing the great seductress,' I say, like I'm disappointed.

'I would, if Macbeth was anyone other than Mark Delaney.' She sounds like she hates the guy.

'You want to give it your all, though, don't you?' OK, my thought process is pretty basic (she throws herself at him as Lady Macbeth, he won't be able to resist). But I'm desperate.

'Don't worry. When I'm on stage, no one will be able to stop me. Not even Mark Delaney.'

I smile. 'He won't know what hit him.'

'To hell with him.'

'Really?'

'Really.'

And I wonder if she honestly believes that.

***

}|{

Saturday, and Mike drives me and Marsha into town. We trawl the shops for buttons, fabrics, ribbons, fake gems and, surprise, surprise, belts. It's weird. Dublin's my home but it takes a New Yorker to show it to me. She brings me places I never knew existed: up and down backstreets, in and out of tiny shops, finding the most perfect treasures. I thought I was a pretty serious shopper. Compared with Marsha though I'm a brand-conscious mall-hopper. She's got imagination, flair. She sees potential in everything. I used to think a button was a button. Or a belt a belt. Now they're jewellery, armour, part of a boot or headpiece. It's fun. We take regular coffee breaks to check our merchandise and plan more. She tells me about some of her clients – total weirdos. I tell her about David. She comes alive.

'I was kind of hoping you two would get together.'

'Really?'

'It was so obvious how into each other you guys are.'

'Really?' I say again, and suck at my smoothie to stop myself smiling.

'So this is your first love?'

I almost choke. 'God. No! No one said anything about love.'

'OK, your first serious relationship?'

I'm still thinking about that, when . . .

'Ah, nothing like first love.' She sighs. 'Nothing. Ever again.'

I make a face. 'Isn't that kind of depressing?'

'Eh. Yeah.'

We laugh.

'OK, so I don't want you telling The Rockstar.'

'Who?'

'Sorry. My dad.'

'Oh, right,' she says, nodding by just raising her chin.

'And you'd better not tell him I call him The Rockstar, either.'

'I wouldn't do that.'

'Good.'

'He might be hurt.'

'Are you kidding?'

'Alex, this may amaze you, but men do have feelings.'

'You don't know him very well, do you?'

'I know he's a good man.'

I laugh. 'Yeah, sure.'

'You know, things aren't always as simple as they look.'

'Except when it comes to The Rockstar.' I get up, gather my bags. Talking about him always makes me want to shop.

But when someone asks you if your relationship is serious, it makes you stop, wonder, really look at it. As we wander around the shops, I think about the person I'm spending so much time with.

Am I seriously into him?

That would be a 'yes'.

Do I seriously want to be with him all the time?

Another 'yes'.

Do I seriously think about him more than anyone else?

Absolutely, yes.

Sometimes, I can't believe we've been going out eight weeks. But mostly it feels like we've been together forever, that I know him completely, that it's always been the two of us. When I'm with him, I'm happy. When I'm not, I'm thinking about him. I'm wondering what he's doing. I'm wondering if he's thinking of me. When we are together, I don't want it to end, I don't want him to leave. I'd love if we

}{{

could sleep together. I don't mean sex. I mean curling up together, falling asleep together and waking up next to each other. I've never seen him sleep. I'd really love to. He'd be so cute. I look at Marsha now, lifting up some fabric to the light. I wonder if I should ask her about sex. What I should do. But no. She could go back to The Rockstar.

I try to imagine what she'd say.

'Oh, just go ahead. But wear protection.'

Thing is, I'm not Marsha.

When I was a kid, my dad would read me stories of fairies, princesses in towers and cobblers who worked through the night to produce magic shoes. Well, Marsha turns out to be one of those cobblers. She works flat out. Like a seamstress on speed. I help her as much as I can, but I've school. In five days, she has run up Rachel's three costumes. I feel guilty.

'Marsha, stop, please. I really didn't mean you to work this hard. We still have time.' Not much, though.

She looks up from the sewing machine. 'Honey, sometimes people need to work.'

Which makes me feel even more guilty, like I'm using her pain. Or something. 'Let me do something. Please.'

She gives me the job of ripping out these big stitches at the end of the dresses. I'm probably saving her, like, three minutes. Of course, it takes me a hell of a lot longer. But I'm happy. It's kind of relaxing. I can see why Gran does it now.

'It's good to hear you hum,' she says.

'I'm humming?'

'Humming away like a honey bee.'

I look at her and smile. She's actually kind of sweet.

'Thank you, Marsha,' I say. 'For everything.'

She winks at me. 'For nothing.'

Because she's working so hard, I decide to, too. Next day, at school, I ask Ms Hall for time off to complete the costumes. It's Transition Year. They're pretty flexible with time if it's for something worthwhile. Still, Ms Hall is Ms Hall. She looks at me dubiously. So I show her the photos I took of the costumes so far. She looks at me like I've transformed into Cinderella. And lets me off. Which is just as well. We've only got four more days till Opening Night.

I put everything on hold. School. Friends. Even David. For the next four days, the only person I see is Marsha. And there's something nice about that.

16
SMUG

Opening Night. Tension's high. Behind stage, people are whispering, rushing around, sweating. Everyone wants to get it right, even people like me who weren't into it at first. You'd swear we were on Broadway. I'm hurrying between everyone, making sure they take to the boards looking like they should. Marsha and I are so proud of our costumes. They're like our children. We don't even allow ourselves favourites. Marsha's out in the audience with a camcorder. She came an hour early to get front-row seats. I told her it wasn't a fashion show. She said it was for her. The Rockstar isn't here. I didn't tell him about it and asked Marsha not to either. He might have felt he had to show up.

It's David's turn to go on. Even under the make-up, he looks pale. I kiss him good luck and smile at the fabric we chose for him, which has tiny waves on it so he'd feel at home.

Only once do I slip out into the audience. For Rachel's performance. I stand in the aisle, waiting for her to appear. When she does, you can hear everyone taking a breath. It's not just her beauty. It's her presence, the way she holds herself, owns the character. She is Lady Macbeth. And when she sidles up to Mark Delaney, all passionate and tactile, with big eyes and heaving chest, he looks like he might pass out. He really does look like he'd do anything for her. Kill, even. Kissing was not in the script. But he's grabbing her and bending her back with a kiss that goes on and on. Everyone's going wild. Clapping. Whooping. Cheering. Stamping their feet. And as they walk offstage, looking happier than they should (given that they're planning murder), Mark takes Rachel's hand and holds it like he'll never let go.

It's late when we finish and we've another night tomorrow, so no one really hangs around. I have to collect all the abandoned costumes and hang them, ready to go for tomorrow, so I'm one of the last to leave. I ask Mike to take (a very proud and happy) Marsha home. David stays back to help. It's romantic, just the two of us, surrounded by costumes. It feels like ages since I've seen him. I watch him trying to get a belt to balance on a hanger. I could eat him up. I sneak up behind him, snake my arms around his waist and breathe him in.

'So,' I say to him, all hopeful, 'd'you think this is it?'

'What?'

'Rachel and Mark?'

'I don't know, Cupid,' he smiles, 'but I think they left together.'

'Yes!' I punch the air.

'Don't ever change,' he says and kisses me.

Next day, on the DART, Rachel's beaming.

'Spill,' I say.

}|{

She looks around at the throng. 'Wait till we get off.'

'OK, but tell me one thing – it's good news, right?'

Her smile widens. 'It's good news.'

Getting off the DART, we bump into Sarah. We fall into step together.

'So,' Sarah says, 'did that snog turn into anything interesting?'

Rachel smiles. 'Define interesting.'

'OK, that's a yes,' Sarah says.

'Knew he wouldn't be able to resist that costume,' I say.

'Excuse me,' Rachel says, clearly happy. 'Did he kiss a costume? Is he going out with a costume?'

'Going out with?!' I scream and throw myself at her. When I finally let her go, I expect Sarah to get in there for a hug. But she's just standing silent. Her face grim.

'What's wrong?' I ask.

'Nothing.'

'Sarah?' Rachel asks, concerned.

Sarah takes a huge breath and blows it out. 'It's nothing. Just that everyone's going out with someone now. Except me.'

Rachel's voice is gentle but definite when she says, 'You'll meet someone.'

But it's like Sarah doesn't hear. 'You'll all be heading out together in couples and I'll be stuck by myself.'

She's getting totally carried away here. 'Who said anything about heading out together?'

But Rachel looks at me. Then at Sarah. 'Even if we ever did, you don't think we'd go without you?'

'Hel-lo! I'm not going out on my own with two couples. I'm not that sad.'

This is going nowhere. She's talking about stuff that will probably never happen. 'Look,' I say, 'We'd better get a move on or we'll be late.'

We start to walk. I want to ask Rachel about last night, but can't, not with Sarah like she is.

'What about Simon?' Sarah says suddenly.

'Simon Kelleher?' I ask. I always assumed there was another reason Sarah didn't go out with Simon. He's Simon.

'Simon is a queue-skipper,' Rachel says. She has a thing about people skipping queues.

'So?'

'He's the kind of guy to elbow you on a football field,' I add in a burst of creativity.

'Easy for you to say,' Sarah snaps. 'You've got someone.'

'You will too,' Rachel says.

'Sure.'

'Come on. You know you will,' says Rachel.

Another pause. 'No one likes me.'

Oh for God's sake.

'Sarah,' Rachel persists, 'you're extremely popular.'

'So how come the only guy who's ever asked me out is Simon Kelleher?'

'Now you're talking him down,' I say. Because, seriously.

'No, I'm not. I'm just saying he's no Dave McFadden. He's no Mark Delaney.'

'Exactly,' I say. 'So don't waste your time.'

'Do you know how smug you sound?' she says.

What? 'I'm just being honest.'

'Smug.'

'OK. Whatever.' I give up. Just because Rachel and I are now going out with people, our advice is suddenly rubbish.

Whatever we say is going to sound 'smug' to Sarah. Silence falls between us.

We approach the school. I start to look forward to seeing David. Now that Rachel and Mark are together, there's no reason we can't sit together at lunch, I think happily. Then I remember Sarah.

'I don't suppose you want to sit with the guys at lunch, then,' I say.

She looks at me. 'Why not?'

Oh my God. What have we just been talking about?

'Simon might be there,' she says, casually.

School is all about *Macbeth*. We dissect our first performance and prepare for our next. The costumes, though, are done, so I'm just hanging around. Observing. Rachel and Mark look so happy. So relaxed. As if they've been studying for some huge exam that's now over. They look so good together. Like they fit. I want to hear it all, so when Rachel takes a toilet break and I see that Sarah's busy, I hop up. In the corridor, I call her. She stops and waits, smiling, because she knows what I'm up to.

'Leave nothing out,' I say.

'He was so nice, Alex.' She looks at me like she can't believe it. 'He wasn't trying to be funny or smart or anything. He was just upfront. He said he backed off because he didn't want to be turned down again. And he did think I was gloating, telling everyone how hard he was trying to go out with me. But that in the end he just gave in. I felt terrible that he thought I was such a bitch. I explained everything. How I thought he was just messing with me, how embarrassed I was when Sarah brought it up and how I was about to say yes when she did. He was so sweet, Ali. I never thought Mark Delaney would be sensitive. But he is. When he asked me out, I didn't have to think.'

I hug her. 'I'm so happy for you.'

'I was such a fool.'

'No you weren't.'

'I just never knew how nice he was.'

'Well, now you do.'

She smiles. 'I can see why David hangs out with him.'

We sit with the guys at lunch, and Sarah not only flirts with Simon but with all the guys. It's like she wants to be the most attractive person at the table. Witty, funny, talented. She's exhausting. But at least I can sit beside David and feel his leg against mine. And nudge him with my knee when she gets totally ridiculous.

'So what do you think?' she asks afterwards. 'Do you think he noticed?'

'I think he noticed,' I say. He'd want to have been blind, deaf and dumb not to.

'D'you think he'll ask me out?'

'I don't know, Sarah, maybe,' I say.

'I was funny enough, though, wasn't I?'

'You were fine. I just don't know what's going on in Simon Kelleher's head.'

'Sarah, I wonder if you should be a little bit more subtle, next time,' Rachel suggests. Which is brave, given the reaction she's probably going to get.

And here it comes: 'What do you mean, more subtle?' Sarah's furious.

'Just, sometimes, you're better off playing a little hard to get.'

}|{

'What, you mean like you did? If it wasn't for me, you two wouldn't even have got together.'

Oh my God, I think. They got together in spite of Sarah.

'And, like, who made you the expert all of a sudden?'

17
SPONGEBOB

The day after the play closes, technically, we're supposed to show up at school. I don't know anyone who does, though. David and I have his place to ourselves. We're fooling around on his bed. He's trying to give me a foot massage, but it's so ticklish, I'm squirming and trying to pull away. His phone rings. I reach for it on his locker and hand it to him.

'I'm busy,' he says.

'Might be an emergency.'

It keeps ringing. I shove it towards him again. He takes it with one hand while continuing to drive me mad with the other. He answers it. And his face freezes.

Now would not be a good time for this to be an emergency.

He tells someone he's on his way and hangs up. Then looks at me.

'Bobby's been injured playing hockey.'

'Oh no.' I feel terrible.

He drives too fast. Parks where he shouldn't. And hurries

onto the pitch. Bobby's in the dugout, holding an ice pack to his hand. One of the other kids' mums is with him.

'It's his thumb,' she says. Then more quietly, 'Doesn't look great.'

David sits down beside Bob. I stay back, giving them space. 'You OK, dude?'

Bobby pulls back the ice pack to show him his injury. His thumb looks weird. 'I didn't cry. It really hurt but I didn't cry.'

'What happened?'

'See that asshole over there?' I have to stop myself laughing. 'He whacked me with his stick.'

The coach comes over. 'You might want to get that X-rayed.'

'Yeah, sure, thanks,' David says. 'Come on, Bob, let's go.'

Walking back to the car, David turns to me. 'I'll drop you home.'

'No. I'll go with you.' I'd rather be with David in Casualty than without him at home.

'We'll probably be in there for hours.'

'It's OK.'

Bobby sits in front, silent, head bent, observing his injury. No one talks. It takes almost an hour to cross the city. Casualty is mobbed when we get there. And it's a long wait before Bobby's seen in Triage.

'Are you his next-of-kin?' a nurse asks David.

'Well, our dad is. But he's away on business, so yeah.'

She writes something down, then asks Bobby, 'So who's minding you while your dad's away?'

David straightens right up. 'I'm seventeen. My sister's nineteen. Is there a problem?'

'No. No problem,' she says and starts to blush.

'Can he have something for the pain?' David asks.

'Of course. I was just going to get him something.' She sounds defensive. Then she leaves to get it.

Bobby looks up at David.

'Didn't you like her?' he asks.

And I see it. How important David is to him. Whatever David says goes. If he thinks the nurse is OK, so will Bobby. If not, then too bad for the nurse. I look at Bob. And see a mini David. He's wearing Billabong. Like David does. His hair is spiked. Like David's. He even holds himself like David.

'She's OK,' David says.

Bobby nods.

The nurse returns with the medication. Then it's upstairs to X-Ray. The queue's even worse but moving faster. *SpongeBob SquarePants* is on TV.

'Shouldn't you ring your dad or something?' I ask.

'Later, when we know if it's broken,' he says.

It makes sense. Why worry him if it's not broken?

'My legs are sweating,' Bobby says.

David removes his shin pads.

'I need to go to the loo.'

David finds one.

Around Bobby, he's like a parent. Make that a good parent. Nothing's a hassle for him. He makes everything easy.

The thumb's broken. So it's back to Casualty, where, after another wait, the thumb's wrapped up tight and we get to leave. Bobby'll have to return to the Fracture Clinic to get a cast on. The wonders of the Irish health care system.

Back at their house, their sister, Romy, takes over, getting Bobby something to eat, setting him up on the couch with

}|{

pillows, a duvet and a DVD. David rings his dad, then drives me home.

'Sorry about that,' he says. And I can hear how tired he is.

'Like it was your fault.' I look at him. 'Do you mind having all that responsibility?'

He shrugs. 'If it wasn't for Bob, I'd probably still be moping around, feeling sorry for myself.'

I know what he means. I don't have a Bobby, but I've a Homer, who went on needing me after Mum, needing vaccines and flea treatments and worming and brushing and walking and feeding and training. And loving. Mum knew what she was doing when she got me a puppy. He might just be a dog to everyone else, but to me he's family.

David pulls up at my house. 'Hey. Thanks for coming. It was great having you there.'

I kiss him. 'You're lovely.' Then I jump from the car.

Inside, the door of The Rockstar's office is closed. The house is totally quiet. For a moment, I panic that he's gone, just got up and left. I get like this sometimes, which makes no sense because he might as well be gone, he's so zoned-out. But then I hear strumming from the basement and voices and I know he's hasn't vanished. And I can breathe again.

18
THE LOST WORLD

The shops are overflowing with decorations, and the wind carries an icy chill. I look at the Christmas tree in the Jitter Mug and wonder how I'm going to get through my first Christmas without Mum. Is The Rockstar even going to hang around? I remind myself I have David. To help me through it. To help me through everything.

'Have you found work experience yet?' Rachel asks Sarah and me. In January, we're supposed to experience what it's like to hold down a job.

'No,' we both say together. I don't know about Sarah but I still can't think that far ahead.

'Don't worry,' Rachel says. 'You'll find something.' She was very determined herself. She found a place in the Radiography Department of a local hospital, months ago.

'Might help if we knew what we wanted to be,' Sarah says, kind of miserably. Then she looks at me. 'Your dad could probably bail you out with something.'

'He probably could. If I asked.'

'You're not going to, though, are you?' She smiles, like suddenly she gets my world.

'No. I'm not.'

'Fathers, right?'

'You talking to yours?' I ask.

'Nope.'

We smile.

'Hey! How about that great jewellery shop in Glasthule?' Rachel says.

Sarah makes a face. 'It's tiny. And the only guys who go in there are buying stuff for their girlfriends.'

We laugh.

But Rachel doesn't give up. 'What about you, Alex? You're always in there. You're one of their best customers.'

And because I don't want to think and it's as good as anywhere else, I say, 'Yeah, OK. I'll give it a try.'

I walk up to the shop, confident. But as soon as I get inside, I lose my nerve. The owner's behind the counter, dealing with a customer. I can't just go up to her and ask for work experience. Even if she was free. I mean, what do I know about selling jewellery?

I glance around. I love this place. Love their stuff. It's modern. Pretty, but not too girly. Not too fussy. I pick up this really sweet bracelet for a closer look. It's gorgeous. I try it on. And suddenly I just can't do without it. I take it off and am about to bring it to the till when I notice the woman beside me. She's standing in front of the mirror looking at a necklace she's trying on. She frowns. Lifts up a second one. Then she takes off the first and tries the other. I don't know why she's confused. It's so obvious.

'The second one,' I say.

She looks at me in the mirror, then back at the necklaces. Her face relaxes. 'You're right. You're absolutely right. You know, I knew that. Just didn't trust myself.'

I smile. 'They've earrings too that would be really nice with it. Over here.' I bring her over.

'Thank you,' she says, 'I didn't see them.'

'Sure.'

I let her go to the till first. She looks so happy now.

God, I love shoppers.

She turns around before she leaves and thanks me again. She calls me 'a gem'. I smile goodbye. The bell on the door clinks and she's gone. I hand my bracelet to the owner.

She smiles at me. 'Good choice.'

'I love it,' I say, looking at it while she wraps it.

She looks up. 'So you go to Strandbrook?' she says, looking at my uniform.

I just smile.

'What year are you in?'

'Transition.' And then, out of nowhere, I'm saying, 'Actually, I'm supposed to be looking for work experience.' I go kind of red.

She looks up from the bracelet, her face open. 'Well, I hope you were thinking of here.'

'Really?'

'Absolutely. You're a natural salesperson.'

'I am?'

'That's not the first of my customers you've helped. I've noticed you in here before.' OK, sometimes I get a bit carried away with the whole shopping thing. 'You've a talent for it,' she says.

}I{

I make a face. 'It's kind of easy, though, when you love the stuff.'

'That's my point!' She hands me my bracelet, beautifully wrapped, like they do here. 'But maybe you were thinking of somewhere else?'

'No. No, I wasn't.'

'So, what do you say?'

'Seriously? I'd love to. Thank you.' Could it really be that easy?

'I'm Pat,' she extends her hand.

I shake it. 'Alex.'

'So, Alex,' she smiles. 'When would you like to start?'

'The beginning of January?'

'Perfect. It'll be sale time. I could use an extra pair of hands.'

Next day, we're sitting in the canteen. David, Mark, Sarah, Rachel and me. Simon hasn't sat with us since Mark and Rachel got together. Which is probably a sign he's not interested in Sarah – or at least that he doesn't want everyone to think he is. In any case, it's more relaxed without him. No one showing off. I bite into my pizza and watch Rachel and Mark. Who can't keep their eyes off each other. It's amazing. They've changed so much. Mark's stopped being so cynical about everything. He actually smiles now. And Rache . . . Who'd have guessed the ultimate beauty treatment was sitting two seats in front of her? Everything about her seems to shine. Her hair, skin, even her teeth. And I think how much she deserves this.

'Hey,' Mark says, 'why don't we all meet up, Saturday?'

There's instant silence. Rachel and I look at each other, then at Sarah.

'Whoa,' he says. 'That was greeted with enthusiasm!'

I'm trying to come up with a decent excuse.

But Sarah beats me to it, leaning across the table to Mark and David.

'Do you think you guys could bring, like, a friend?' It's like she's thought this through and decided to turn it into an opportunity. And you've gotta admire her.

David and Mark exchange a glance.

'Eh, yeah, maybe,' says Mark. He looks at Rachel. Who nods encouragement.

Her enthusiasm boosts his. 'I'll make a few calls.'

'Great, thanks,' says Sarah, like it's a done deal.

I glance over at Simon. Does he know his biggest fan is moving on?

It's two days before there's news. But it's positive.

'A friend of Mark's is going to meet up with us, Saturday,' Rachel tells Sarah, walking up from the DART one morning.

Sarah's face lights up. 'Really? Who is he? What's he like?'

'Don't know but he hangs out with Mark so he's proba-bly . . . a total nerd.' She laughs but then sees Sarah's face. 'Only joking. I'm sure he's fine.'

'What does he look like?' Sarah asks.

'No idea.'

'Can you find out?'

'I'm not asking Mark what the guy looks like.'

'OK, I will.'

'Sarah, he's just hanging out with us, OK? You guys might click. You mightn't. Don't get your hopes up. He could be completely not your type.'

'What's he into?'

}|{

Rachel laughs. 'You didn't hear a word I said, did you?'

Sarah doesn't give up. 'It's just that if I know in advance, I'll know what to talk about.'

'Then you'd better ask Mark.'

'How does he know him, anyway?'

'Karate. I think.'

'Ah. So he must be fit,' she says, looking hopeful.

'I don't know. Maybe.'

'God. You're useless,' Sarah says, just as I was beginning to feel sorry for her.

We're on David's bed and we've reached that point again. I want to. But don't. I pull back. Again.

'I'm sorry,' I say, totally frustrated. 'I can't.'

'I don't want you to,' he says, but I know he does.

I wonder what's wrong with me. He's lying there, beautiful. Perfect. I'm aching for him. And still . . . He throws his legs over the side of the bed and I wonder how much more patient I can ask him to be.

We go downstairs. He busies himself putting on pasta. After a while, it becomes easy between us again.

Bobby comes into the kitchen. 'Can I've some?'

'Here, see if it's ready,' David says, scooping out a spoon and blowing on it, reminding me of my father when I was a kid. I'd forgotten he did that.

'Ready,' Bobby says.

And as David pours microwaved red sauce from a jar onto the pasta (Barbara would be appalled), I wonder when I will be ready. Will I just wake up some day and know?

* * *

Sarah goes all out. Straightens her hair. Borrows money from me to get more highlights and a spray-on tan. Rachel gives her money for a manicure. She spends hours in Dundrum, shopping. When we hook up, Saturday, she does look amazing. OK, maybe slightly too amazing for the amusements in Bray but then you can never look too good, right? We're meant to meet Mark's friend, Peter, outside the amusements. But he's not there. We wait around for a while, freezing.

'Maybe he's inside,' Sarah suggests, hopefully.

We go in and wait near the entrance while Mark goes to look for Peter. After a few minutes, he comes back alone, with his mobile at his ear. He hangs up. And his face does the talking.

'Some family thing. Apparently.'

Sarah tries not to let her disappointment show.

'What kind of loser is he anyway?' I say, so she knows it's his problem and not hers. Then I remember he's Mark's friend. 'Sorry, Mark.'

'No, you're right. He should at least have called before now.'

'Well, his loss,' Rachel says.

And from that moment, without anyone saying anything, without even a look passing between us, we all make sure that Sarah's not the odd one out. I avoid David. Rachel avoids Mark. David asks Sarah if she's been here before, and suggests she try out the virtual motorbikes.

We go upstairs. It's dark. The noise of gunfire competes with music. All around, people are lost in their games. A little boy has a bazooka on his shoulder and is wiping out life. An overweight woman dressed like a biker is on a virtual rollercoaster, screaming. Sarah asks David if he'll race her on the motorbikes.

'Sure.'

The rest of us hit the air hockey table.

Rachel looks back at Sarah. 'Don't know what we were worried about. She's fine.'

We take it in turns to play each other. Then I start to feel like an extra. I wander off to find the others. They're not at the bikes any more. But they're not far. David's standing in front of a large screen, legs spread, arms outstretched, a pink gun in his hand. Sarah's beside him. I go over, stand on the other side, and watch what's happening. He's coming under serious fire, guys in combat gear springing up all over the place. I bite my fingers to stop a scream. He just turns his gun on its side and shoots non-stop. Then he calmly reloads.

He'd be good in a war situation, I think, imagining him telling me to 'get down!'

'Will I keep going?' he asks suddenly. 'Or will I quit? Quick.' He has a coin poised over the slot. I'm about to tell him to keep going when I realise he's looking to Sarah for the answer. I wonder if he's even noticed I'm here.

'Keep going,' Sarah shouts. Then, as if in slow motion, she leans back and looks at me with this really smug expression, like it's some kind of victory that he asked her, not me.

I walk away. Sit into a game nearby. 'The Lost World'. And, though I'm so not into being chased by dinosaurs right now, I drop in the coins and start to play. I don't last long. So I go again. After a few minutes, someone arrives beside the machine. I recognise David's jeans. But keep on playing. He stoops to watch until Game Over comes up on screen.

'Hey,' he says then.

'Hey.' My voice is flat.

'Shove over.' He sits in beside me. 'How did you do?'

'Lost after two seconds.'

'It's a hard one.'

It feels cosy in here, just the two of us in the dark, away from everyone.

'So. You're Mr Popularity all of a sudden,' I say, turning to look at him.

He shrugs. 'Don't ask me why.'

'Could be all the attention you're giving her.' I hear the edge in my voice.

He must too because his face goes all serious and he looks at me for a long time. 'Sarah's your friend. I was trying to make her feel included. For you.'

And I see that suddenly. But am too embarrassed to admit it.

'Want a game?' I say instead.

'Sure.'

After that we stay together, just the two of us shooting hoops, playing air hockey and racing motorbikes towards an ever-changing horizon. We laugh. Touch. We're ourselves again. And I can't believe I doubted him.

The DART is practically empty. David and I are first on. We sit beside each other, opposite two empty seats. Across the aisle are another four places. I'm not exactly thrilled when Sarah sits opposite David, leaving Mark and Rachel to take the seats across the aisle. When the train gets moving, she smiles at David.

'I like the way you hold a gun.' Oh my God. It's totally suggestive.

David laughs awkwardly. 'You mean that pink gun?'

'Yeah, but pink is so you.'

I roll my eyes. When really I want to slap her. What is she doing?

She crosses her legs slowly. Her dress is so short it's total-ly provocative. David looks out the window. And I'm think-ing, *what kind of friend does that, especially when you've gone out of your way to include her*? I just sit there, glaring at her, but she doesn't see it. Because, at no point in the whole DART ride, does she look at me.

I'm glad when the next stop's mine. I get up and say bye to Rachel and Mark. Ignore Sarah. Easy, given that she's ignoring me. David walks me to the door.

'I'll come with you,' he says.

'No. You'll be late.' His father is bringing them to a restaurant.

'Dad won't mind.'

I smile. 'Of course he will. Look, I'm fine. I'll call you later. OK?'

'Why don't I get off, pretend to go with you and get back on another carriage?'

I laugh. 'She's not that scary.'

'Trust me, she is.'

'Just sit with Rachel and Mark when you go back.'

'Don't worry. I was going to.'

Of course, Sarah will join them. At least he won't be alone with her though.

The doors open. We kiss quickly and I get off. 'Enjoy tonight,' I call.

For a moment it looks like he's going to come after me. And I so want him to. But he lifts a hand and the doors close in front of him. I stay on the platform watching the DART head towards town. I imagine how it will pan out from here. Mark and Rachel will get off at the same stop. And David will be left alone with the nympho. I trust him 100 per cent. Still, I wish she'd never come.

I spend the rest of the evening telling myself to forget about it. She was being ridiculous, embarrassing herself more than anyone else. I'll rise above. I watch the three *Bourne* movies back to back. By the time I get to bed, I'm so punch-drunk I fall straight to sleep.

19
Toyota Corolla

Sunday, and I'm dying to see him. When he pulls up out front, I rush to the door.

The Rockstar calls from the office, 'Who's that?'

'Friend from school. Bye!'

'Eh . . .' There's a pause. Then, a resigned, 'Bye.'

Outside, David's coming up the steps. His head is down, his shoulders hunched.

I burst out laughing. 'What's wrong with you?'

He looks up. Without a smile.

And for the first time, I think there might actually be something wrong. I feel guilty for laughing. 'Are you OK?'

'Yeah. Fine.'

He sounds the opposite.

'Did something happen?'

'I'm just not feeling the best.'

He does look pale. 'What did you eat at the restaurant?'

He looks at me strangely. Then says, 'My stomach's OK.'

'Did you sleep at all?' There are dark shadows carved into the skin below his eyes.

'Not really.'

'Maybe you should go home. Lie down.'

'I'm fine.'

He doesn't kiss me. Just turns and starts walking to the car. I follow. He ducks inside. I sit in. Peer at him again. 'It could be flu.'

He starts the engine. 'It's not flu. Let's go.'

I shrug. 'OK.'

But it's not OK. If it was, his hand would be resting on my leg. He'd be telling me about last night, driving along and making me laugh. He'd be waving at the fans outside the gate. Instead, he just drives. The silence between us grows, taking up space in the car. He turns on the radio. It's a programme about the economy. I feel like saying, 'You're not serious.' But then I realise he's not even listening. I stare at him. He looks straight ahead. And I know there's something wrong.

'What is it?' I ask.

'Nothing.'

I take a deep breath. OK, fine. If he's not going to tell me, I'm not going to keep asking. 'Where d'you want to go?'

'I don't know, a movie?'

'Fine,' I say, though, after Jason Bourne, I'm all movied out.

Only when we get there do I realise how perfect his choice is. He can sit beside me, looking straight ahead, not having to open his mouth. Because other people are doing all the talking.

Afterwards, we don't go for a pizza. We don't go anywhere. David drops me straight home. We don't talk. We don't kiss goodbye. And before I even make it to the front door, my eyes are filled with tears.

}|{

Why won't he tell me what's wrong? Why won't he look me in the eye? Is it something I've done? Something I said? Maybe it's because I was hard on him about Sarah yesterday. But he was fine when we were saying goodbye. Could she have said something to him after I left? Or, worse, done something? I shake that thought from my head. Whatever about Sarah, I know David. And I trust him. Completely. Maybe it's something totally different, nothing to do with Sarah at all. What, though? And why won't he tell me? These are the thoughts spinning round in my head all night.

* * *

In the morning, I catch the DART, semi-conscious. I wake right up, though, when I see Sarah getting on. She spots me and makes her way over, smiling like nothing's happened. Unfortunately, the woman beside me gets up for the next stop and Sarah perches herself like a princess, on the same puke-green upholstery she was sitting on the last time I saw her. I tell myself to rise above, but she looks so immune, like she can do and say anything to anyone.

'Don't ever do that again,' I say.

'What?' she asks like a wide-eyed Barbie.

'You know damn well what.'

She gives me a look that says, 'Get over yourself'.

'Friends don't do that, Sarah. Friends don't come on to your boyfriend. Would I do it to you? Would Rachel?'

She looks as cheerful as ever. 'Be kinda hard, seeing as I don't have a boyfriend.'

'You are unbelievable.'

'And you are overreacting.' She bends her fingers and examines her nails.

}|{

'What is your problem?' I whisper. 'Why does everything have to be about you? You're not going out with someone, so what? Half the world's single. And they manage to cope without moving in on other people's boyfriends. You know what? I'm tired of the Poor Sarah routine. You can keep it.'

I get up and walk to the door, where I stand, fuming, until it opens at our stop. Then I'm out, powering up the hill, passing groups of people in uniform. And I find it weird, as I storm towards the school, and see Tiptoes carefully reversing her Toyota Corolla into a space, that something she said at the beginning of the term has come to make so much sense. What is a friend? Not someone who moves in on your boyfriend. Not someone who only thinks of herself. OK, her parents have split up. That doesn't give her the right to treat me like that. A real friend wouldn't. No matter what's going on in their lives.

David's late for school. He apologises and takes his seat. He glances back at me and smiles. But it's a different smile. It's flat and blank and it's hiding something. I watch him all morning, staring out the window, failing to hear the teacher calling him, apologising. It's like all I've heard from him this morning is 'sorry'.

At break, we all go to the canteen as usual. I don't look at Sarah. But I watch how David is with her. He is different: quiet, withdrawn. But then, he's different with everyone. He's somewhere else. I have to get away. I get up and leave my tray behind as if I'm coming back. But I go to my locker, grab my coat and go outside. It's windy, cold and grey but I need air, and anything's better than having to be where Sarah is. Even where David is, right now. I drag my scarf

}|{

across my face, shove my hands into my pockets, put my head down and walk. Fast.

I don't know how much time has passed before I hear Rachel calling me. I stop and turn. She catches up.

'I saw you from the window. You OK?'

I look at her. 'No.'

She takes a deep breath. 'Look, I know what she did was dumb but she's like that sometimes. Needing to be centre of attention. She wasn't being malicious. Sarah never is.'

'I don't care about Sarah,' I snap. 'Something's wrong with David.'

'What d'you mean? What's wrong?'

'I don't know. He won't tell me. Was everything OK on the DART after I left?'

She looks surprised, then frowns, thinking back. 'Yeah, we all sat together. Sarah was doing her usual attention-grabbing thing, but we ignored her.'

'Did Mark get off the DART with you?'

'Yeah, why? Oh my God, you don't think . . ?' She looks shocked.

'No. No, I don't.'

'David wouldn't.'

'I know.' I take a deep breath. Wish I knew what it was.

'Want me to ask Mark, see if he knows anything?'

'No! Say nothing. Let me figure it out. Or let David tell me. In the meantime, don't ask me to be buddy-buddy with Sarah because it's not going to happen, OK?'

She looks at me for a long time, then nods. 'OK.' But I know what she's thinking – where does that leave the three of us, and where does it leave her and Sarah?

'Look, about Sarah,' I say. 'I'll be civil with her, if it's easier for you.'

}I{

She looks relieved. 'Thanks.'

But then I get annoyed because it's just too easy for Sarah. 'For the record, why are you taking her side? You know she was a total bitch.'

She looks shocked. 'I'm not taking sides. I just don't want us all to fall out. We've been friends since, like, First Year. And I know she can be a bit . . . silly sometimes but she's actually a really sweet person and I know she wouldn't hurt you on purpose. She's not like that.'

'Then why did she do it?'

'I don't know. Things never go right for her. That guy Peter not showing up, it's just, like, typical. I mean, who, of all of us, is the real romantic? And who is on her own? She hangs out with all these rich kids but her parents struggle to make her fees. Her mum gives her a pretty tough time. And now her parents have split up.'

'So you think I should just feel sorry for her?'

'No. But I think we should cut her some slack, right now. That's all.'

Rachel is just so sweet that I soften. 'You realise you're a total softie?'

She smiles. 'Probably.'

'Look. Like I said, I'll be civil. Just don't expect me to be the same as usual. She still did what she did.'

She nods. Then checks her watch. 'Jesus, we better get back.'

We turn around and pick up the pace. Which wouldn't be hard.

Then she looks at me. 'It'll be OK, Alex. Whatever it is, it'll be OK.'

But I know David. And I know it's not OK.

20
AERONAUTICS

It's Christmas Eve, and rain is falling instead of snow. We sit in Starbucks, silent, like a couple who've had a fight. But there's been no fight. This is how it's been between us for over a week: David pretending nothing's wrong, me pretending to believe him. I fiddle with the marshmallow swizzle stick he insisted on getting for my hot chocolate, which, for a moment, made me feel like he still cared. I watch his profile as he stares out the window. Until I can't take it anymore. I put down the swizzle stick. It seems ridiculous now.

'OK,' I say. 'Get it over with.'

'What?' He looks surprised.

'This. Us. You've obviously had enough. So end it. I won't break.' I might, though.

Now he looks sad. 'The last thing I want is for this to be over.'

'Then what is it? Tell me.'

'After Christmas, OK? Let's just have Christmas.'

Oh God, so there really is something. No more pretending. 'No. Tell me now.'

}|{

His lips press together. He looks away.

'David.'

He turns back. And when I see his face I want to tell him to stop, don't say it.

'I'm going away,' he says quietly. 'My dad's lost his job. We're going back to the States.'

It's a slap across the face, a punch in the stomach, a bomb going off in Starbucks.

'He told us that night in the restaurant.'

I can't believe it.

'Things are tough in aeronautics,' he says. 'There's more security on the military side –'

'Stop. Stop talking about aeronautics. God.' I'm pulling the sleeves of my hoodie down over my hands. I'm trying to think. Outside, shoppers hurry by in the rain, umbrellas bumping off each other, life going on as normal. That's all I want. Life as normal. I look back at him.

'Stay,' I say. 'There must be a way.' Then, I have it. It's so easy! 'You could board!' He'd have to change school, but he'd still be here, still in Dublin.

If he looked sad before, he looks flattened now. 'I can't leave Bob.' He says it like he's considered all the options and ended up with this unarguable fact.

I argue anyway. 'He could board too!'

'He's nine.'

I know that. And I also know that it would be impossible for Bobby without David. Still, I say, 'But he'll have Romy over there.'

'No. Romy's staying here to finish her Leaving Cert. She's staying with a friend.'

'What about you? He can't take you out in the middle of a school year.'

'It's Transition Year. He knows we do nothing.'

'But you could stay if you found somewhere to, right? You and Bobby could stay?' They could stay with me. I could convince The Rockstar . . .

'He wants Bob with him.'

I stare at him. 'So that's it? You're going.' Nothing I can do, or say.

He nods.

'When?'

He swallows. 'Just over two weeks.'

'Two weeks!'

'He took a week to tell us. And I took a week to tell you. I'm sorry.' He reaches for my hand and looks into my eyes like he wants me to really believe what he's about to say. 'I'll come back, Alex. When I've finished school, I'll come back for you.'

More than anything, I want to believe him. But I know about life. And plans. And he should too.

'You'll come back?'

'Yes.'

'On your own?'

'Yes.'

'In two and a half years?'

'In two and a half years.'

But he's forgotten something. 'Who'll we even be in two and a half years?' I never thought I'd change. Then I lost my mum. And even dying didn't take two and a half years. Who says we'll even be alive?

'Alex, listen –'

'No. Because in two and a half years, Bobby'll still only be eleven. You won't leave him. Don't fool yourself. Don't fool me.'

'I'm not fooling anyone. I've it all worked out. I'm going to build a life for him in San Diego. I've it all planned out . . .'

And there's the problem, right there. After everything he's been through, he still believes in plans. I turn my face to the wall. I think of Marsha, who planned to stay married and whose relationship couldn't take the distance. I think of my mum, who planned to stay alive and couldn't even last a year. I think of him promising I'd never lose him, and here he is, telling me he's leaving. And yes, he probably really believes we'll stay in touch, stay as close as ever, but that's not the way it happens. I've had friends leave. They promise to stay in touch. They start off all enthusiastic but the emails get shorter and the gap between them grows. You can tell it's becoming a chore. The only thing keeping them going is guilt. And, finally, even guilt isn't enough. So, if he's going, let him go, quick and fast. Because I can't lose anybody else bit by bit. I won't. I take a deep breath and turn back to him.

'It's over,' I say. 'Let's just face facts.' But I'm looking into the face that's dearest to me in the world and a pain is starting in my chest.

'No,' he says, with such conviction that the people next to us glance our way. 'It's not over. Because I'm not giving up on you. I'm not giving up on us.'

I look at his features one at a time, trying to memorise each one, because I know what it's like for a face to become a blur. My throat burns and my eyes sting. I look away to hide tears that insist on coming. But he takes my chin between his finger and thumb and turns my head, so I'm looking into his eyes. 'Alex. You trust me, don't you?'

My tears spill over. And I nod. He gets up and comes over

to my little piece of couch. He hugs me so tight. But it's not enough. Because I do trust him. But not life. Which gets in the way. Always. To blow your plans into pieces so small you can't ever get them back together again, plans you didn't know you had until they were gone. I pull back. Ignoring tears that are streaming now, I look into those eyes I know so well.

'It's over, David.'

'No.'

'Please. It's not going to work. So let's not put ourselves through it.'

'It is going to work. We'll make it work. We just have to be patient. We can do it.'

He is so convinced. So positive. So strong. And that's when I realise, I love him. I absolutely love him. Every little thing about him. His smile. His eyes. The freckle on his eye-lid. The fact that he's a tub of Mr Zog's Sex Wax at home. I even love the way he is with Bobby. I love everything that makes him David. And I'm telling him it's over. I get up and start to walk. Because if I don't get away right now, I'll change my mind.

Outside, David catches up. 'Alex. Don't do this. Please just trust me. Trust us.'

I wrap my arms around myself. 'I need to go home now.' I need to climb into bed, curl up in a ball, with my knees right up to my chest and squeeze.

'OK,' he says. 'But we'll talk tomorrow, right?'

I nod, but really can't think about tomorrow.

* * *

I feel cold. So cold, I'm shaking. I'm in bed, curled up, back where I was nine months ago. Only worse, because now I feel guilty for missing him more than my own mother. I close my eyes. I need to sleep, put everything from my mind till tomorrow. But I see his face behind my eyelids, the most beautiful face in the world, the face that will fade from my memory, no matter how impossible that seems now. My throat burns, and I'm off again. Loud, wailing sobs I try to silence. I'm crying for him. I'm crying for Mum. And, stupidly, I'm crying for all those things I'll lose eventually. Homer. The Rockstar. Rachel. I'm crying so much, I don't think I'll ever stop.

21
PUDDLE

I'm falling into a puddle. Only it's not a puddle, because my feet can't feel the bottom. I'm going down. My boots are filling with dirty brown water. They're dragging me deeper. Behind me, David's diving in. But it's too late. It's gone dark. I've run out of air. I wake on Christmas Day, gasping. A phone is ringing. It's mine. Croaking and vibrating on the locker beside me. I watch it until it goes silent again. Then turn over, away from it. Away from everything. Everyone. Homer places his head on the bed, right up to my face. He looks at me with sad chocolate eyes, like he can read my mind. So I turn from him too. All I want is to fall back to sleep. Block everything out. Feel nothing. Ever again. If I'd kept up my guard, kept him out, not listened, not trusted, I'd be OK now. A guy in my class would be going back to the States. That would be it.

So I'm shutting down. Turning off. Going back to sleep.

If the phone would let me. It's him, I know. Trying to change my mind. It won't work.

Finally, I get sense and turn off the phone.

Now someone's knocking on the door. I cover my head with the duvet.

'Alex?' It's The Rockstar.

I don't move.

'Dinner's ready.'

I turn in the bed and sigh like I'm asleep.

'Homer. Come on, better let you out.' A moment passes. 'Homer, come on now, good boy.' Silence. 'OK, I'll leave the door open. Come down when you want,' he says, like he's talking to a person. Then he's gone.

Minutes later, another knock. Someone moves over the carpet and slides what I guess must be a tray onto the bed-side locker, because I smell food.

'No, Homer, not for you,' says Barbara. 'No.'

At last, she leaves. I get up, take the Coke from the tray and carry everything else out to the landing. Homer follows, looking up at me with great big, you-know-you-love-me eyes.

'Alright, go on then.'

I put the tray on the floor, wish him Happy Christmas, go back to my room and close the door. I am, finally, on the cusp of sleep when there's another knock. The door opens, and I feel like screaming.

'Alex? You awake?' It's Marsha.

I make my breaths even and heavy.

'Brought some sustenance,' she says.

I make my breathing deeper still.

'Toblerone,' she says. After a few minutes, I feel her sit at the edge of the bed. 'Christmas is a bitch, isn't it, when you've lost someone you love?' She's thinking about my mum. She's thinking about her ex-husband. She doesn't

even know about David. And she won't. It still takes at least
five minutes before I finally feel her weight lift from the bed.

'I'll just leave it here, then, the Toblerone.' There's silence
for a moment, then, from the door, she says, 'I'm not going
to say anything as dumb as Happy Christmas, but I hope
you're feeling better soon.'

As soon as I'm sure she's gone, I get up and lock the door.

On Stephen's Day, I'm left in peace until noon when The
Rockstar bangs on the door. I'd forgotten I'd locked it. If I
don't open it fast, it'll be a big deal – locked doors always
are in this house.

'Sorry,' I say.

He hands me the phone. 'For you. Rachel.'

I put it to my ear and look at him as if to say, 'You can go
now.'

He does.

'What's up?' she asks. 'Why aren't you answering your
phone?'

I can't motivate myself to talk. Just walk back to bed and
flop onto it.

'Want to go out?' she asks.

'No. Thanks.'

'How about I come over?'

'No.'

There's a pause. 'Mark told me . . . I'm so sorry, Ali.'

If I talk, I'll cry. So I don't.

'You sure you don't want company?'

'Yep.'

Another pause. 'OK. But if you change your mind, call
me. OK? Any time.'

Stupidly, I nod. I hang up, leave the phone out on the landing and go back to bed. For the rest of the day, I see no one. Food's delivered, and, apart from the Cokes, is taken away untouched. Hours blur together. I don't know when Marsha comes in, but she catches me coming back from the en suite, so I can't adopt my usual strategy of faking sleep.

'Hey,' she says. 'I'm glad you're up. David's downstairs.'

My heart thuds against my chest. So I harden it. 'I'm asleep.'

She gives me a look.

'Please, Marsha. Just tell him I'm asleep.'

She squints at me. 'You've been in bed two days now. This isn't just about your mum is it? You two have argued, haven't you?'

'Marsha, please. Just tell him, OK?' I get back into bed.

'OK. Whatever.' She shrugs and leaves.

Two minutes later, she's back. Looking a bit too happy. 'He says he'll wait in the car till you wake.'

'I. Won't. Be. Waking.'

She looks shocked. 'You can't have him wait out there for ever.'

'Try me.' I pull the duvet over my head.

'Where's your heart?'

On the floor.

'Look. He's sorry – whatever he did – or he wouldn't be here.' I hear her moving around and hope she's leaving. 'Aw, look at him, down there,' she says from the window, her voice going all soft, like she's talking about a puppy. When I don't respond, she says, 'You're a pretty hard nut, aren't you?'

'Hard nut' is exactly what I'm trying for here.

'OK, well I'm going down to tell him you don't want to see him.'

}|{

I say nothing.

'I'm not having him wait out there for ever.'

Finally, she leaves.

I try not to think of him down there, waiting in his car, listening to her say I don't want to see him. I try not to think of his face. But I can't help it. I want to run to the window, tell him I'll wait, I'll hope, I'll believe. And maybe I would if I was this bright, optimistic person, who'd never been let down, who believed in the future, in possibility and happy-ever-afters. But I'm none of the above. So I go back to bed. And try to pretend he's not there, to pretend he never was.

Then Marsha's back. 'He says he'll wait.'

I groan.

'Trust me, Alex. This time you will lose him.'

'Already have.'

He waits for two hours, two of the longest hours in my life, spent talking myself out of rushing down and climbing into his arms. The hardest part is when his car starts up. I have to really fight then. I close my eyes, wrap my arms around my knees and squeeze. And as the sound of the engine fades, the hollowness expands inside me, like spilled water. But I will not cry.

22
VITAMIN C

Next morning, my Christmas presents are at the end of my bed, a carefully wrapped bundle at my feet. I get up and walk to the wardrobe. I open the door. Then, one by one, I put the presents away. I go back to bed. Then, I harden my heart, freeze it back up. I am Ice Queen. I am cold. Next day, I delete David McFadden from my life. I remove him from my phone – his number, his texts, the photos we took at the zoo. How happy we looked; how stupid I was. I change my screensaver, from a picture of him massaging my foot to an ice-capped mountain. I delete all our MSNs, emails. On Facebook, he is no longer a friend. One by one, all photos of him go. And when I start to cry, I remind myself, I feel nothing. I feel nothing. I feel nothing. I feel nothing. From my iPhone I delete every track that reminds me of him. Pretty soon, I've none left. Not even Nina Simone. David McFadden no longer exists. He never did.

I shut down all communication. Keep my phone off. Put away my laptop. Hide out in my room. The Rockstar does his duty every so often, and asks if I'm OK. Marsha stops by for one-sided conversations at the edge of my bed. Then,

}{

on Day Four, I have a visitor.

Cool air from outside wafts into the room with Rachel. It smells so fresh. And she seems so alive, so alert, hair glossier than ever, eyes more sparkly, skin glowing. And I know it's because of Mark. Because she's happy.

'Hey,' she says, hanging by the door like she doesn't want to intrude.

'I'm kind of tired, Rache,' I say, hoping she'll get the message.

'I can't believe it, Alex,' she says, coming in. 'Everything was going so well.'

Sympathy's dangerous. So I ice up. 'Yeah, well, that's life, right?'

'I know, but it just seems so unfair.'

I need to stop this. 'Rachel, I'm not feeling the best.'

'Is that why you aren't returning anyone's calls?'

I close my eyes. 'I just want to be alone.'

There's a pause. 'I get that, Alex. I really do. But you can't cut everyone off.'

Watch me.

'You need people.'

Absolutely wrong there.

'At least talk to David. In nine days he'll be gone.'

Nine days! The ache inside me spreads. But I can deal with it. I can handle this. Nine days is good. The sooner he goes, the easier it'll be to forget he was ever here.

'Just listen to what he has to say. Hear him out.'

My jaw tightens.

'Don't give up on what you've got. Don't let it go.'

My teeth are gritted so tight when I say, 'Rachel, please. I'm tired.'

'OK, I'm going. But think about it, OK? What you're walking away from.'

I nod. Just so she'll go.

And finally she does.

Next day, I wake with my head throbbing, my nose running and my eyes stinging. This is what I get for lying to Rachel.

'Alright, let's have look at you,' Marsha says. Because you can't hide anything from Marsha.

'I'm fine,' I say, and, with disastrous timing, I sneeze.

'You'll be finer when I'm finished with you.'

I stare at her. What's she even doing here? She's not my mother.

She touches my forehead with the back of her fingers. 'You hot and cold?'

I nod.

'Blocked nose?'

'D'you need to ask?' I say in a disgustingly nasal voice.

'Headache?' she asks.

I nod, only because she might go away to get me some painkillers.

'Back in a minute,' she says and is gone. Minutes later, she reappears with a tray full of stuff. She puts it on the locker. 'Right, knock these back.' In one hand, she holds out painkillers and vitamins; in the other, a glass of orange juice. It's homemade, warm and sweet with bits of orange floating in it. It tastes like my mum used to make.

'Did you make this?'

She raises an eyebrow. 'You don't think I'd deprive Barbara of the pleasure. Now, put your head over the bowl and the towel over your head, then breathe in through your nose.'

'I just need sleep.'

She stands, arms folded, eyebrow up.

And I know that the only way to get rid of her is to do what she asks.

I'm beginning to look like a bag lady. My hair is uncombed and stuck to my head. I've been living in the same T-shirt and trackie bottoms for days. I could do with a shower. And opening a window or two. But I can't get out of bed.

Next day, The Rockstar appears.

'How's the cold?' he asks lightly, as if that's all this is. A cold.

I shrug with one shoulder.

'Plenty of OJ,' he prescribes. Rockstars don't use proper words, like 'orange juice'.

'Listen, I just came to say, I have to go to London for a few days.'

I almost laugh. He's so predictable.

'Marsha'll be here.'

'Does she know that babysitting's part of her job description now? Maybe you need to give her a raise.'

He smiles awkwardly. 'I just meant if you want someone to talk to. Of course, Mike's here. And Barbara. For anything you need. Any problems.' How about a broken heart? They got anything for that?

'Great,' I say.

He leaves that night. Why hang around?

The following morning, there's a knock on the door. It opens to reveal Marsha. And David. He looks pale and serious.

'Oh Jesus,' I say, feeling the energy drain from me. Sitting in bed, I draw my knees up to my chest and squeeze.

'I'll leave you two to it,' Marsha says, and I wonder why The Rockstar pays for security with her around.

David comes in. Closing the door behind him. He starts walking towards me.

'I know what you're doing,' he says. 'And I'm not going to let you.'

My heart is pumping like a broken machine.

He stops walking. 'I love you,' he says.

It's like everything stops. I look at him standing there and know with such force that I don't just love him back but love him with every single bone in my body, every hair on my head, every breath that I take. And that is why I have to say, 'I don't love you.' Eyes closed, I force it out. Because better to snap suddenly in two than shatter slowly into a million pieces. Better for both of us.

But he just looks at me, 'I don't believe you.'

'That's pretty arrogant.'

'No. It's pretty honest. I'm leaving in just over a week. Let's make the most of it, let's spend our last few days together.'

I have to kill this. I have to do it. 'What makes you think you're so special?' I demand, kneeling up on the bed, pretending to be indignant, pretending he's this arrogant person. But I know what makes him special. His smile. His eyes. His face. The randomness of the few freckles he has. His sense of humour. His honesty. Honesty that is making this so hard. He starts walking again, towards the bed, holding my eyes with his. If he kisses me, I'll melt. Oh God. I'll cave in.

}I{

'Stop.'

He doesn't.

'Stop or I'll scream.'

He does stop. He stops and looks at me like I've just accused him of something, and he can't believe it. He takes a step back.

'I give up,' he says, more angry than sad. 'I give up.' Then he is walking away. And I wish with all my heart he'd given up before I had to hurt him.

It's better this way, I tell myself. For him. For me. But when he walks out the door, all I can think is, *I'll never see him again*.

I cry myself out. And have to wait for over an hour before my face looks any way normal. Then I go looking for Marsha. I find her in Dad's office, sketching designs.

'No more visitors,' I say firmly. 'No more phone calls.'

She looks up. 'What's going on?'

'Nothing. You said yourself, Christmas is a bitch. Well, it is.'

She puts down her felt-tip. 'This isn't about Christmas, though, is it?'

I close my eyes, take a deep breath. 'Look, I just want to be on my own for a while, OK? I just want peace.'

'David's a good guy.'

I have to stop myself covering my ears. 'Marsha. I don't need to hear this.'

She looks at me for a long time. 'You've lost him, haven't you?'

I take a deep breath. I keep my voice steady, free of emotion. 'Yes I have. And now I want to be alone. OK?'

She stands up and opens her arms.

I don't move.

'Marsha. I'm OK,' I say, like I'm totally in control. 'I'm going back upstairs to have a shower, to open the windows. Then I'm going to eat something.' Because these are the things that make people think you're OK. This I know.

But there's something in her eyes. And I start to panic.

'Don't tell The Rockstar about this.'

'He's your dad.'

'And you're my friend. I'm asking you not to tell him. He doesn't know I was going out with anyone. So what's the point? David's leaving. He's going back to the States. I'll get over it. Let's just leave everything as it is, please. I don't want him to know.' I don't want him pretending he cares.

Then the phone's ringing. She looks at me and answers it.

'Oh, yes. Hi. One moment and I'll check.' She covers the mouthpiece. 'Are you here for your gran?'

My stomach tightens. I've been avoiding her, unable to tell her about David. (She'd have too much to say.) But she's the only one who needs me.

'Last phone call,' I whisper to her. I put my hand out for the phone.

'Hey, Gran.'

'Good Lord. You sound terrible,' she says. 'Are you alright?'

'I've a cold. It's fine.' I look at Marsha to let her know I'm leaving with the phone. Then I do.

'I'll pop some Vitamin C in the post.'

'Honestly, Gran. It's nothing.' I don't want her having to go out to buy vitamins.

'You'll get it in a day or two. Take it.'

'OK,' I say, because it's easier to agree.

And By The Way . . .

}|{

'I'll email some links on building your immunity, OK?'

'OK. Thanks.'

'Read them.'

'I will.' I start to walk up the stairs.

'Is your father around?' she asks.

I pause. 'He's in London.'

'Oh, for goodness sake. Who's there with you?'

'Marsha.'

'Is that the cook?'

'No, the stylist.'

'Jesus, Mary and Joseph!'

'It's OK. Mike's here. And Barbara, the cook. I'm not alone.'

'I'll come over.'

'Gran, he's back tonight,' I lie. 'I'll be fine.' She hates coming over. She's about as happy with The Rockstar as I am.

'Are you sure?' she asks.

'Totally.' I get to my room and close the door.

'OK, well, drink lots and get plenty of rest. I'll pop round in a few days.'

'No, I'll come to you . . . How are you?'

'Fine. Just worried about you.'

I feel guilty again. 'It's just a cold.'

'Are you in your bed?'

'Yep,' I say, sitting on it so I don't have to lie again.

'Good girl. You take care of yourself, alright?'

'OK. Thanks, Gran.'

We hang up. And I'm crying again.

23
MY OTHER LIFE

For the rest of the week, I hear from no one. I should be happy. It's what I wanted. But I'm not happy. I miss David so much. And he's not even gone. The Rockstar returns from London. So I get up and have that shower. Open those windows. Change my clothes. I even go out. To bring Homer for a walk. Cold air on my face wakes me up. I squint in the glare of daylight, like someone who has emerged from a cave.

I'm not walking him on Killiney Hill. Or the beach.

Poor Homer. Bringing him along the road means using the lead. Which he hates. We both do. He tugs me forward, I tug him back. It's a battle.

It starts to drizzle. And it's so cold. Then Homer crosses in front of me suddenly to get a stick that's lying on the edge of the path. I stumble forward.

'Homer, God!' I shout at him.

He cowers.

We walk on, and the drizzle turns to rain. I don't care. I'm not going back.

}|{

The tug-of-war continues.

'I should have had you trained,' I say to him.

He ignores me. Then he spots a dog on the other side of the road and runs out onto it, pulling me with him.

I wrench him back. 'Heel!' I shout. Which is stupid. I never taught him to come to heel. He's no idea what I'm talking about. He looks up at me like he's sorry.

'That's it, buddy, we're going home.'

We're supposed to go back to school a day before the work experience starts to make sure everyone's set up. The teacher knows I am, so I don't go in. I can't face anyone. Especially not David. Though he probably won't turn up either. It's only days now, before he leaves. And he certainly won't want to see me.

Next day, I get up early. There's no sign of Marsha or The Rockstar, which is a relief. I force some cornflakes down. Then catch Barbara looking at me like I've had some kind of relapse. I force a smile. And go out to Mike. When he sees me, he jumps from the car with what seems like great energy. He opens the door for me with a smile.

'Good to see you back on your feet.'

'Thanks.' This time my smile is genuine. Because I know that will be the limit of his conversation for the entire time we're out.

He drops me at the car park close to the shop.

And as I walk towards it, I feel glad that in this place no one knows me. I walk through that door, just another girl on work experience, not someone with problems, worries, issues.

'Hey, Alex,' Pat says. 'Welcome.' She actually hugs me.

I smile. Like I'm happy. Like everything's easy. 'Thanks.'

'Come on. Let me show you the ropes before things get busy.'

It's good to have to concentrate. It's good to have a challenge. It's good not to have time to think. The morning goes fast. I'm good with customers – not pushy, just helpful. I genuinely care that they go away happy. And they seem to pick up on that. Some even compliment Pat on me. By lunchtime, I'm tired. But good tired. I leave the shop but have nowhere to go, so I get a takeaway coffee and walk down to the sea.

In the afternoon, the shop gets a little bit quieter. And Pat, unfortunately, starts to get chatty. I don't set out to fool anyone except, maybe, myself. It starts with a compliment. Pat tells me I'm good with people.

'My daughter, Emily, won't go shopping with me anymore,' she says wistfully. And I don't know why she's telling me that. I used to be exactly like her daughter, when I had a mum, turning her down in favour of Rachel and Sarah. If I'd known there was a deadline, that our time together had a limit . . .

'Do you go shopping with your mum?' she asks, as if she should judge everything by me.

I clear the lump in my throat. I'm not telling her about Mum. I'm not bringing my life here. If I do, how can I escape it?

'Sometimes,' I say.

'Where d'you go?'

'Dundrum,' I say, imagining the life I'd like. 'Mum's pretty hopeless. I have to find stuff for her. She'll look at a rail and see nothing. I make her try things on. She doesn't realise how pretty she is.' She never did.

}{{

I can't believe how much information can be requested and passed over in one afternoon. By the time I'm leaving, I've a father who's an engineer. He hassles me about homework and boys and keeping my room tidy. I've a brother who broke his thumb playing hockey. And I've a friend, Rachel, who climbs mountains.

On Tuesday, I know what I want to do when I leave school – medicine.

On Wednesday, I have a boyfriend. But it's not serious.

On Thursday, my real life invades. Rachel walks in. I slip behind a display. And watch through the glass as she approaches the counter. Pat looks up from pricing some necklaces. I don't hear what Rachel says, but I do hear Pat.

'Not at all.' Her eyes scan the shop. Doesn't take long. 'There you are! Someone here would like a quick word.' She smiles at Rachel.

'It's OK,' I say. 'I can call Rachel after work.' Because I don't want a quick word, a slow word, or any kind of word.

'So this is Rachel,' Pat says, looking impressed.

Rachel looks at me, totally stunned that I've told anyone about her.

I come hurrying forward.

'Why don't you two grab a quick coffee?' Pat says. 'Go on.'

'Thanks,' I say, grabbing my bag from behind the counter, before she can bring up mountain climbing.

'I'd better not stay long,' I say to Rachel, outside. 'Don't want to take advantage.'

Rachel looks straight at me. 'Don't worry, I won't take up much of your time.' Ice.

'I didn't mean it like that.'

'You don't return my calls. You won't see me. It's OK, Alex, I get the message.'

'So why are you here?' I say, to really hammer it home. To push her away for good.

She doesn't flinch. 'His flight's at ten tomorrow morning.'

I wrap my arms around myself. 'So?'

'So. This is your last chance.'

I don't tell her what I did with my last chance. 'Tell me why this is your business,' I say instead. Because I don't need anyone.

'Stop! OK?' she says so suddenly, so loudly, that people passing turn to look. 'You need people. Alex, if you don't say goodbye, you will be sorry.'

'Look. I have to go back.'

'Alex. Open your eyes. Look what's happening. You're totally isolating yourself.'

Exactly, I think.

She throws her hands up. 'OK. Fine. But, just so you know, there comes a point when people stop trying.'

'Good,' I say, to make sure that this is it. The end.

'Goodbye, Alex.'

I let her go without a word. I tighten my arms around myself. Then I force a smile on my face and return to the shop. I'll keep busy. I'll be fine.

'That was quick,' Pat says, cheerfully.

I just smile wider.

'So that was Rachel?' she says.

'Eh. Yeah.' I pick up a cloth and start cleaning a glass cabinet, my back to her.

'She does look fit. Mind you, I'm not sure I'd be in a hurry to let my kids up the side of a cliff.'

}|{

I rub the cloth round in a circle. Round and round, over the same bit of glass. But then I catch my reflection and look so sad I turn away suddenly. I bump right into Pat. She laughs. Then sees my face.

'Are you OK?'

'Yeah, fine. Thanks.'

'You don't look so well.'

'Migraine.'

'Oh, well, in that case, go home.'

'It's OK.'

'You don't have a choice here, Alex. I get migraines. I know what they're like. Hang on.' She goes behind the counter. Roots in her bag. Takes out a box of tablets. She hands me two. 'Take these now, while you can still absorb them.'

I hold out my hand for them. Then she hands me a bottle of water.

'I don't have cooties,' she says, smiling.

I knock back the tablets. 'Thank you.'

'Now go.'

I squint at her. 'Are you sure?'

'Absolutely. Do you want me to call your mum?'

I take out my phone. 'It's OK, thanks, I got it.'

Mike brings me home. I go straight to my room. I take out the laptop and bring it to bed. I watch movies back to back. *Kill Bill* followed by the sequel. Then *Pulp Fiction*. At some point, my plan works and I fall asleep without thinking.

24
MISSING KNIGHT

In the morning, my first thought is David. He'll be at the airport now. Checking in. An ache starts in my chest and spreads out. I try to ignore it. Mike drives me to work in the rain. All day, I keep my head down, my mind blank. I smile extra hard at customers – until I catch my reflection and realise how scary I look. I try to concentrate, but give one woman too much change, another an empty jewellery box. I drop an earring onto the floor and step on it when I try to find it. By four o'clock, I've apologised so much, I'm annoying myself. Pat asks if I want to leave early.

So I leave early.

I stand outside the shop. Take a deep breath. And just start walking. One foot in front of the other. My steps form a rhythm. And carry me to the sea. It roars loud, wild and rebellious. And I think, *there must have been a storm last night*. Waves rear up like angry horses. There's salt in the air, mist in my face. And for just one moment, I close my eyes, breathe it in and think of David – who is now over the sea somewhere, travelling hundreds of miles an hour, away from

}|{

me. Then I'm walking fast, along the coast, my feet pounding the ground. Then I'm running, past Sandycove beach and up the hill towards the Forty Foot, the infamous 'gentlemen's bathing place' that had to give in to pressure and allow women bathers. (Big of them, right?) I stop, out of breath, watching waves explode like fireworks against the rocks. I go down the steps to the changing area. People swim here all year round. Today it is deserted. I climb the rocky outcrop. Spray covers me, landing on my hair like cold fingertips. I forget time. Zone out. It's just me and the sea.

I almost don't hear them at first, the voices. When I do, I keep my face turned to the sea. I don't know how long they've been there, when I hear one of them shout, 'Alex? Is that you?'

Reluctantly, I look down. It's Sarah's brother, Louis, at the base of the rock – my rock – looking up at me.

'What are you doing up there? One freak wave and you're history.' He starts to climb up.

I look out to sea.

'Come on down,' he says, reaching me. 'You're getting soaked. Here, give me your hand. Let me help.'

'I don't want help.' A wave crashes overhead, spraying us.

'Jesus! Are you on a suicide mission or something?'

'Go away, Louis.'

'Come on . . . We've got booze.' He nods to his two mates, back at base. One is passing a naggin to the other. 'What're you doing anyway?' he asks, when I don't respond. 'Not like you to bunk off.'

'How would you know?'

I start to climb down. Away from him. All I want is to be alone. That's all. It's not much.

'Careful,' he says, negotiating his way down beside me.

I reach the bottom. 'See you, Louis.'

I have to pass his mates to leave. All they say is, 'Hey', but somehow he ends up introducing us.

'This is Alex,' he says to them, cheerfully, like we're at a party or something. To me, he says, 'Johnny. Rob.'

I raise my chin. They raise theirs. Louis puts out his hand for the naggin. Rob passes it over. Louis takes a swig and gives it to me. And I'm thinking, alcohol kills pain, right? I knock it back. It's like swallowing fire. I spit it out like dragon breath. Then they're laughing. I hand the naggin back to Louis and I'm walking away.

'Hey! Where you going?'

I run up the steps.

'Alex, stop. Hang on.' He's coming after me.

I stop. 'What?'

'There's a party later . . . If you want to come.'

'Do I look like I want to party?' I say.

'Maybe you look like you need to party,' he smiles. 'Here, can I borrow your phone for a sec?'

I look at him.

'It's an emergency.'

I doubt that. Still, I pass him my phone because I know that the sooner I do the sooner I can go. I fold my arms so he gets the message to hurry. He starts pressing keys. Then looks up and hands it back.

'There!' he says. 'If you change your mind, you have my number.'

I roll my eyes. 'Some emergency.'

'Alex, you really should get out of those clothes.' Weird, Louis advising the removal of clothes without being suggestive.

}|{

I look down and notice, for the first time, that I'm soaked through. And, just like a cartoon character who only falls once she realises she's run off the cliff, suddenly I feel the cold. It's like an invasion, coming through me, right to my bones. My teeth start to chatter. Like someone's flicked a switch, I'm shaking all over. How did I let myself get so wet?

'Here.' He's taking off his coat.

'I don't want your coat.'

He holds it out to me. 'Come on,' he says, like an adult humouring a child.

It's warm from his body and too big for me. The sleeves come down over my hands. Then, the weirdest thing, he zips me up, right to the neck. And just for one moment I'm a child again, and my father is protecting me from the world.

'Thanks,' I say, and my voice sounds hoarse, even to me.

'How'll you get home?'

I remember Mike. Check my watch. 'Someone's picking me up in the village at six.'

'You better go then.'

'Thanks for the coat. I'll get it back to you.'

'Whenever.'

I get to the car park just before Mike. When he sees me, he jumps from the Jeep and strides over to me.

'What happened you?' he asks, all concerned.

'I went for a walk. The sea's kind of wild so I got a bit wet. Can we go?'

'Of course. Come on.' In the car he blasts up the heat. 'Where did you get the coat?' He's looking at me closely in the rear-view mirror.

'Some guy I know let me borrow it.'

He squints. 'You sure you're OK?'

'Yeah, yeah, fine.' I look out the window.

When we get home, he doesn't go to park, as usual, but abandons the car and comes in with me.

'You better get out of those wet things. I'll ask Barbara to put on some soup for you.'

'I'm not hungry.'

'Alex. This isn't about hunger. Your lips are blue. You're shaking all over.'

Right now, it seems easier to just do what he says. So I go up, take off the coat and get straight into the shower, still in my clothes. I stand under it for ages trying to warm up. Eventually, I undress. The only reason I finally come out is that I know Mike will be waiting with the soup. I wrap up warm in extra layers and come downstairs in two pairs of socks and my Uggs, still freezing. When Mike sees me, he hands me the soup.

'Here, you better bring it back up. You can't go around with wet hair.'

Mum used to say that.

I go to my room, make myself drink the soup, then dry my hair.

It's not long before The Rockstar appears.

'Mike tells me you got wet. What happened?'

I sigh deeply. 'I went for a walk by the sea. I got wet. No big deal.'

'How are you feeling?' he asks, which must kill him. The Rockstar never talks about feelings.

'Never better,' I say sarcastically.

'Do you need anything from me?'

'No.' Which is just as well.

}|{

'Should I call the doctor?'

'No.'

'How's the work experience going?' he asks, like the problem might be there.

'Fine. Good. I like it.'

'OK, well, I think you'd better get an early night.' He comes up to me and does something he hasn't done in a very long time. He kisses me on the forehead.

'Ugh, gross,' I say.

And, just in time, he backs off.

I don't know why I go to his room. Not to apologise. That's for sure. Maybe to say goodnight. It's the first time he's shown any concern for me in such a long time. And I threw it back in his face. He doesn't sleep in their old bedroom any more, the place I used to go to kiss them goodnight, even at fifteen, when Mum would sometimes pretend to get stuck in a hug, unable to let go. I don't knock. Just walk in.

I stop dead. Not believing. I close my eyes. And start to back away. I bump into the door, whacking my head. I open my eyes. And Marsha is looking at me.

'Oh no,' she says.

My father's head slowly turns.

And I'm gone. Running. Down the stairs, through the hall. Homer thinks it's a game and starts to race along beside me, looking up and barking. I order him back. He whines. I burst through the front door, slamming it behind me. I race out across the lawn. The security lights snap on. I run through the gate that leads down to the sea and am plunged into darkness. I make my way down the narrow path, stumbling, tripping. There's this: I've just seen my

父亲 having sex. There's this: it was with Marsha. There's this: I thought she was my friend. Mostly, though, there's this: he's forgotten my mum.

I race along the beach in the dark. To my left, I hear the waves crash to the shore like they always do, like nothing's changed. I run and run, my eyes finally adjusting to the dark. The moon comes out from behind a cloud. A bird calls from somewhere I can't see. I keep running.

Finally, I have to stop. I collapse onto the sand, trying to catch my breath, gripping the pain in my side. How could he do this? To Mum? To me? I used to hate Marsha. Why didn't I keep it that way? She never cared about me. Just him. Oh my God, I hate her. But not as much as I hate him.

I start to get cold. The kind of cold you get when you cool down after exercise. The kind of cold you get when it's January and you're out without a coat. The kind of cold you get when you've already frozen to death earlier in the day. I need to get off the beach. I need to get indoors. But I've left without money. Without a plan. I check my pockets. All I have is my phone.

Who can you call when you've cut off all your friends? Who can you call when you're escaping from your family? Finally, because I've no other choice, I call the last number entered on my phone. Luckily, I always have my phone on private so I don't have to worry about Louis getting my number.

'If you want me at that party, pick me up from Killiney Beach.'

'Alex?'

Is the guy slow? 'Yes, it's Alex. Do you want me to go or not?'

'Yeah, sure. But I don't have a car.'

'Find one.'

'What time will I meet you?'

'Now.'

'Now?'

'Now.'

He laughs. 'You're full of surprises. OK. Give me twenty minutes.'

I wonder if I'll have died of hypothermia by then. I pull up the hoods on my two hoodies. I rub my hands together, then run them up and down my arms. I jog on the spot. Finally, I see him coming onto the beach. He looks around uncertainly. Calls my name. I come up behind him.

'Hey.'

'Jesus Christ!'

I laugh.

'What are you doing on Killiney Beach at eleven at night?' he asks. 'What is it with you and the sea?'

'Let's go.'

We walk quickly off the beach to the waiting taxi.

Getting in, his hand brushes off mine. He looks at me. 'You're freezing. Again.'

I remember a scene I want to forget, the scene that brought me to the beach. 'Kiss me.'

He doesn't hesitate. His mouth is warm, and, for a second, I do forget.

Then I'm pulling back. 'Thanks.'

He laughs. 'You're welcome.'

'Where to?' asks an unimpressed taxi driver.

Louis gives him an address. Then puts an arm around my shoulders and kisses me again.

* * *

We get out of the taxi. Louis takes off his leather jacket and gives it to me.

'If this keeps up,' he says, 'I'm going to run out of clothes.'

The house, a massive Georgian pile, is lit up with purple lighting. There are bouncers at the gate. They're wearing tuxes, like something out of *The Blues Brothers*. They look me up and down. Compared to other arriving guests, I'm totally scruffy in my two hoodies, my trackie bottoms and Uggs. Louis puts an arm around me and walks me forward. They open the gates with, 'Have a good night.'

We walk up the drive, stones crunching underfoot. Music's coming from the back of the house, where, behind the garage, I see the roof of a marquee.

'So,' Louis says, looking me over slowly, like he's amused. 'No short skirt. No make-up. Hair a total mess. You're seriously trying to impress me here.'

I tug at his T-shirt, which says, 'National Pornographic'.

'Who're you trying to impress with that?'

He looks down at it, then back up with a bad-boy expression. 'My mum.'

I think, *here's one person who won't want a piece of my soul.*

'You realise you're with a seriously dangerous guy here.' He raises an eyebrow. 'Half vampire, half werewolf.'

'I guess that explains the unibrow.'

He bursts out laughing. 'You're funny.'

We get to the marquee. I keep his jacket on. He keeps me to himself all night. Gets rid of Rob and the other guy when they come over. He gets closer and closer, until he's lifting a strand of my hair, twisting it round a finger and slowly unwinding it. Then he's kissing me, and my mind is emptying again, the ache is going. Too soon, he lets me go.

}|{

'Back in a sec,' he says.

My eyes follow him through the crowd. He's saying something to the guy whose party it is. They look over at me. Then at each other again. Then he's back, taking my hand and pulling me towards the house. In the hall, there's no knight in shining armour.

In the bedroom, he closes the door and comes slowly towards me, eyes holding mine. I stand facing him. I let him come. He runs his fingers through my hair to the back of my head, cupping it in his hands. His lips almost touching mine, he says, 'First time I saw you –'

I cut him off. 'Got protection?' I say it like I'm tough, like I've done this a million times and I'm not scared. I say it like I'm in charge.

He laughs again. 'God, I love you.'

And that's it, right there, the kind of love I need: a love that distracts, that takes away the pain, that promises nothing. A love that's not love at all.

I close my eyes and let it happen.

It's over quickly. I wonder what all the fuss is about. He lies beside me, chest rising and falling, rising and falling. I don't know this person. I close my eyes. Think of my mum, driving me to ballet, fencing, tennis: all those things I wanted so badly to do, then quit as soon as I started. I think about the day she picked me up from school and said, 'I feel like carrying someone today,' and did, though, really, I was too big. I think about lying on the sand beside David looking up at the sky, making pictures out of clouds. I think about . . .

'Are you OK?'

I turn my head. 'What?'

'You're crying.'

'I am not.'

He runs a thumb along my cheek. It comes back wet.

'Those aren't tears.'

No one else would believe me. 'So, you're OK?' Louis asks.

'Of course I'm OK.'

He breaks into a smile. 'Good!'

I ignore him. Just look at the ceiling, the blankness of it.

'Mind if I smoke?' he asks.

'Knock yourself out.'

He lights up then passes me the cigarette like we're sharing a peace pipe. I take a drag. And hand it back slowly, trying not to gag. We're quiet for a long time. He blows smoke rings and I watch them wobble to the ceiling.

'So,' he says, 'whatever happened with that guy at Sarah's party?' And, just like that, the pain is back. 'You know the guy, good-looking in a surfer-dude sort of way.'

'I don't know any surfer dudes,' I say, grabbing at my clothes.

'What are you doing?'

'What does it look like?' I shove my arms into my first hoodie and yank it down.

'Why, though?'

I ignore him. Hurry into the second hoodie.

He flings back the covers. I look away.

'So,' he says, dragging on his jeans. 'Not that I make a habit of this or anything but . . . can I've your number?'

I have to think fast. 'I'll call you,' I say, not planning to. I want to forget about Louis. Forget I was ever here.

He's grinning. 'You don't talk. You don't give out your number . . . You sure you're not a guy?'

I head for the door. 'You'd better fix the bed.'

'Oh, right, yeah.' He flings the duvet back.

I don't wait. On the way downstairs, I turn on my phone to call a cab. Messages pop up on the screen. Loads of messages, and missed calls. Some from Mike's number, some from a withheld one – home. The last call was three minutes ago. I close my eyes. Do I really want to go back? Then Louis is beside me. I remember I've no money. But I'm not asking him. I feel cheap enough already.

'I'll see you, OK?' I say.

He looks at me for a moment, like he knows it's the brush-off it is. He shrugs. Smiles. 'Sure.'

He walks back to the party.

Out on one of the busiest streets in South Dublin, I flag down a taxi. I sit in the back and start trying to forget the biggest mistake of my life. Outside, people sway unsteadily home from parties. One girl is in her bare feet, carrying her shoes. Her boyfriend's jacket sits across her shoulders. It reminds me of a time I sat in a fairy-tale garden and shared a bench with a knight. Silent tears glide down my face.

25
ACCIDENT

Before the taxi even stops, the front door of our house swings open. It's Mike with The Rockstar right behind him. They're running down the steps. Wearily, I open the door of the cab.

'Thank God,' says The Rockstar. Like he cares.

'Have you got money? I need it for the cab,' I say, coldly. This seems to throw him. He stops, roots in his pocket and produces a crumpled twenty. It could be a hanky for all the respect he shows it. I snatch it off him and give it to the driver. I tell him to keep the change. It's a lot. But The Rockstar has too much anyway and needs to share it around a bit. I slam the door shut, walk past The Rockstar.

'Are you OK?' Mike asks me, and I soften when I see how worried he looks.

'Yeah. Sorry,' I say to him. But only him.

'It's OK, Mike,' The Rockstar says. 'I'll take it from here.'

Mike looks at him, and, for a moment, I think he's going to object but he just looks at me and says, 'OK. I'll see you tomorrow, Alex. Good to have you back.'

}|{

Then he turns and disappears into the house.

'Where were you?' The Rockstar asks.

'What do you care?' I hurry up the steps and through the front door.

But he keeps up. 'It's three in the morning. I've been desperate . . .'

'Yeah, well, I'm back now.'

He closes the door behind him.

I reach the stairs.

'Alex, wait. Let me explain. About earlier. I'm sorry . . . It was an accident.'

Oh for God's sake! I swivel round. 'So, what, you, like, accidentally fell into bed with her? Your clothes accidentally flew off? And you accidentally ended up on top of her. Is that it?'

He has the decency to look guilty. 'What I mean is, it wasn't planned. It didn't mean anything. Two lonely people in the wrong place at the wrong time.' He shakes his head, as if it's useless trying to explain. 'I'm sorry, I don't expect you to understand –'

'Oh, I understand. I understand loneliness. I get loneliness. What I don't get is how quickly a person can forget his wife for the first lonely woman he happens to accidentally fall into bed with.'

'Alex. It was a mistake. It'll never happen again. I swear.' He puts his hand to his heart, like a soldier pledging allegiance.

'I'm going to bed.'

'Wait. I need to know. Where were you?'

'Out.'

'Clearly you were out. Where out? And who with, until three in the morning?'

)I(

I start walking.

'Alex!'

And suddenly I'm sick of the concerned-parent act. I turn to face him. 'You really want to know?' It's a dare.

'Yes, Alex, I really want to know. We were calling everywhere. I was about to contact the police.'

'Alright, since you ask. I was out having meaningless sex with a guy you wouldn't approve of.' I sound proud. I feel the opposite.

'What?'

I repeat every word – making my voice cheerful.

'I heard you.' He says it so quietly.

'It's OK. It didn't mean anything.' I throw his words back at him.

'You're serious, aren't you?' he asks slowly.

'Oh, no, it's not serious. And I haven't decided if it was a mistake. Or an accident.'

He sinks into the chair beside the phone. 'Go to your room,' he says without looking at me.

'Sure,' I say, happy for shocking him, for getting a reaction. But sad too, like I've lost something.

I climb into bed, still in my clothes. I just want to sleep. For ever. But then, from downstairs, I hear his voice, raised and angry. I go to the door. Stand out on the landing.

'You were supposed to be watching her,' he says. 'You were supposed to be keeping her safe.'

Mike says nothing.

'How could you let her disappear like that? Anything could have happened.'

Anything did happen, that's his problem. And now he's

blaming Mike. I creep downstairs. I stand outside his office door.

'I can't tolerate this, Mike. I can't risk it happening again. I have to know that she's safe twenty-four hours a day.' He sounds emotional, close to the edge. 'I've one daughter. One daughter. I will not put her at risk.' There's a long pause. 'You're going to have to find yourself another job, Mike. I'm giving you a month's notice.'

Oh my God. He can't do that.

'Fine,' Mike finally speaks. 'But save me all that "one daughter" bull.'

'Excuse me?'

'You've a lovely kid there, a fantastic kid, but you don't give her the time of day. You don't even know her.'

'Don't tell me I don't know my own daughter.'

'OK, what does she do when she's upset?' It's a challenge.

'I don't have to answer to you.'

'She shops. She blows the money you dole out on her instead of your time.'

'I don't need this.' I hear The Rockstar's chair slide back.

'Alex lost her mother. You're all she's got. But you spend your time working. No wonder she's gone off the rails.' I was right behind him till 'off the rails'. 'Do yourself a favour. Do Alex a favour and take a long, hard look in the mirror. Because you are the problem here.' Then Mike surprises me by coming through the door. I stand back. But it's too late. He sees me. And stops.

'Sorry,' he says. 'You weren't meant to hear that.'

'No, I'm sorry. This is all my fault. If I hadn't run off –'

His smile looks forced. 'Needed a change of scene anyway.'

I'm straight into the office. 'Fire Mike and I'm out of

here. I don't know where I'll go, but I swear to God I will go.'

He drops his head into his hands. 'Jesus!' comes out as a sigh.

'You'd better hire him back right now or I swear to God –'

He looks up. 'Mike's job is to protect you.'

'Isn't yours?'

He's nothing to say to that, so I keep going, while I have the moral high ground. 'Mike is the best at what he does. As far as he was concerned, I was home. Safe. This is not his fault.'

'I'm not having him speak to me like that.'

'So you're just going to fire him?'

He sighs deeply. Then puts his hands up. 'OK. OK. Fine. Mike can stay . . .'

A sudden thought hits me. 'What if he doesn't want to now? You have to apologise. Ask him back. Mike's the best. You have to treat him right.'

'Alex, I know that, OK?' He sounds tired. 'Now, go to bed. It's been a long night.'

'I want to talk to him first.' I walk out.

'Five minutes,' he calls after me.

I find Mike in the security office, staring at a screen which shows the front gate. His shoulders are slouched. Mike never slouches.

'I'm sorry, Mike.'

He swivels round in his chair. Smiles like he's not bothered. 'I'll find something else.'

'But he's not firing you! He's sorry. He's coming to apologise.'

'After what I said?'

'You just told the truth . . . Thanks, by the way. I didn't think you noticed.'

'I should have said something long ago, not waited till he fired me.'

'So, you'll stay?' I ask. Because I have to know.

He looks at me for a long time. 'No more vanishing acts?'

'No more vanishing acts.' I cross my heart like I used to do when I was little.

He smiles. And, before I can stop myself, I throw my arms around him.

26
THAT BOY

In the morning, The Rockstar's in the kitchen when I come down, standing at the window, staring out. I ignore him and go for my cornflakes.

'Oh, hi,' he says, coming away from the window.

His hair is sticking up all over the place. The lines on his face stand out like branches against the sky. The shadows under his eyes are dark smudges. Good, he didn't sleep either.

'Can we talk?' he asks.

I ignore him, just sit at the table and look into my cereal. If he wants to talk, let him.

He sits opposite. 'Marsha left today. She's gone back to the States.'

I pretend not to hear.

'Alex, the last thing anybody wanted was to hurt you.'

I start to count cornflakes. Eventually, he'll have to leave. There's a long silence. 'Do you think I let you down?'

I'm so surprised, I look up. He's looking at me like he's hoping I'll say no. Well, if he thinks I'm going to lie, here,

}|{

he can forget it. He closes his eyes, like he's heard the worst news.

'Mike's right,' he sighs deeply. 'I have let you down.' His eyes fill with regret. But there's something else. It's not The Rockstar looking at me now but my father. 'I've lost you, haven't I?' he asks. And it's like everything's changed, like I'm not his little girl any more.

I swallow.

'Alex, I'm sorry.'

Does he really think it's that simple? A quick 'I'm sorry' and everything will be OK? Someone else could do with a 'sorry', but she'll never be able to hear it.

'Is that it?' I ask, like I'm bored. I slide my chair back.

'No,' he says. 'That's not it. This boy. Do you love him?'

'Louis?' I laugh, loud and harsh. 'Did you love The Stylist?'

He looks sick. 'Tell me, at least, that you took precautions.'

'Oh my God. I can't believe you asked me that. Did I ask you if you took "precautions" with her?' And, what, does he think I'm a complete retard?

He takes a deep breath like he's trying to be patient. 'Alex, I have to make sure you're safe. I'm your father.'

'Since, like, when, a few minutes ago?' But the real question is: how long is he planning to stay a father – another five seconds?

'I want you to stop seeing that boy.'

'What boy?'

'Don't act cute. The boy you were with last night.'

'I'm not seeing him.'

'Right, well, make sure you don't.'

'Oh yeah, and, like, you're Mr Authority all of a sudden?'
I glare at him, the switch-on dad, and decide that, actually,
I will see Louis again – just to spite him.

'I can be Mr Authority if I have to be.'

'Yeah, right.'

'OK. Enough. You're grounded, young lady.'

I burst out laughing. He's never grounded me in his life. I
get up and head for the door. But just before walking
through, I stop and turn. 'Oh and by the way – grounding
only works for people who have a life.'

I run upstairs. In my room, I look up Louis's number on my
mobile. He answers on the fifth ring. He sounds groggy, like
he was still asleep. And I wonder what I'm doing.

'Yeah?'

I think of The Rockstar and urge myself forward. 'It's
Alex.'

'Well, hel-lo.' It's like he's suddenly sitting up.

'Want to meet up sometime?' I can't believe I'm doing
this.

There's a pause. 'I got that wrong.'

'What?'

'Didn't think you'd call.'

'So, when?' Damn. I remember Mike. Can't risk him getting fired again. 'I'll call you straight back.'

I run downstairs. The Rockstar's in his office, lying on his
black leather couch with a wet cloth over his face. And I hate
to disturb but – 'So, what exactly do you mean by grounded?'

He takes off the cloth and sits up. He looks exhausted.

'I mean that when you come in from school –'

'Work,' I say, just to annoy him.

}|{

'OK, work. When you come in from work, you stay in.'

'How long for?'

'The rest of the evening.'

I roll my eyes. 'How long am I grounded for?'

'Oh, right.' After some hesitation, he opts for a week. He could sound more sure, like he did when I was a kid and he'd no problem saying no.

'OK,' I say, and walk straight out.

On my way back upstairs, I try to work out a time I'm free and not expected home.

I call Louis back. 'Lunchtime, Monday.'

He laughs. 'You think you could be more specific?'

'Look, I'm grounded. It's the only time I've got.'

I hear the smile in his voice when he says, 'Naughty girl, were we?'

'Louis, are we doing this or not?'

'We're doing this.' There's a long pause. 'OK. Come to my place. There'll be no one around.'

I know what that means. I also know that this was never about tea and a chat.

'Can't stay long,' I say, to make sure of that.

'Ah,' he says, like he's smiling. 'Forgot, there, for a minute you were the guy in the relationship.'

'What relationship?' I ask, warily.

'See what I mean?' He laughs. 'Don't worry, Alex, I'm as allergic to commitment as the next guy. You're safe with me.'

'Good.' I hang up, look at the phone and wonder where the real Alex has gone.

The movie I pick to get me through the afternoon is *Reservoir Dogs*. Nothing in it that could remind me of my life. Just plain old bank robbery and murder. Blood and guts by men in black suits. I'm just wondering if I should skip the torture scene when Mike calls my mobile. My gran's just pulled up in a taxi. I get up immediately. I hurry upstairs, worried that something's wrong.

She's getting out of the taxi. I run down the steps. She waves hello but when she sees me, she's the one who looks worried.

'You've lost weight,' she says. 'And I've never seen you so pale.'

'I'm fine. Is everything OK?' She looks OK.

'You sound exhausted,' she says, peering at me. 'I hope you're not getting ME.' Gran has three medical encyclopedias. And doesn't need an excuse to use them.

'It was just a cold,' I remind her.

'Come here. Let me have a look at you.' She drags down my lower lids like I'm a child, and peers in. 'You might be anaemic.' Her concern makes me want to cry. 'I think you're all right,' she says, 'but I'll get you on a course of iron, just to be on the safe side.' She frowns. 'Might make you a bit constipated –'

'Gran!'

'What?' she asks innocently. 'Someone should be looking after you.' I think she hates him. Which makes two of us.

So it's awkward when we bump into him in the hall.

'Grace,' he says, extending his hand, 'good to see you.'

She shakes it without a smile, which is so not Gran. 'John. How are you? Working hard?'

For a moment he doesn't reply. Then, he turns to me. 'Too hard,' he says, like it's an apology. Then he's looking at Gran. 'Grace. Can I get you tea, coffee?'

}|{

'No, thank you. Alex will look after me.'

'All right, good.'

Then, just as it looks like he's going to make a getaway, Gran asks, 'Have you been feeding her at all?'

His Adam's apple shoots up. His eyes sweep to me like he's expecting to see a skeleton. He shifts uncomfortably, the man with the platinum sales and MTV Video Music Awards.

And then, Gran is moving away. 'Right, well, I think it's time for the library,' she says to me.

'Right, well, good to see you,' he says and, for once, he doesn't rush off, but waits until we walk away.

The library is Gran's favourite room, the smallest and cosiest in the house. She helped Mum decorate it. I think it reminds her of that time. I shut the door behind us and light the fire that is always set.

'I think I need a sherry after that,' she says. It's not like her to be harsh.

I get the sherry. It seems to revive her. I pour myself a Coke so she's not drinking alone.

'So, how's my favourite American?' she asks, reminding me why I've been avoiding her.

I look into my Coke and mumble, 'Not sure.'

'What do you mean you're not sure?'

Might as well tell her; she'll get it out of me anyway. 'David's gone back to live in the States.'

'What?'

She heard.

'Why?'

'Gran, I don't want to talk about it.'

'OK, but why did he go back to the States?'

I answer only because I know she won't give up. 'His father lost his job.'

'Are you telling me that, after all those children have been through, he's uprooted them again because he lost his job? What's wrong with the man? I mean, how hard did he try to find another one here?'

I shrug.

'When did he lose his job?'

'A few weeks ago.'

'So he didn't try at all. Has he actually got a job in the States or did he just run back there with his tail between his legs when things got tough?'

'David said there's more security on the military side –'

She tut-tuts. 'The man's a coward. I mean, what kind of world would it be if we all let fear make our decisions for us?'

'Gran, can we not talk about this?'

She looks at me and her face softens. 'I'm sorry. He was just such a nice boy. And so good to you. You'll miss him.'

Understatement.

'Come here, give your old Gran a hug. No wonder you're miserable.'

I close my eyes. She smells safe and familiar, and I almost give in, I almost cry. But I keep my jaw set. And I stay on track.

When Gran goes, I return her sherry glass to the kitchen. Just inside the door, I stop. I'm about to back up when he sees me. He's standing at the hob, wearing Mum's red-and-white spotted apron and consulting one of her old cookery books. He looks up and smiles.

}|{

'What would you like for dinner?'

I'm cautious. 'Where's Barbara?'

'I gave her the rest of the day off.'

'But you don't know how to cook.'

'Of course I do.'

'Look, it's OK,' I say. 'I'll make myself a sandwich later.'

'How about curry? You used to love curry.'

'Mum's curry.'

'I can make Mum's curry.'

Just before I walk out on him, I say, 'And what's that going to do, bring her back?'

He makes the curry anyway. And guilt makes me sit down with him to eat it. It's just the two of us. No Marsha. No Barbara. No Mike. And none of the general hangers-on. For once, I could do with them here. I put an elbow on the table, between us, so I don't have to look at him.

'So,' he says. 'Grace is looking well.'

I can ignore that. It wasn't a question.

'How's she doing?'

I look right at him when I say, 'She misses Mum.' I let it hang there so he'll get the message – he should miss her too.

Victory! He looks guilty. His eyes return to his meal. After a while, though, he tries again, 'So, how's the work experience going?'

'Fine,' I say into the curry, which, weirdly, is good enough to remind me of Mum.

'What are they like, the people you work with?'

'Fine.'

'I should call in sometime and buy something. Support them.'

I look up suddenly. 'Don't!' He's supposed to be an engineer.

He takes a deep breath. Then says, 'OK.' He looks so hurt, I almost explain. Then I remember how things are. How they will always be.

And that's it for conversation.

Until he's taking my plate away.

'Do you think we should get you a course of vitamins, or something, you know, after the cold?'

When I recover from the shock, I say, 'It's OK. Gran got me some.'

'Really?' He looks guilty, like it was something he should have taken care of. 'Oh. Right. OK.'

After a few minutes' silence, he gets up and carries his plate to the sink.

If it was anyone else, I'd help clear up.

* * *

Sunday morning. When I come down for breakfast, he's sitting at the kitchen table with a newspaper open, like normal dads do. He could almost be an engineer. He looks up and smiles.

'Would you like an omelette?'

I feel like telling him to stop trying. 'Where's Barbara?'

'Having a lie-in.'

I go get my cereal. 'Haven't you work to do?'

'It's the weekend.'

'Hasn't stopped you before.'

He looks at me for a long time. 'And I'm sorry about that.'

I shrug, sit at the other end of the table and pour my golden flakes of corn.

He gets up, goes to the hob and starts to make himself an

omelette. And, suddenly, I do have a memory of him cooking. Frying something. I close my eyes and try to remember the smell. Burgers. That's what it was. Burgers. I was very small. But I remember – he used to make burgers. Good burgers. I'd forgotten that. He joins me at my end of the table and peppers his omelette.

'I was thinking,' he says. 'Would you like to bring Homer for a walk after breakfast?'

At the word 'walk' Homer's head and ears pop up.

'What, you mean with you?' Weird.

'Yeah. I was thinking we could bring him to the beach. Retrievers like water, don't they?'

'It's OK. I'm just going to walk along the road. And the path isn't wide enough for us all.'

'No problem,' he says, but his smile looks like it took a lot of effort.

27
TRIANGULAR SANDWICHES

He can't tell me what to do. Not anymore. He can't just waltz back into my life and order me around. He's lost the right.

This is the conversation I have with myself on the DART, on the way to Louis. Because this is the conversation I need to have to get me there. So many times, I plan to get off at the next stop and go back to the shop, forget the whole thing. But, somehow, my feet take me there.

Louis opens the door, looking like he just got out of bed. His hair is all over the place. His black T-shirt and denims look like they've been slept in. And he's in his bare feet. I ignore his smile and walk past him. Weird, coming into Sarah's house. For this.

'So,' he says, following me in. 'How are you?' He says it like he feels he should.

'Louis, there's no need to make conversation.'

He laughs. 'God, I love you!' He grabs my hand and starts towards the stairs, energised suddenly.

I've never seen his room before. It's pretty plain, just an

}|{

old drum kit in one corner and a punch bag in another. There are clothes on the floor and a half-eaten pizza on his desk. He hasn't bothered to make the bed. Holding my eyes, he starts to strip. My gut reaction is to turn away, but I make myself not. Then he is with me, and it starts. I don't set out to think of David. But the mouth on mine is his. The touch of a hand, his. The whisper in my ear, his. I've worked so hard to push him from my life, from my mind. I can let myself have this, can't I? Just for one second?

But the second becomes a minute. And then I'm falling, letting myself go, having what I denied myself for so long, going over the edge with him, giving myself to him, to us.

And then it's over. Too quickly. I open my eyes. And it's Louis, not David lying beside me. He looks relaxed and goofy. And maybe even a bit vulnerable. I feel guilty. For him. And for David. He offers me the famous cigarette. I take it out of guilt. He doesn't talk (which helps), just blows smoke rings like an extra young Marlboro Man. I lie, watching ring after ring defy gravity.

He rolls his head to look at me. And smiles. 'You were really into it today.'

I'm very still. 'Was I?' I feel myself blush.

He turns on his side and moves his face right up to mine. 'Hope you're not beginning to like me.' He grins.

'Fat chance.'

He laughs.

I make a point of looking at my watch. 'Look, I gotta go.'

'What's the rush?' he asks, lazily.

I start to grab my things. 'Haven't you lectures or something?'

His smile is lazy. Like James Dean. He says nothing. Just

swings himself from the bed and drags on his jeans. 'I'll walk you out.'

'Such a gent.'

At the front door, he asks, 'Don't I get a kiss goodbye?'

I land a quick peck on his cheek.

He laughs and shakes his head. 'You're weird.' It's the most sensible thing he's ever said. 'So, tomorrow?' he asks.

I shrug.

Back at the shop, I work hard, doing things that don't really need doing: cleaning glass that's not smudged, rearranging perfectly fine displays. I'm extra helpful with customers. But it doesn't stop the guilt. At six, Mike's waiting outside to take me home for Day Three in the Big Brother House, Day Three of Being Grounded.

The house is unusually quiet. No music. No conversations. An empty office. No buzz whatsoever. But the biggest surprise is waiting in the kitchen – my father unloading the dishwasher.

'Where's Barbara?'

His head pops up. 'Gave her the week off,' he says, cheerfully.

'Why?'

'So, how was work?' he asks.

Speaking of work, 'Haven't you an album coming out?'

'Where does this go?' He holds up a dish.

I shrug. 'The album,' I remind him.

'Don't worry about it. I'm not.'

This is seriously weird.

He knocks the dishwasher closed with a knee. I go to the fridge for a Coke.

'So. What are you up to?' he asks.

}|{

Getting the hell out of here, I think. It comes out as, 'Going to my room.'

'You know, Alex, if you ever want me to come watch a game of hockey or anything –'

I stare at him. 'One: you'd look like a total perv. Two: I've quit.'

He seems to think for a moment. 'Marsha mentioned some play . . .'

'Weeks ago.'

'OK. Right.'

'Look. You don't have to do this, OK?'

'What?'

'Whatever you're doing.'

'I'm just trying –'

'Well, don't. OK? Just go back to work.' Because he will, sooner or later, and I don't want to get used to this.

In the morning, he's at the island, putting ham between two slices of buttered bread.

'What're you doing?'

He looks up and smiles. 'Making your lunch.'

I watch him slice the sandwiches into triangles, the way I used to have them when I was a kid. It's the kind of thing that would kill your street cred. But weird that he remembers.

'You don't have to do that.'

'I want to.'

I shrug. And take the sandwiches he's carefully wrapped in tinfoil. He'll get tired of playing dad soon. Then we'll all know where we stand.

* * *

Louis passes me the cigarette. I pass it back without inhaling. This is the nicest bit. Maybe the only nice bit. Lying together. But not a couple.

'You and me,' he points the cigarette at me then at himself, 'we're the same. We know what we want and go after it.'

I feel like laughing because most of the time I don't know what I want. And if I ever do, I run from it. I turn on my side, my back to him so he knows not to talk. He traces a finger slowly along my spine. It feels intimate.

'Stop!'

He doesn't. I turn to face him, seriously ticked off. But he just kisses me. 'Let's go again.'

I look at him, the guy I once thought was dangerous. 'Will that shut you up?'

He laughs. 'Alex Newman, I think you might just be the perfect woman.'

Give me until I'm walking out the door and I'll feel the opposite.

All the way back on the DART, I wonder why I keep going back to him when I always feel so bad afterwards. It doesn't make sense. In the shop, I catch Pat looking at me and know she's wondering where the happy-go-lucky person she hired has gone. So I become that person and push everything from my mind. When I get home, I'm exhausted from the effort. Walking through the hall, I feel my shoulders relax. At least, here, I can be myself. But then, my father hands me a letter with a US postage stamp. My heart thumps hard. Until I see that it's from New York.

'It's from Marsha,' he says.

I hand it back.

'Come on, Alex. Hear her out. She's always had a lot of time for you –'

I give him a 'yeah, right' look.

'Just see what she has to say, then do what you like. Ignore it. Tear it to pieces. But you should read it.'

And, only because I know it won't change a thing, I do.

Dear Alex

I am so sorry. I never meant for anything like this to happen. I admire your father so much. He's been so good to me. Sometimes, people are just so lonely and sad, they do things they'd never normally do. I'm not excusing myself here. I hate what this has meant for you and your dad. I want you to know that I valued the friendship we had so much. You're an amazing person. I mean that. I won't be back – this is where you cheer – I'm giving up as a stylist. I'm going to start again as a fashion designer. I want to thank you for that. It was you who made me see what I really enjoy and what I'm good at. Good luck in everything you do, Alex.

Love Marsha

P.S. I'm only going to say one thing about your father – he is a good man.

I hand it back to him. 'Doesn't change a thing.'

* * *

But later, when I'm lying in bed, I think about the one line that jumped up and smacked me on the face. 'Sometimes, people are just so lonely and sad, they do things they'd never normally do.' I think of Louis. And for the first time, maybe I understand what's going on. Doesn't make me like myself any more, though.

I live three lives now. At work, I am one person. With Louis, another. At home, someone else. Sometimes people aren't happy with that. Take Louis. Always wanting to talk. Always wanting to know more.

'What's your favourite Simpsons character?' he asks, one day.

I laugh. Because if there's one question likely to make me talk, it's this. Still, I don't talk.

'Let me guess,' he starts.

'I don't watch *The Simpsons*,' I say, to cut him off.

He takes a long drag on the cigarette. 'Then why call your dog Homer?'

I sit up. 'Who told you about Homer?'

'My sister just happens to be one of your friends.'

'You haven't talked to her about me, have you?'

'Relax,' he says calmly, the way he says everything. 'I haven't talked to anyone about you. I just have ears.'

'Right, well, for the record, don't talk to her, OK?'

He fakes hurt. 'Don't you want people to know about us?'

'There is no "us".'

He looks down the bed, as if to say, 'What's this, then?'

'OK, enough! I'm getting up.' But I'm stuck between him and the wall and have to wait for him to move. He doesn't. So I start to climb over him.

Mistake. He grabs me around the waist and pulls me down.

'OK,' he says, smirking, 'I get it. This isn't serious. Now come here.'

Then there's Pat, a grown woman, who talks to me like we're friends. She's almost as bad as The Stylist.

'That was some lunch,' she says when I get back. She's smiling.

'Sorry,' I say. 'There's just something I have to do at lunchtime.'

'As long as you're having fun.'

And it occurs to me that maybe she's being sarcastic. 'I could work Saturdays to make up time.'

'Absolutely not!' She laughs. 'I was only joking.'

'It's not like I'm doing anything anyway.'

'You're sixteen, Alex. I'm pretty sure there's lots you do on a Saturday.' She looks kind of wistful.

'No, seriously. I'd be happy to work.'

'You are not working Saturdays. I don't mind you taking your time at lunch, seriously. You deserve it. I love having you here. And you're great for business.'

'Are you sure, because –'

'I'm sure,' she cuts across me. Then she stoops behind the counter. Next thing I know, she's handing me a small, gift-wrapped box. 'Here,' she says, 'something small.'

'For me?' I touch my heart. And there I go again. Someone shows me the tiniest kindness and I feel like crying.

'I saw you looking at it this morning.'

It's this really cute necklace – a silver chain with a square pendant that has a tiny heart at the centre, which moves. I look at her. 'Are you sure?'

She smiles and lifts it from the box. 'Here, let me put it on.'

'Thank you so much.'

'Alex, don't give it a second thought. You wear this, and, mark my words, people will buy them. You're a beautiful-looking girl.'

I am totally stunned.

But the amazing thing is, she's right: we sell three of those exact necklaces the same afternoon. And I find it hard to believe that anyone would want something just because I'm wearing it.

At about four, I'm arranging a display when I sense some-one behind me. I turn.

'Hi!' booms a woman in a pale-pink tracksuit, blonde hair piled on top of her head.

'Sorry, I didn't see you there.' I glance over at Pat who was supposed to be free for customers. She looks back at me and shrugs.

'I'm looking for a ring,' the woman says. Her accent is – I don't know – Australian?

'Of course.' I smile.

'An engagement ring.'

This isn't the kind of shop that sells engagement rings, and you'd know that the minute you walk in. Everything's modern and funky. There's nothing that I know of that's over 200 euro. Still, it must be an exciting time, so I congrat-ulate her.

'Oh, I'm not engaged,' she says.

I squint at her. Like, what?

'But I will be,' she adds, beaming.

I wonder if the guy knows this.

'I'm sorry,' I say. 'But we don't really sell engagement rings. It's mostly costume jewellery.'

}|{

'Where did you get that?' she asks, pointing at my hand. Her nails are bitten right down.

I look at the ring my mum had made for me out of one of the diamonds from her engagement ring. I never take it off. After Homer, it's the most precious thing I have.

'It was a gift,' I say quietly, slipping my hand out of sight. 'From someone very special.'

I squint at her. 'I'm sorry, but do I know you?'

She takes a step back. 'No, no. It's just, a present like that . . . must have come from someone special. That's all.'

Suddenly, I need her out of my face. 'Actually, I'm just here on work experience. Let me get you the owner. She might be able to help.' I look over at Pat.

'No. It's fine. She can't help. You don't do engagement rings.' She backs away. And, as quickly as she came, she's gone.

Pat comes over. 'Someone you know?'

'No.'

'Really? I was sure she knew you. She came in and walked straight by me as if she wanted to talk to you specifically.'

I look at the empty doorway. 'She wanted an engagement ring.'

'On her own?'

'She was kind of weird.'

28
THE BLACK HORSEMAN

One day, Mike pulls up outside the house, beside a car I recognise in the same way Frodo, from *The Lord of the Rings,* would recognise one of the black horsemen. One look at it and everything stops. I'm back ten months, to when the clock stopped and nothing else mattered. Mike and I exchange a glance.

'I'm sure it's nothing,' he says.

I want to tell him to reverse, get the hell out of here. I also want to rush in.

The front door opens. And the Black Horseman emerges, doctor's bag in his hand. I remember that bag – as not carrying the solution. I look from him to my father. Then, slowly, I get out of the car.

'Hello, Alex.' The doctor says it with pity in his voice, like I'm the same person I was back then.

'Hi,' I manage but just want him gone.

'Well, I'd better be off. You take care,' he says to my father, the way an undertaker might say, 'Don't die.'

I watch him walk to his car. Then watch my father. His

}{(

face looks tense and lined, like he's in pain. Suddenly, I'm cold.

'What is it? What's wrong?'

'It's just my back.'

'Just' his back? Why did he have to say 'just'? Mum had back pain. It wasn't 'just' her back. 'What's wrong with it?'

'Slipped disc.'

'Have you had an X-ray?'

'No need.'

'Then how d'you know what it is?'

'I've all the symptoms of a disc.'

'You need an X-ray. An ultrasound. Maybe even a CT scan.' I know the drill.

His face softens. 'Alex, this is a disc problem. Nothing more.'

'How d'you know? How can you be sure? I mean –'

'It's a common problem,' he says, firm now. Then adds, 'For people my age.' He smiles because normally he never admits his age.

'I'd still like you to have the tests. Please, Dad,' I say, surprising us both. I don't know when I last called him that.

He nods. 'OK. I'll have tests.'

'Thank you.'

I hurry to my room, where I fling my bag aside, ignore Homer and open my laptop. I google 'back pain' and 'causes'. No mention of cancer, so I change my search. 'Back pain' and 'cancer'. That produces results. 'See,' I feel like saying to the Black Horseman. 'He needs the tests.'

I come back down.

'How did you slip your disc?' I ask, watching his expression carefully.

'Tying my shoe. Can you believe that?'

That's exactly what I'm wondering, can I believe it? 'Did he give you painkillers?'

He nods. 'And Valium to relax the muscles.'

'Did you take them?'

'Yeah.'

'Maybe you should lie down.'

'He said I'm better off moving around.'

'Maybe we should change doctor.' It's not like he was any good last time.

'Alex. It's a disc. I'd put money on it.'

'How about your life?'

Louis stands at the door of his house. Watching me.

'What's up?' he asks.

'Nothing.' I walk past him.

He follows. Sticks his face in mine. 'No. There's definitely something. You're worried.'

'Louis, the only thing I'm worried about is that you won't shut up.'

'Let's not do it today,' he says.

'What?'

'I'll make you lunch instead.'

'Right, I'm going.' I head for the door.

He laughs. 'Alright, alright. But I'm going to feel used and dirty.'

I look at him. And he bursts out laughing. I hit him. He grabs me, throws me over his shoulder like he's some sort of caveman and carries me upstairs. Where I do stop worrying. For a while. I feel like thanking him.

* * *

}|{

When I get home that evening, my father is sitting at the kitchen table, reading a cookery book. He has it up to his face, and I don't know whether it's because he can't bend over the book or because he's going blind. He's wearing blackout shades – indoors – so the blind theory isn't all that crazy. He's also wearing grey tracksuit bottoms, a navy hoodie and flip-flops (in January). He's also got serious 5 o'clock shadow.

'Who's the new stylist?' I ask, dropping my bag and heading for the fridge.

'My back.'

I turn. 'What?'

'Nothing else is comfortable. And I can't bend to tie laces.'

'So, explain the shades.'

'I always wear shades.'

'Yeah, but you can usually see your eyes through them. You look like a mobster.'

He puts a hand to them. 'The shades are staying.'

He gets up from the chair, grimacing as he straightens, placing a hand on his lower back.

I frown. 'Have you had the tests yet?'

He looks guilty. 'They take a while to set up.'

'Have you set them up?'

'On my list.'

I give him a look.

'OK. First thing tomorrow. Promise.' He makes his way to the island, walking like an old man. 'So, what would you like for dinner?'

'Get Barbara back. Seriously, look at you. You can't even bend down.'

He holds the counter, slowly squats down, bending at his knees, keeping his back straight. 'Voilà,' he says.

I shake my head. And go upstairs to my computer. There must be better advice on back pain than 'keep moving'.

In the morning, he still hasn't shaved. He looks seriously grizzly.

I make no comment. Just eat the porridge he insisted on making me.

'Why don't I drive you to work today?' he asks.

I look up, surprised. 'Why? We've Mike.'

He eases himself into the chair opposite. 'When was the last time I dropped you anywhere? I'm your dad. I'm supposed to be giving you lifts. And moaning about it.' He smiles.

'What about the album?'

'What about it?'

'Don't you have to work on it?'

'The album'll get done.' He takes a spoon of porridge, lifting it all the way to his mouth rather than leaning towards it.

I look at him incredulously.

'So, am I dropping you off?' he asks.

I shrug. 'Alright, then.'

'Great!' he says, like he's just topped the charts.

He grimaces getting into the car.

'This isn't good for your back, is it?' I ask.

'Honestly?'

'Honestly.'

'No. It's terrible.' He chuckles.

}|{

'I'll go get Mike.'

'No. I'm in now. I'll let Mike collect you.' Pain crosses his face when he presses on the clutch.

'Dad!'

'I'm fine.'

'OK, just so you know,' I warn him. 'The first question I'll ask when I get in is about the tests.'

'OK, Boss.'

Louis lies on his side, looking at me.

'You're beautiful, you know that?'

I turn slowly. 'You'd better not mean anything by that.'

He laughs. 'What? So I can't give you a compliment?'

'No.'

'OK, then, you're pig ugly.'

'That's better.'

He laughs.

29
SMALL, HAIRY ANIMAL

I can't believe how fast his hair grows. I can detect four colours in his beard now: red, grey, brown and black. Picture that with flip-flops, trackie bottoms and shades. I try to be kind.

'The beard has to go, Dad.'

'It's not a beard.'

'Then what is it, a small, hairy animal? Beards are so not in right now. At least, that kind of beard.'

He looks up from chopping vegetables. 'It's not a fashion statement.'

'That's for sure.'

'If anything, it's an anti-fashion statement.'

'Okaaay,' I say. 'And that would be great if you didn't look like Steve Carell in *Evan Almighty*. Seriously, with the flip-flops. All you're missing's the robe.'

'A robe?' he says, like it's an ingenious idea.

'OK. Just get rid of the shades. Seriously, Dad. You're not a rapper.'

He smiles. 'Can't a man try something new?'

'The flip-flops are new. The facial hair is new. Just leave the shades, OK?'

He just smiles.

'OK. Suit yourself,' I say casually. I lean forward to steal from his chopping board. 'What you cooking?'

'Stir-fry.'

'Want a hand?'

He hands me a knife, but instead of taking it, I whip off the shades. 'See, you don't need –' I start to say, but never get to finish. His eyes are red. Seriously red. And swollen. Like he's been crying. Which couldn't be right. He doesn't do crying. I should know.

'Are you OK?'

He snaps the shades back on and smiles. 'Onions!'

I look down. 'Spring onions?'

He ignores that.

I look at him closely. 'Did you set up those tests?'

'Yep.' He says it too lightly.

'For when?'

'Tomorrow.'

I try to stare him down. But end up staring at my reflection in his shades.

'Tomorrow, I promise.'

Next day, soon as I get home, I ask what the X-ray showed.

'Slipped disc.'

'Just a slipped disc?'

'Just a slipped disc.'

'Can I see it?'

'What, the X-ray?'

'Yeah.'

}|{

'I don't have it.'

'Where is it?'

'I don't know. I think I might have left it in the hospital.'

'Dad!' God.

'It's the Valium. It's making me stupid.'

'You'll have to ring them. You're supposed to keep the X-rays.' Doesn't he remember anything? Then again, he wasn't around.

'OK,' he says. 'I'll ring them.'

'When?'

'First thing.'

'OK. Because I want to see them.'

I've compiled a pretty decent file on back pain and slipped discs. He needs a hardboard under his mattress. He needs to go for walks. Swimming is good. But not all types of stroke. I've a printout of all the different gadgets that could help: a special car seat, a roll to support his lower back, a type of belt that releases heat. When he's over the worst, Pilates could help strengthen the muscles that support the spine. I collect up the sheets and slot them into the folder. I head downstairs.

The one time I want to find him, I can't. I check the kitchen first (which shows how much things have changed around here). I try the office and the basement and am glad to find them deserted. I go outside because he's been wandering around the garden on his own a lot lately. It's only when I'm out here, freezing, that I see him – inside. He's getting into the pool, climbing down slowly, like each step causes huge pain. The door to the pool is locked in winter so I have to go back in through the house.

When I reach the pool, he has managed to get in. He's

standing waist-deep, his back to me. I'm about to call out, when I realise something's not right. He's shaking. His whole body is shaking. Then, he drops his head into his hands. A loud sob echoes off the tiled walls. Oh my God. He's crying – my father, who never cries, who doesn't know how. I back away, my mind playing catch-up. He lied about the tests. This is more than 'just' his back. He's hiding behind shades – because he doesn't want me to know. He's stopped shaving – because what's the point? He's being nice to me – because he's not going to be around.

I run to my room, drop the printout in the bin and sink onto the bed. From somewhere deep inside comes a wail. I pull my knees to my chest and wrap my arms around them. But it's useless. I can't hold it in. Loud, noisy sobs break free, then I'm crying like my heart is broken. And maybe it is. Down in the pool is the man who gave me piggybacks, taught me to cycle, read me once-upon-a-times. How easily I blocked all that out – so I could hate him. Tears flood my face, an avalanche of salt water – and snot. My body shakes. I hug myself tighter. But just can't stop.

I don't know how long I've been like this when I hear a quiet knock on the door. I press my lips together. Swipe tears from my face. Wipe my nose with one sleeve and then the other. I say nothing and hope he'll go away. He knocks again. Then the door slowly opens.

At the sight of my face, I expect him to turn and run. But he doesn't. He comes in.

'Alex. What's wrong? What is it?' He comes and sits on the edge of the bed. He grimaces, holds his back, then stands again. He turns around to face me, then lowers himself onto his knees, like a child saying his prayers at his bedside.

'You can take off the shades, now, Dad. I know.'

He looks confused. 'Know what?'

'It's not your back, is it? You're ill. Seriously ill. And you don't want me to know.'

'I don't know what you're talking about.'

'I saw you in the pool. I'm not stupid. You don't cry. You never cry. This is it, isn't it? Tell me. I'm not a kid any more.' But I feel like a kid. I feel small and vulnerable and in need of comfort. 'And take off those freaking shades.'

He does, lowering them onto the bed. 'I'm not sick, Alex. Sometimes, I wish I was.'

'How can you even say that?'

'I'm sorry. But if I could swap places with her, I would. Like that.' He snaps his fingers.

And I feel guilty, because there were times I wished it had been him.

'You want to know why I'm so upset? Because I failed you both. So incredibly.'

So he's not dying?

'I've been hiding, Alex, running away.'

What's he talking about?

'I couldn't face it. Any of it. Mum's pain. The fact that there was nothing I could do to save her. The reality of her being gone.'

This is about Mum?

'I blocked it out. Pretended it wasn't happening. Lost myself in work.' I want to tell him to slow down. Go back. Repeat everything. But I say nothing. Just try to keep up. 'Every time I looked at you, I saw Mum. I also saw your pain, and I couldn't handle it. So I kept away. From my own daughter!'

But this isn't about me. 'Mum needed you. She loved you so much, and she had to die without you. You could have been there. You should have been.'

He drops his head into his hands. 'I know. I. Know.'

'You should have said goodbye.'

He looks at me, like his heart is breaking. 'I couldn't, Alex. I couldn't let her go. She was ready. She accepted it. I couldn't. And as long as I live, I'll never forgive myself.'

Good, I think. 'She needed you. We needed you.'

'You needed me to be strong. But I couldn't go into that room and be strong. I couldn't pretend.'

'No one wanted you to.'

'No one wanted me to go in there and beg her not to die, not to leave us, but that's what I'd have done.'

'At least it'd have shown you cared.'

He stares at me like I've hit him. 'I cared. God, I cared. Your mother was my life. She was everything. The only one who made sense of my stupid, crazy existence. The only one who really understood me. No one will ever know how much I loved her. And now, I have to face it. She's gone, and she's never coming back. I'll never see her again. Never touch her. Never hold her.'

Welcome to my world, I think as he breaks down.

I imagined this. I wanted it. I thought it was all I wanted. For him to be sorry. For him to cry. But I never imagined how hard it would be to see him so lost without her.

'I'm sorry,' he says, finally. 'I've been the worst dad. But I never stopped loving you, Alex, never stopped caring. That's why I got the experts, people who knew about grief, who knew how to listen, who knew what to say. To give you what I couldn't.'

Doesn't he see? 'I didn't want experts. I wanted you. You were all I'd left.'

'And I'm sorry. So, so sorry. I love you. So much. I always have. I want you to know that.' He reaches out his hand for mine.

'I'm tired,' I say. 'I need to think.'

He drops his head. 'OK.' He leans back and pushes himself into standing position. 'I'm sorry,' he says again, and then leaves, looking like a man who has lost everything.

The good thing about dogs is that they're simple. If they love you, they want to be with you. They wag their tails. Lick you. Jump up. You know where you stand. When Homer comes over and nuzzles me with his wet nose, I don't send him away.

'I'm sorry,' I say. 'For being so mean, for taking it out on you. Tomorrow we'll go to the beach. You can chase seagulls and bark at the waves. I'm sorry, Homesy.'

I put my arms around him and my head against his neck. I close my eyes and try to adjust to my shifted life. My father's not dying. He loved my mother. He loves me. He doesn't know everything. And he's not always right. There goes gravity – again.

30
CARROT CAKE

At breakfast, I hand him the printout.

He puts down his spoon. 'What's this?'

'Just some stuff on backs.'

He glances through the pages. Looks up and smiles. 'Thank you.' He's still wearing the glasses. And the beard is getting scary. He slept in their old room last night. I heard him cry. We don't talk about that. We don't talk at all.

Mikes drives me to work. It's my last day there. And while a part of me is kind of sad about that, another part feels it's time to move on. At lunch, instead of taking the DART to Louis, I find myself walking to the sea. I sit on the wall at Sandycove beach and watch tiny waves wash in and out. I lose myself in their rhythm and think about last night, everything Dad said. I wish I had Mum here now, to tell her that he loved her. But then, she always knew. It was me who raged against him. She who defended. She who told me that it was 'his way'. I just didn't believe her. She was fooling herself, I thought, avoiding the truth that he'd moved on. How could she have had so much faith in him? How could she have been so sure? And why couldn't I be like her? Instead of being like my father: cutting and running.

'I'm sorry,' I whisper to the sea, as if the waves can carry my message around the world to him, to David.

Pat tries to give me money. For a 'shopping spree' with my mum.

'Thank you so much,' I say, touched. 'But I can't take it. We're not meant to.'

'I thought you might say that. So, Plan B.' She hands me a gift-wrapped box. 'Something small,' she says.

It's a matching set. Earrings, necklace, bracelet. And I know exactly how much it costs. 'It's too much.'

'If you don't take it, I'll be offended. I mean that.' I look at her. She's just so sweet. I wish her daughter spent more time with her.

'Thank you so much, Pat.' I actually hug her. What's getting into me?

When I get home, Streak's car is outside. My heart sinks. Because my father must be returning to work. But his office is empty. And when I go into the kitchen, I see them in the garden, sitting on the far wall, in the same spot Marsha chose to read her divorce papers. Dad's head is bent, and Streak's arm is around him. Suddenly, I want to protect him from this – from the grief, the loss, the pain. But I can't go back there. I can't let his grief make mine raw again. So thank you, Streak, for your arm. For your presence beside him. For your ears. And your wisdom in staying quiet and letting him talk.

I turn from the window. I pick up the phone and call Rachel.

}I{

'I'm sorry,' I say.

'You should be. You were a complete bitch.'

'I know. Sorry.' It's not easy to explain. So I quote Mike. 'I kind of went off the rails there for a while.'

There's a long pause, then a cautious, 'You back on them now?'

'Think so.'

'Good,' she says, like it's an order.

'How are things with you?' I ask.

'OK. Sarah's driving me mad, though.'

'Don't suppose you're free to come over?'

'Now?'

'Only if it suits. I'm kinda grounded.'

'Seriously?'

'Seriously.'

The minute we see each other, we hug. And I promise myself I'll never hurt her again.

'I'm sorry,' I say, just so she's sure.

She pulls back. 'I presume you did the same to David?'

I look away. 'It's better this way.'

'To hurt the guy you love?'

I turn back. 'Who says I love him?'

She gives me this look. A typical Rachel, no-nonsense look. And something inside me gives. I close my eyes. 'OK. I admit it. I love him. I love him so much, Rache.'

'So why not trust him?'

'I do trust him. But not life. He promised he'd never leave. And he's gone. I can't trust in good things happening. They never do. Not to me.' And, after managing not to for so long, I start to cry.

}|{

She hugs me. And, for a long time, neither of us speaks.

'Maybe you're right,' she says, finally. 'I haven't been through what you have. I've no clue.'

But I don't feel right. Not anymore. 'I'm such a mess.'

'No you're not.'

She doesn't know what I've done. She doesn't know about Louis. And I can't tell her. She'd hate me. Like I hate me.

'I found my dad in bed with The Stylist.'

'Oh my God. When?'

'The day David left.'

'Oh, Alex.'

'She's gone back to the States.'

'And your dad? I guess you must really hate him now?'

'Actually, we kind of made up.' I explain how he threw himself into work because he couldn't face life without Mum. I explain how he loved her. And how he loves me.

'It makes so much sense,' she says. Then smiles. 'I always liked your dad.'

And I have to admit, I always liked him too. Even when I didn't want to.

But enough about me. 'How was your work experience?' I ask.

'Lots of filing X-rays, so kind of boring. But I got to go up to the wards to track down X-rays too, and that bit was great. I'd have a real look around. I'd watch the doctors and what was going on in the wards. In the nurses' stations I'd listen to discussions about patients, their illnesses and treatment. That bit was great. And the people in X-Ray were so sweet. They never asked what took me so long. They even gave me a cake when I was leaving. How about you? How was the shop?'

)I(

I shrug. There was so much going on in my life, I can't remember a lot. But – 'Pat was lovely. Really sweet. How did Sarah get on?'

She rolls her eyes. 'Miss Grace had to find her something in the end. She and Simon Kelleher got placed up in UCD.'

'Oh my God. She must have been thrilled. Just her and Simon.'

'She's, like, been throwing herself at him ever since. I never thought I've ever feel sorry for Simon Kelleher. But I kind of do.'

'D'you think they'll get together?'

She shrugs. 'If he finally caves in.'

'What does she see in him?'

'Boyfriend potential, I guess.'

Speaking of which: 'How's Mark?'

She breaks into this beautiful smile.

'That good?' I say.

'I think I love him.' She grimaces.

I hug her. Because if anyone deserves love, it's Rache.

We're dropping Rachel home when my phone rings.

'Hey!' Oh, God. It's Louis.

'Can I call you straight back?' I kill the line.

Luckily, we're just pulling up outside Rachel's.

'So, see you Monday,' she says, hugging me.

I smile. 'Monday.'

I wait till I'm home to call him back. 'How did you get my number?'

'And hel-lo to you, too.'

'Seriously, Louis. I asked you not to tell Sarah.'

'I just asked for a number. Could have meant anything.'

'If Sarah wasn't Sarah.'

'Where were you, today?'

'Oh. Sorry. I couldn't make it.'

'We on for tomorrow?'

I have to think. 'Louis. There's a lot going on right now.' All of it in my head. 'Can I call you?'

'Sure,' he says, as chilled as always. And that's the great thing about him. He just doesn't care.

In the morning, my father's still wearing his blackout shades and pretending everything's fine. It's easier this way. For both of us.

'How's the back?'

'Pain in the butt. Literally.'

'Did you try lying on your side with a pillow between your legs?'

He nods. 'It did give me some relief.'

'Some relief?'

'It's a start, believe me.' Then he smiles. 'Last night, I was lying there trying to get comfortable, and I had this flash-back to when Mum was pregnant with you. That's the way she'd be, pillow between her legs, moving around, trying to get comfortable.'

'She slept like that?'

'For the last month or two.'

I think about that, the three of us snuggled up together, me there, but not yet.

'It was a great time,' he says, his face softening, 'maybe even the best, everything ahead of us, you to look forward to.' His expression changes. 'Seems so long ago.' It's a whisper. He clears his throat.

)|(

I don't think, just reach out and squeeze his hand. 'I'm still here.'

He takes off the glasses. 'And I'm sorry for not appreciating that until it was too late. For ignoring you till I lost you.'

I look him in the eye. 'You haven't lost me.'

Saturday, I call to my gran, feeling like Little Red Riding Hood bringing cake to her gran. Dad made her a carrot cake.

'Your father made that?'

'He's OK, Gran. He's sorry.' I tell her everything.

She looks at me. 'Maybe I'll have some of that carrot cake, after all,' she says. She cuts herself a huge wedge, like she's feeling guilty for being so hard on him.

'Tell him I loved it.'

'Maybe you should eat some first.'

'Tell him anyway.'

I smile. 'OK.'

For a while, we just chill, sipping tea and eating cake. Then she asks, 'So, how's David getting on in San Diego?'

I try to hedge by giving a little shrug.

'What's that supposed to mean?'

'Nothing. We're just not in touch.'

She puts down her fork. 'What? Why not?'

'It's easier.'

'Easier?' She sounds dubious.

'We can get on with our lives.'

Now she's squinting at me. 'Whose idea was this?'

I shrug again, poke at the cake.

'David wanted to stay in touch, didn't he?' she asks. And when I don't answer, she adds, 'He did. Didn't he?'

'OK, yeah, he did. But what's the point? It was going to end anyway, sooner or later.'

'How do you know that?'

'Because everything does.'

She looks at me. 'Not true,' she says, gently. 'I still have you, haven't I?'

I force a smile.

'You know, you could have just played it by ear –' she starts again.

'Gran! Playing it by ear is something you do when you don't care either way. Then, when it doesn't work out, you're not flattened.'

'You love him, don't you?'

I look away.

'Then don't give up on him.'

'Too late.'

She comes over and sits beside me. 'Alex. Bad things happen, but you have to trust that good things do too.'

I don't have to trust anything.

'That boy loved you . . . But you know that, don't you?'

I shrug.

'Did you tell him you love him?'

'Who says I do?'

'This is your gran you're talking to. Now, answer the question.'

'No, I didn't tell him.'

She sighs deeply. 'What am I going to do with you?' But then she smiles, and it's like, no matter what I do, she'll go on loving me. 'Come here,' she says. I move closer, and she hugs me. 'You're a chip off the old block, you know that?' I'm used to people comparing me to mum. But then she says, 'Just like your dad.'

I look at her, totally shocked. I'm not like my dad at all.

'So afraid of being hurt you run from people.'

I stare at her as I start to get it.

She looks at me. 'You miss David, don't you? You just won't let yourself admit it.'

I look down.

'Be honest with yourself, Alex. No matter how scary it is. Because if you can't be honest with yourself, life gets very confusing.'

I stare at her. She knows, I think. She knows about Louis. But how can she?

Maybe she just knows what she's talking about.

31
How OK?

Monday morning, and I'm on the DART with Rachel.

'Here comes Sarah,' she says. 'Be prepared. She's kind of upset about the communication blackout.'

Sarah doesn't smile. She just sits beside Rachel and looks across at me like she has a problem.

'I'm sorry,' I say before she can speak. 'For not returning your calls.'

'And texts. And MSNs. And emails.'

'Sorry. I just got a bit down over Christmas.'

'That's what friends are for.' She holds my eyes, making her point.

'I know. I'm sorry.' I blow out a breath.

'It's OK,' she says suddenly, lightly. Like, apology accepted, let's move on. And that's what I love about her. Instant forgiveness. 'What did you get for Christmas?' she asks me.

'Oh God. I forgot about my presents.'

'What?'

I shrug. 'I put them away. Then forgot about them.'

She looks at me as if to say, 'How's that possible?'

}|{

'Wow. You really must have been down,' she says. She thinks for a moment, then instructs: 'OK. Open them tonight and let us know.'

I smile. 'OK.'

We reach the school. In the corridor, we meet Mark. I haven't seen him since before Christmas. And he must have forgotten I exist because when he says, 'Hey,' he looks only at Rachel and Sarah. I'm kind of surprised but not bothered. We all walk together towards the class.

'Yo, Mark!' Simon calls. And Mark stops to talk to him.

The rest of us carry on. It's almost nine when we reach the classroom, so we just go to our desks. Sitting at mine, my heart plummets. Last time I sat here, my favourite view was the back of David's head. Now, I look over at his empty desk, knowing he won't be in, won't be throwing his bag down, won't be taking his place, glancing back and smiling. I feel the ache starting. But this time, I don't try to stop it. Just let it come. Then Simon flops into David's seat, slips off his shoes and puts his feet up against the radiator. I have to stop myself throwing my pencil case at the back of his head.

Mark passes my desk. And totally blanks me. That's the second time! I look at Rachel to see if she's noticed, but she's rooting in her bag. I glance back at Mark. Who looks away. Oh my God!

Class starts. There's talk of a trip to Uganda to help children there. I know nothing about Uganda. And I guess I should. So I listen.

At break, I follow Rachel to the loo.

'What's wrong with Mark?' I ask as she washes her hands. 'Did I do something to him?'

}|{

Our eyes meet in the giant mirror over the sinks. She looks embarrassed.

'Don't mind him. He's just being stupid.' She turns off the tap and goes to dry her hands.

I follow. 'So there is something.'

She turns. 'He just thinks he's being loyal to David.' She rolls her eyes at that.

'What d'you mean?'

'The way it ended between you.'

Finally, I get it. 'You mean the way I ended it?'

'Alex, I know how hard it was for you after losing your mum. I tried to explain that to Mark but he just sees it from David's point of view.'

'Which is?'

She shrugs. 'He lost his mum too. And you walked out on him.'

And that's it, right there: the truth. Like a wall of sound coming at me.

'Look, Alex. This is none of his business. Don't worry about it, OK? You know guys. Tomorrow he'll have forgotten about it. Seriously.'

'No. He's right. He's absolutely right. David lost his mum, too. And I shut him out. Like my father shut me out. I knew what that was like and I still did it to him. He'd never have done that to me.' And he'd never have gone off with someone else, the way I did.

'David'll be fine,' Rachel says.

'No. I was horrible to him. He told me he loved me, and I threw it back in his face. The things I said.'

'You were trying to protect yourself.'

And him. But. 'You don't know what I said.'

'I do. Mark told me.'

I look at her. 'I never meant to hurt him, Rache. I just wanted to cut out all that pain. But I'm so sorry for everything I said to him.'

'Then tell him.'

'How can I when I'm sorry for hurting him but not for ending it?'

'You're not sorry you ended it?' She looks shocked.

'Rachel, nothing's changed. Life is still life. I can't trust in it again. I won't.'

'I don't know what to say.'

Amy walks into the bathroom and takes a long look at us. 'Uh-oh, looks heavy,' she says, smiling.

'Let's go,' Rachel says.

Out on the corridor, I stop. 'Rache.'

She stops. Turns.

I pause, so she knows what's coming is important. 'What you have with Mark . . . Treasure it, OK? I mean, really treasure it. Fight for it.'

She looks guilty. But nods. Then, she says, 'You'll meet someone else.'

'No.' I don't want anyone else. David was the one. The way Dad was for Mum.

We go back to the canteen. And it's no coincidence that Mark leaves at exactly the same time.

'I'll see you later,' he says to Rachel. And is gone.

'Where were you?' Sarah's asking. 'I was about to send out a search party.' She glances at Simon when she says this, checking for a reaction.

He has eyes only for his ham roll.

Sarah looks at me. 'So,' she says. 'Why did Louis want your number?'

I blush. 'My number?'

}|{

Rachel looks at me.

'Yeah. Your number,' Sarah says, staring me down.

'How should I know?'

'Didn't he call you?' She looks surprised. 'Louis doesn't ask for things he doesn't want.'

'If Louis calls, you'll be the first to know,' I lie. And know suddenly what I have to do.

I arrange to meet him at the Forty Foot. It seems right to end it where it started. Not that there really was an 'it'. Louis's not going to care. I'm like a battery to him – easily replaced.

I arrive on time. But he's already there. He waves when he sees me and stands.

'Hey,' he says. He hugs me. Which is weird.

We sit side by side, looking at the sea, which is darkening as the sun sets. I wonder what words to use.

'So,' he says, before I can use any, 'I thought we could go out. On a date. A proper date.'

I stare at him.

He laughs. 'Don't look so shocked.'

'Louis –'

'It works like this. I bring you to a restaurant, nothing too fancy. I slag you a bit. You slag me back. I bring you home, we kiss goodnight –'

'Louis. I don't think we should go on a date.'

He looks disappointed but not surprised. 'Even if I promise not to talk?'

I want to hug him. 'You know I don't want a relationship.'

'Did someone say "relationship"?' He looks around. 'No. I think dinner was the proposition.' He looks kind of adorable like this.

}|{

'I'm kind of messed up, Louis.'

'You're the sanest person I know.'

'You don't know me.'

'I think I do.' His smile is crooked. And in his own Louis way, I love him. 'OK. Forget dinner,' he says. 'Bad idea. When am I seeing you again? It's been a while.'

'That's the thing. I don't think we should, any more.'

He looks away. I see him swallow. When he turns back, he says, 'There's someone else, isn't there?'

I'm surprised by the question. Even more surprised by the answer. 'Yes.'

'Surfer boy?'

'Surfer boy – who's now living in San Diego and hates my guts.'

'Some consolation, I guess.' His smile is crooked. 'But, hang on,' he says, 'if he's not here, and he hates your so-called guts –'

'It's over. Totally over. But I haven't been honest with myself for a long time now. And I need to do that. I need to miss him. I owe him that. I owe myself that.' I squint. 'If that makes any sense.'

'Eh. No.' He smiles.

'Louis, you're a great guy . . .'

'No. I'm not. But I was becoming a better guy.'

'I like you. I really like you. But –'

'OK. Stop there. You love this guy, right?'

I press my lips together. Nod.

'Then don't tell me how much you like me, OK?'

I blush. 'Sorry.'

And then he goes all bad-boy again. 'Don't suppose there's any chance of a sympathy shag?'

I burst out laughing. 'Don't suppose there's any chance of us staying friends?'

His turn to laugh.

'I'll miss you,' I say.

'You're weird.'

'Finally, we agree.'

I've deleted everything. Photos. Texts. Emails. All I can get back are the songs. I download Nina Simone, Gorillaz and everything else I've deleted. I lie on my bed listening to sounds and letting myself remember. Our first kiss, stolen by him, behind flapping sails . . . hearing that he'd always liked me . . . the hospital trip with Bobby and how gentle he was with him . . . the freckle on his eyelid . . .another on the sole of his foot . . . his touch on my skin . . . the curl of the hair at the base of his neck, his smile, his laugh . . . Mr Zog's Sex Wax . . .

I sit up. Remembering. I still have the presents I got him for Christmas – Mr Zog's Christmas stocking and Mr Zog's hoodie. I get up. Go to the wardrobe and take them out. I strip off the wrapping, put on the hoodie and roll up the sleeves. I look at myself in the mirror and let myself miss him. Then I go back to the wardrobe and take out all the other gift-wrapped presents. And put them on the bed. One by one, I go through them. The gift I got the man formerly known as The Rockstar: a personal organiser. It was a hint. The gift I got the person I thought was a friend: a pretty cool belt, actually. The gifts I got Rachel (a medical en-cyclopedia she didn't already have – harder than you'd imagine) and Sarah (a year's subscription to *Kiss* magazine). I take the last two out and put them in my bag. I throw the belt in the bin. And decide to shop for a new present for Dad.

}|{

Then I take out the gifts I never opened. A day with a personal shopper, from The Stylist. I know who'd like that. I put it aside for Sarah, then go to the bin and fish out the belt for her too. Rachel won't mind. It's an unwritten rule. All unwanted presents go to Sarah who hasn't half the stuff we have and really does appreciate them. From The Rockstar, I get a bunch of clothes, individually wrapped, probably selected by The Stylist. The last present has different wrapping. I read the note attached and my heart starts to pound. All I can think is: How? I try to work it out. That day he called and I wouldn't see him . . . He must have left it with Marsha. But why didn't she just give it to me straight away rather than include it with all the other gifts? Probably knew what I'd do with it.

When I open it up and see what it is, I can't believe it. It is the exact necklace Pat gave to me because she saw me admiring it. I imagine him going into the shop. Did he ask for help? Or did he know, automatically, what I'd like? And as my eyes fill, I know the answer.

Next day, the weirdest thing. Sarah gets me on her own in school. She looks awkward, which is so not like her.

'I'm sorry,' she says. 'About David.'

'Oh. OK. Right. Thanks.'

She looks down at her Dubes. 'I mean, I know you're not into deep conversations and that. But I just wanted to say, like, shame. You know?'

'Thanks.'

'I wanted to tell you yesterday when you got back after Christmas, but there was always someone around.'

I nod.

}|{

'Alex?'

'Yeah?'

And then she starts to speak so quickly, not even stopping for a breath, like this is something she's been holding in for a long time. 'I'm so sorry for flirting with David that time in Bray. I let on it was no big deal. Because I didn't want it to be. But I did flirt with him. I don't know why. I know he's caliente but I don't fancy him. And the last thing I'd ever want is to upset you. I just think I was so down about that guy not showing up . . . But I swear to God I didn't do it on purpose. I mean, if I'd thought about it for just one second, I'd never have done it. I swear.'

'It's OK, Sarah. Forget it.'

'Are you sure because I've just been, like, totally hating myself about it, you know? You're my best friend, well you and Rache, both of you, and you're like, so important to me, and I'd never want to upset you. And I want to say sorry for every time I've, like, put my foot in it about your mum. I don't know how I do it but I keep doing it, and the more I try not to, the more I do it. And I'm, like, so sorry –'

I smile. 'It's OK. Seriously. Don't worry about it. OK?'

She nods. Then asks one more time if I'm sure.

'Come here,' I say. And we hug.

32
THE NAKED GUN

Being grounded is not supposed to be a picnic. But, for me, it is. I like that there's someone who wants me back by a certain time. Who actually cares that I'm walking in the door. Who is in the kitchen when I come in. And asks how my day went. He walks the dog with me, now. I help him with dinner. We watch movies together. I never see him work. For the first time in ages, I like being home. I also like having an excuse to stay there when someone calls, asking me out. Which is why I decided to stay grounded. I don't say anything, just carry on living my new routine.

One day, Dad stops wearing the shades. Soon, the beard goes. Then, on the eve of my mum's anniversary, comes the third surprise: he suggests we do something to mark it.

I feel my whole face brighten. 'Really?'

'Maybe we could watch a movie she liked – or something?'

'*The Naked Gun*!' I say, straight out. She always loved it. He looks at me. 'How did you know?'

'What?'

'It was our movie.'

'Was it?'

'We saw it on our first date.'

'Really? I never knew that.'

'And our next.'

I look at him.

'And our next.'

I laugh. 'What?'

'We just kept going back. I thought she was only after me for the movie.'

I try to imagine them young.

'She used to call me her knight in shining armour.'

I think of David. 'What did you rescue her from?'

He waves a hand. 'Oh, some boring old accountant who was sniffing around.'

'Sniffing around? Seriously, Dad.' But I want to hear all about them then, in love, happy. 'So why did she pick you over the accountant?' I say it like it was a really dumb move. But it's OK. He knows I'm joking.

He shakes his head like it's still a mystery. 'She was way out of my league.'

I think of David stealing that kiss. 'Maybe she thought you were cheeky? Maybe she liked that you wouldn't be put off?'

He looks surprised that I would know this. 'Maybe,' he says.

'Were you in a band then?'

'Ah, some garage band, totally hopeless and going nowhere.'

'I'd love to see some really old pictures of when you started going out.'

He smiles. 'You make it sound like it was BC!'

* * *

}|{

I plan it out. Do it right. The way Mum would have. I make popcorn from kernels. Pour tall glasses of Kombucha and ice. Turn off all phones. Close the blinds. Dad has to sit on a hard chair for his back. So I put it next to the couch and place the popcorn between us. We clink our glasses. Because this is a tribute.

'To Mum.'

'To Mum.'

I laugh in all the right places. So does Dad. Leslie Nielsen's face helps. I can't help missing her, though, especially at her favourite bits. The opening credits. Lieutenant Frank Drebin's car taking off without him and catching fire. ('Did anyone get a look at the driver?') And, of course, the driving lesson that turned into a car chase. It's weird how the funniest parts of a movie can make you saddest. I do a good job of pretending, though. Dad's laughter turns to tears when Frank Drebin starts to frisk the baseball players. He disappears for a while.

When he returns, he's not hiding behind glasses any more and he's carrying a box of old photos.

I turn off the DVD, open the blinds and land on the box like a hawk. They were so young and skinny. With flared jeans. And long hair. Their teeth were so white. God, they smiled a lot. And did a huge amount of gazing into each other's eyes.

Then, I'm wondering. Did we look that good together? Were we always smiling?

Later, we bring Homer to Killiney Beach.

'You go on ahead,' I say to Dad.

I sit on the sand and pick up pebbles. I don't set them out on the back of my hand, but I remember the time I did, when I placed him at the centre of my universe. After all that's happened, I still don't regret that.

'How about a game of chess?' Dad suggests, after dinner.

'Chess?'

'I saw the board in your room.'

How could he? I always hide it. 'What were you doing in my room?'

He takes a deep breath. 'The night you went missing, I was desperate, searching for some clue of where you might have gone.' I feel guilty, then. 'When I saw the chessboard, I remembered how it used to be between us.' His eyes are sad – until he catches me looking and makes his face bright. 'I'm surprised you kept it.'

'It's just a chessboard,' I say, defensively.

'So, want to beat the pants off me?'

'Since you put it like that, yeah.' But I'm smiling.

We set up in the library and light the fire. He gives me the white pieces, like he used to. But I twist the board around.

'You'll need the head start.'

He laughs, looks at the board for a few seconds, then advances one of his pawns two paces. My fingers close around one of my knights. He looks up, surprised, because that used to be his strategy, starting with the knights. I keep my eyes on the board. He moves another pawn. I try to work out his plan of attack and unfold my own at the same time. I start by taking his bishop. Three moves later, I'm lifting his queen, surprised at how easy it is.

'I'd forgotten how good you were,' he says.

I was never good then. It's years of imaginary games, years of using knights, thinking like he does, that's what has me so 'good'.

'Best of three,' he says when he loses.

He improves with play, as if it's coming back to him. I remember how much I used to enjoy these battles.

And then, out of the blue, I'm asking, 'So, The Stylist? What was that about?' I've no idea where this has come from. And I wish it would go back. I don't look up. He stops moving, his castle suspended in the air. I feel his eyes on me, and, finally, I lift mine.

'It was about missing your mother. And not admitting it.'

I think of Louis. And David. And how weird it is that my life keeps overlapping with my father's. Maybe Gran was right.

'I wasn't unfaithful,' he says. 'But I feel like I was.'

'Yeah,' I say, knowing what he means.

But he misunderstands. 'Alex, no one will ever replace your mother.'

'I know.' Just as certainly as I know that no one will ever replace David. You can't block out a person as important as that, no matter how hard you try.

Monday, on the DART, I ask Rachel how Bobby's settling in.

'Who?'

I blush. 'David's brother.'

She looks at me a little too long. 'I don't know.'

Suddenly, I need an excuse to be talking about him. 'I was just thinking they should get him a dog, you know, to help him settle in.'

'Why are you doing this?'

'What?'

'Bringing David up.'

'I'm not. It was just an idea, for Bobby.'

'Who you wouldn't be thinking about if you weren't thinking about David.'

Trust Rachel to suss me out. 'OK. I admit, he's on my mind a bit. But only because I'm hoping he's OK.'

'He's OK.'

'Is he, though? I mean, how's he getting on over there? Is he OK?'

She looks at me as if maybe this isn't a good idea. 'Yeah, he's OK.'

Suddenly, it's not enough. 'How OK, though? I mean, has he friends? What's the school like?'

She holds my eyes with hers. 'Do you really want to do this?'

I close my eyes. Breathe in. 'No.' A moment passes. 'I just sometimes wish I could say sorry. That's all.'

'But you said –'

'I know. I'd just like him to know. Without it coming from me. You know?' I look at her. 'D'you think that if you explained to Mark how genuinely sorry I am, it might get passed on?'

She eyeballs me. 'Alex. It's not an apology unless you make it.'

I sigh. 'I know.' I look out the window, at the sea – choppy, grey and cold. It's not the one that separates us but it feels like it is.

'Why don't you write to him? At least if you write you can say what you want to say without getting into a conversation.'

My stomach tightens. 'No.' Because I can't open things up between us again. And he won't want me to.

'I'll text you his address anyway.'

I sigh. Look out the window.

'Don't look now,' Rachel whispers, 'but there's a woman over there who keeps staring at you.'

'Where?'

'Across the aisle, two seats back, by the window. Pink tracksuit.'

Pink tracksuit?

'I said don't look.'

'Oh my God! She was in the shop when I was working there.'

The woman looks startled that we've sprung her. But gives me a little wave, like she knows me.

'Do you think she fancies you?' Rachel jokes.

'Rachel! Stop! God! She was buying an engagement ring.' Thankfully.

'Weird tracksuit.'

'Weird woman.'

I'm in the screening room with Dad. We've just watched *The Naked Gun 2½*. Dad's staring at the screen, watching the credits roll. I know he's missing her. I know there's nothing I can say.

'I wish I could just say sorry,' he says. It's like he's wished so hard, he's said it out loud and doesn't even notice. But then he turns to me. 'If I could just have her back for a day, there's so much I'd tell her.'

'Me too.'

'I loved her so much,' he says, and his voice breaks.

'She knew that, Dad.'

He looks at me. 'Yeah – until I walked out on her.'

I get up, grab the zapper and turn off the DVD. 'No,' I say

firmly, standing in front of him. 'She knew, even then. It was me who doubted you. Never her. She stood up for you, every time, told me you loved her, that this was your way. I didn't believe her. But she was right. She loved you, Dad, right to the end.' I tell him this to make him feel better. But he starts to cry.

'I didn't deserve her.'

I go to him. Sit on the arm of the couch beside his chair. 'Yes, you did,' I say, so strongly. 'I know why you ran, why you turned away. I did the same to someone I loved. I couldn't face him leaving, so I cut him off, pretended he never existed. I totally messed up.'

He's looking at me, very still, like he's afraid to say anything in case I stop talking.

'That's how I ended up with Louis.'

'Louis?'

'That guy you didn't want me to see.'

'Tell me about the other guy, the one you loved.'

'David.'

'David.'

And soon he knows everything. How we got together . . . how annoying he was at first . . . how he taught me to be happy without feeling guilty about Mum . . . how I ended it . . . and how sorry I am for the way I did.

'Tell him.'

'What?'

'That you're sorry. He deserves that much.'

'I can't.'

'That's the point! You can! Some of us never get a second chance.'

And even though I do see that, so clearly, I say, 'He hates me.'

'And how would an apology make that worse?'

'He might think I want to get back with him.'

'Alex, you're running ahead of yourself here. I'm just talking about sorry, about being fair to the guy. I think you owe him that.'

I drop my head. And I know he's right.

'Good,' he says, like I've agreed. 'At least something good can come from my mistakes.'

And I hug him because – whatever about me – he'll never get to say sorry to Mum.

I don't decide to write to David. But I decide to try. Upstairs, I open my laptop. For a long time, I just sit staring at it. Talking myself down. But then I think of Dad not having a choice. I take a deep breath. And type our address. At least I don't have to think about that. Then I close my eyes, take another deep breath and start to type. I don't look at the keys. I don't look at the screen because if I think about what I'm saying, that'll be it.

Dear David,

I'm so sorry. There's no excuse for what I did, how I treated you. I didn't mean to hurt you. I said what I said so you'd leave – so I wouldn't give in. I thought it would be easier – for both of us – to end it quickly. I know you said you'd come back and I know you really believed you would. But nothing ever pans out in life, does it? This way, you can get on with your life, not be held back by me. You probably totally get that now. But what I said, what I did, was unforgivable. I

*don't want you to forgive me though. I just want you
to know that I'm sorry. With all my heart. I owe you
so much, David, and I really hope everything's working out for you in San Diego. I hope it feels like home
again. David, I wish you so much luck. In everything
you do. Always.*

Love Alex

I delete the 'Dear' and the 'Love' before I read over it again.
Then I go over it. And over it. Finally, I decide I'm only making it worse so I print it off and sign it before I change my
mind. I bring it downstairs. My father has an envelope and
stamp ready. I handwrite the address from Rachel's text.

'I'll post it,' he says, like he knows I'll change my mind.

And, faced with a postbox, I probably would.

'I wrote to David,' I tell Rachel when she gets on the DART.

She looks cautious. 'I thought you said you weren't going
to.'

'I know, but I needed to say sorry. I owed him that.'

'OK.' But she doesn't sound OK.

'What?'

'I just thought you were worried he'd think you want to
get back with him.'

'No. I was careful.' Really careful. But I start to panic. Was
I careful enough? What did I write exactly? 'I just said sorry.
And I explained why I pushed him away. And why I still think
that was the right thing. No. It's OK. It's definitely OK.'

'And you don't expect anything?' she asks, still cautious.

'No. God. No. You know I don't.'

'Not even him to write back?'

'No!'

'That's all right then.' Finally, she looks relieved.

But suddenly I'm not. 'Oh God. You don't think he'll think I expect him to write back?'

'No. Not from what you said. No.'

'OK.' But my stomach's in a knot. I knew I shouldn't have written it.

33
GRAND MASTER

Days pass. I stop worrying. Tell myself it was good to set the record straight, apologise. But then I imagine him getting the letter, opening it, reading it. And I start to freak. What'll he think? What'll he do? Oh God. This was a total mistake. I'm supposed to be remembering what we had, not wondering if he'll get back to me.

Two weeks, and I hear nothing. I remind myself that that was the plan. But, in weaker moments, of which there are many, I wonder why he isn't replying. Didn't he get it? Maybe he got it and didn't open it. Maybe he does hate me and just isn't getting back. I know only one thing for sure: I shouldn't have written that letter.

I don't ask Dad if there's post for me. Though I'm dying to. I don't ask Rachel if she's heard anything. Because she'd kill me. But I am wondering what happened. Because David understood. He always understood.

I go into Facebook. His profile pic is new. I stare at that face, so familiar yet so changed. His hair is longer now and lighter, his skin darker, his teeth whiter. I thought I wasn't strong. But I must have been. To let him go.

I look at his 'Friends'. Rachel's there. Mark, of course. Sarah. Even Simon Kelleher. There are new faces. Guys. Girls.

I'm not there. It still hurts.

I have to use Sarah's password ('caliente') to access his wall. It makes me feel like a stalker. And I know it's a mistake. Even before I do it.

Any photo that I was in is gone. All evidence that I ever existed, wiped out. He has deleted me from his life. The way I deleted him. Now I know what it feels like. Like a punch in the stomach. Good. I deserve it.

'He forgot me pretty quickly, didn't he?' I say to Rachel, next day, at the same time I realise I've no right.

'How can you say that? I mean, seriously. How?' She looks so angry, Rachel, who doesn't do anger. 'You ended it. And, yeah, I know why but, seriously, Alex, you broke his heart. What do you expect? Of course he moved on. He had to. I didn't want to have to spell it out. But there it is. I'm sorry.'

It's hard to breathe. Hard to believe how stupid I've been. How did I think that one letter would make a difference to him after what I did?

'He didn't write back, did he?' Dad asks one day when I'm feeling particularly crap.

'No.'

'Then tell him you love him.'

'No!'

'Why not? Look at you, you're miserable.'

'Only because I wrote that stupid letter. I should have let it alone.'

}|{

'You did the right thing.'

'I was getting over him.'

He gives me a look that says 'yeah, right.'

'I was.'

'I don't see why you have to get over him at all! You're alive, he's alive. You love each other –'

'Stop, Dad, please. It's too late. It's over.'

'Is he dead?'

My eyes widen.

'Then it's not too late.'

'He didn't answer my letter.'

'Then write another. And another. And another. And, for God's sake, tell him you love him.'

'He's on the other side of the world.'

'So?'

'We're teenagers.'

'So were Romeo and Juliet.'

'Who died.'

He looks straight at me. 'You just don't want this, do you?'

'No, I don't.' Because nothing's changed. He's over there. I'm over here. With a big ocean and life in the way.

Everyone's talking about Uganda. Most of the class are going. Rachel and Mark can't wait. Rachel doesn't talk about it though, because Sarah and I aren't going. Sarah's parents can't afford the trip. And I didn't tell Dad about it. He'd have tried to get me to go. And I know it's silly – nothing would happen him if I went – but I still couldn't leave him. Now, I'm glad, because I'm here when his back sorts itself out, when one day he just gets into the pool and

swims, and something clicks. He's tried physiotherapists, a
healer, a chiropractor, a 'body balancer' (whatever that is),
a hospital consultant and two osteopaths. And just like that,
it's over. He's still careful, but he doesn't guard his every
movement. He doesn't look rigid. And the pain's gone from
his face. I'd take that over Uganda any day.

In the Jitter Mug one day after school, Sarah has some news.
    'Simon Kelleher asked me out!'
    'That's great!' I say.
    'I thought you didn't like him.'
    'Sarah. You're the one going out with him. Not me.
You're happy, I'm happy.'
    'You think I'm mad, don't you?'
    'No!'
    'You think he's not as good as Mark or David.'
    'Sarah. It's not a competition. You like the guy. You're
going out with him. Be happy.'
    'I am happy.'
    'Good.'

That Friday, Dad and I are chopping vegetables together.
    'Why aren't you going out any more?' he asks.
    'There's not much on,' I lie. Sarah's asked me to go to the
rugby club with Simon and a friend of his.
    Dad looks doubtful. 'I only grounded you for a week.'
    'I know that.'
    'I don't want you giving up on your pals.'
    'I'm not.'
    'So why not go out tonight?'
    'I don't feel like it.'

'It'd be good for you, though, to have some fun.'

And, maybe, I think, he'll stop nagging me about David if he thinks I'm happy here.

'All right, then, I'll go.'

We meet Simon and his friend, Anakin, outside the rugby club. Anakin looks like he grew up in a commune. Extremely skinny with Rapunzel hair – blonde, straight and down to his ass. His goatee reminds me of Jesus. But he has a nice smile. He looks gentle. And totally out of place. Sarah and Simon lead the way inside, like A-listers now that they've found each other. Brad and Angelina. But the other way round, obviously.

I try to make Anakin feel more at home. 'So what kind of music you into?'

'The Dubliners.'

And I thought I'd weird taste.

'Sarah tells me you play chess,' he says, and I think maybe he's not shy after all.

'Eh, yeah. Sometimes.'

'Maybe we could have a game.' He pulls an electronic gadget out of his jacket.

'Here?'

'Yeah, why not?'

He's obviously never been here before.

Inside, Sarah finds seats. Simon heads for the bar. It's an easy order. All Cokes. Except for Anakin who just wants water.

Sarah leans towards him. 'Not sure how water's going to taste with vodka.' From her bag she produces a naggin.

'I don't drink,' Anakin says.

'Great! More for everyone else!' She looks like nothing

}|{

could get her down tonight, sitting so straight with her bum sticking out, looking around, moving to the music.

Simon gets back with the drinks. Sarah takes her glass below the table and pours vodka into it. She takes Simon's glass and does the same. He smiles over at me. She reaches for my glass.

'I'm fine,' I say with a smile.

'Go on.'

'It's OK, thanks.'

She rolls her eyes. Then shouts something at Simon.

Anakin taps my shoulder. I look at him.

'Ready?' He has the electronic thing out.

I stare at him. Then look at Sarah and Simon. And decide, what the hell?

'Jesus H. Christ,' Sarah says when she sees what's going on.

Sarah and Simon disappear for most of the night. After my fifth game, I'm seriously thinking of going home when Sarah appears again. She grabs my hand and pulls me up.

'We're going to the loo.'

I look back at Anakin and shrug.

As soon as we hit the Ladies, Sarah leans towards me conspiratorially. 'We're going to do it.'

'What?'

She looks at me like I'm an idiot. 'It.'

'Oh. Right. OK. Sorry.' And I hate to burst her bubble but, 'Don't you think you should wait?'

'For what?'

And the only reason I go out on a limb here is I wish I could take back what happened with Louis. 'I don't know. Love?'

She bursts out laughing. 'Why?'

'Because then it would mean something,' I say passion-
ately. 'It would be special.' Not something to file away under
Big Mistake.

Her eyes pop open. 'Oh my God. You did it with David!
Didn't you?'

I colour. 'No.'

'Then what do you know?'

Just that I totally messed up.

'Look. We're off, OK? So – good luck with the nerd.'

'He's Simon's friend, Sarah.'

'Don't remind me,' she says, and with a faultless swirl,
she's gone.

When I get back to Anakin, the others have gone. He's playing away on his gadget, looking like something out of *The
Lord of the Rings* with the hair.

'Mind if we go?' I ask. Mike should be outside by now
anyway.

He looks up and smiles. 'Sure.' He puts away the gadget.
He walks me to the car.

'Well, bye,' I say, 'And thanks for the games.'

'You're not going as far as Monkstown, are you?' he asks.

'Eh, yeah.'

'Mind if I take a ride?'

'Sure.'

Anakin talks about chess – about playing Russians online, how he was beaten by an eight-year-old. And how he'd
love to be a grand master. I'm kind of tired and, I realise all
of a sudden, not that into chess. But I let him talk on and
on like some kid obsessed with trains, or Lego or something.

}|{

'Who was that guy?' Mike asks, when he finally gets out at Monkstown.

'I've no idea. Anakin something.'

'Ah,' he says, as if that explains it.

Next morning, I wake early. I look out the window and see nothing. Fog has blown in overnight. I wrap up, get Homer and walk to Killiney Hill. It's eerily quiet. Nothing moves. All I can see is what's right in front of me. But I really do see it. Cobwebs covered in moisture. Drops suspended from branches. And Homer, like a ghost, disappearing in and out of view. He looks like one of the white tigers in Singapore Zoo.

We get totally soaked.

When we get back, Dad's in the kitchen.

'You know what I think we need?' he says, looking out at the fog.

'Porridge?'

He laughs. 'A holiday. A complete break. Just the two of us.'

'Really?'

'I think a change of scene would do us good.'

I think about escaping from Sarah. From school. From the cold. 'Where would we go?'

'Doesn't matter. The main thing is to get away, spend some time together, no one in the way.'

'You mean, no Mike, no Barbara, no anyone, just us?'

'Just us.'

That would be amazing. 'But what about work? You've missed loads of time already.'

'I've spoken with Ed. We're putting things back a bit.'

'An album release, a world tour?'

'It's not open heart surgery.'

'No but –'

'If a person's wife dies, he's expected to take compassion-ate leave, right?'

'Of course –'

'Well, this is mine. Everything else can wait – except you. You've waited long enough. Let's have our holiday.'

I hug him. 'Thanks, Dad.'

The following Monday, I don't mind when Sarah looks at me like she has one up on me, like she knows something I don't, like she's part of some secret club. Nothing bothers me today, because Dad is booking the tickets and telling the principal that he's taking me out of school.

34
ON THE BEACH

Two weeks later, Mike drops us to the airport. Dad has a share in a private jet, but this holiday is about being normal, doing things the way normal people do. So he has grown the beard again, reverted to a tracksuit and pulled the type of hat fly-fishermen wear down over his face, on the basis that the holiday won't stay normal if he's spotted by fans. So I walk with this strange-looking man to the check-in desks. I still don't know where we're going. He wouldn't tell me. Now, though, I see the screen and he can't hide it any more. I feel suddenly sick. I stare at him. Of all places.

'Oh my God. Don't tell me you've set something up.'

'I'd never do that.'

'Then why San Diego?'

He shrugs. 'Just giving you an opportunity, if you want to take it.'

'I don't.'

'Fine. Then we'll just have a good time.'

'If we go.'

'San Diego's a big place.'

){{

I'd be thinking about him the whole time, hoping I
wouldn't bump into him, hoping I would. It'd be a night-
mare.

'You'd better decide, Alex. We've cut it a bit fine.'

'I can't believe you did this.' But when I see his face I see
the truth. He was thinking of me. He really has changed.
He's sorry. And he's trying. Which decides me. 'OK. We'll
go. But this is a holiday, like you promised. Just the two of
us. No one else. And no diversions.'

He puts an arm around me and pulls me to him. 'That's
all I want. Time with my little girl.'

I'm sixteen. And I like being called his 'little girl'.
Seriously sad.

'You should have told me,' I say, when we've settled into our
seats.

'You'd never have come.'

'We could have gone somewhere else.' Somewhere
uncomplicated.

'Would that have been living?' he asks with a smile.

'Dad, I'm not going to see him.'

'And that's fine. I just wanted to give you the chance. Is
your seat belt fastened?'

'Yep.' I take out my mobile to turn it off. It rings before I
can.

'Alex?'

It's Gran. 'Are you on the plane yet?'

'You knew about this?'

I look at Dad. Who smiles.

'Of course I knew.' That they've been speaking is great.

'You be careful, now,' she says. 'Listen to all that safety information. I told your father to get an aisle seat, near a wing.'

'Gran, planes are safer than cars.'

'So, watch the roads. They drive on the wrong side over there.'

I smile. It's so not like her to fuss. But then it hits me. She lost her only daughter. I'm all she's left. And I'm off to San Diego.

'I'll be careful,' I say. 'But Gran?'

'What?'

'You watch too much *CSI*.'

The air hostess flirts with Dad – so obviously his disguise isn't 100 per cent foolproof. Either that or she's into hippies. She's subtle about it, though. I don't think he even notices. She reminds me of someone.

'How's The Stylist doing?' I ask.

He closes the in-flight magazine he'd started to flick through. 'I don't know,' he says, turning to look at me. 'We haven't been in touch.'

'Because of me?'

He clears his throat. 'Because of the situation.' He pauses, puts down the magazine. 'You liked her, though, didn't you?'

'She was OK.'

'She was genuinely fond of you.'

'Yeah well, you know me – irresistible.'

And maybe some day I'll write back to her. Because now I know that she just messed up. Like me.

Mum would have loved the beach house, all modern and sleek with granite walls and windows. It's in a totally private cove. When we arrive, the sun is setting. The car glides forward through a tropical garden that could be Paradise. I roll down the window and listen to the surf. Dad was right.

This was a good idea.

He has nothing organised, no sightseeing trips, no whirl-wind tours.

'I thought we could turn into beach bums for three weeks,' he says.

Sounds perfect. Just hanging out. Lying around. Soaking up the sun. Not bumping into anyone.

For the first few days, we stick to the beach house and the cove. We read. Swim. Dad goes running. After a few days, we explore other beaches. Pacific Beach. Ocean Beach. Mission Beach. We watch surfers, rollerbladers, skateboarders, bikers. We walk boardwalks. Drink coffee. Wear hoodies, board shorts and flip-flops. We fit right in.

One day, we travel to the Children's Beach in La Jolla. Seals and sea lions bask in the sun, their skin glistening. I take a tip from them, close my eyes, turn my face to the sky and forget everything.

'I'm going to quit,' Dad says.

I turn to him. 'What?'

'The band.'

'You can't. You've been together for years. It's what you do.'

'I've had enough.'

I look at him suspiciously. 'Has this anything to do with me?'

'No.'

'I don't believe you.'

'Look, Alex. It's not like I need the money. I never have to work again in my life.'

'But music is your life.'

'No. You are.'

'Who says you have to decide between us?'

'I do.'

'But that's mad.'

'No, it's not. I can still write songs. Just for other people.'

'Dad. What you have with Streak and the guys – it's special. It just works. It's you. It's all of you. You can't quit. I don't want you to. I especially don't want you to for me.'

He looks at me.

'I'm serious. I'd hate myself if you quit. I would.'

He says nothing.

'Come on, Dad. You know it's mad. And wrong.'

'Alex, I'm sorry.'

'I know you're sorry. And I forgive you. OK? Just don't give up the band.'

'Why don't you think about it?'

'I don't need to. So forget it, OK? Seriously bad idea.'

He grimaces. 'Are you sure?'

'One hundred and ten per cent. OK?'

'OK.'

'Thank you, Alex.'

'Don't be stupid.'

There are things you see when the sky is blue. Planes cutting through it in a straight white line. Swallows swooping and diving. A pale, half-moon, up early. The sun, obviously. The sky itself. I love California.

I watch Dad run off along our own private cove. I lie back on the towel, close my eyes and enjoy the tingle of the sun on my skin. I try not to think of David. A shadow falls over me. I wonder how Dad could be back so quickly. I shade my eyes and squint up. But it's not my father. It's a woman. In

a pink tracksuit. I sit up, move back. Because this is weird.
How could she be here, on a totally private beach in
America? And is that all she has to wear?

'Hi!' she says cheerfully. And it hits me like a slap. I was
wrong. Her accent isn't Australian, it's South African.

I glance along the beach. Where is he?

She sticks out her hand. Seems excited. 'I never introduced myself. I'm Sarah, a friend of your father's.'

She might be Sarah. But she's no friend. My mind starts
to race. Back to the shop. She wasn't a customer – she was
just trying to get close to me. Because it's the closest she
could get to Dad. Oh my God! The engagement ring! It was
for him! Just how mad is she, this person who now wants to
shake my hand? I stand up. Act cool. So I can work out what
to do. Slowly, I extend my hand. Hers is clammy. I can't help
it, I drop it like it's a snake.

'Must have been a tough year for you – after your mum.'

I look along the beach again. And see him. But he's so far
in the distance I can't work out whether he's still running
away or back.

'She really loved him, didn't she?'

Suddenly, I need to be away from her. 'Look, I'm sorry but
I gotta go. Why don't you give Dad a call?' I reach for my
towel.

'I hated her,' she says.

To hell with the towel. I take a step back.

She takes one forward.

Would it be stupid to run?

Then I hear Dad calling me. He's sprinting up the beach
towards us. I've never been so relieved to see him.

'Back off!' he's telling her, so firmly that I back off myself.

}|{

He steps in front of me, blocking me from her. The back
of his T-shirt is covered in sweat. He's breathing so fast, his
whole back moves with every breath.

'John,' she says, breaking into a smile. 'How are you?'

Nuts, I think. Totally and completely nuts.

'Look, this has gone too far. You don't involve my daughter.'

'I was just saying hi.'

'OK, there's a barring order –'

She laughs.

'Alex, we're going.' He puts an arm around me and begins
to walk. He steps it up to a stride, but it doesn't feel fast
enough to me. We need to get in the house. And fast.

'Don't turn your back on me,' she practically screams. 'I
won't be ignored.'

His arm keeps me walking when I seriously want to run.
'Don't look back,' he says. The problem with not looking
back is you can't see her. And I'm not sure that's a good
idea. 'Keep walking. We're nearly there.'

It happens so fast. Suddenly, she's behind us. I don't know
how she moved so fast, so quietly – but she's here, arm
raised, then coming down in a blur, hard and fast against
my father's back. He looks at me in shock, his face turning
white.

'Jesus Christ,' comes out so slowly.

For one second, all three of us stand perfectly still. Then
she drops something in the sand. I see blood. And the knife
that drew it. I lose it completely. I run at her, screaming,
pushing her back with the flat of both hands, calling her a
psycho freak. But Dad is dropping to his knees, the red stain
on his T-shirt growing like an opening flower. I rush to him.

He's breathing fast but it's different than before, it's like he's getting no air. His eyes are wide and terrified.

'Oh God,' I say, because there's a noise coming from his back – the noise of air – and I know that's not right. He's lying on the sand now, like he's no energy left. I want to stop the bleeding but don't know how. I'm calling for help. Screaming.

Two security guards are running towards us.

'Hurry, please hurry.' And I'm thinking, *don't die. Please don't die.*

When the guards see him, they drop to their knees on either side of him. One reaches for the clean white shirt Dad left on the towel earlier. He shakes it out and folds it fast, placing it over the wound and pressing. In seconds it turns red. The other guard is on the phone, calling for help. He sounds as panicked as I feel. I start to pray. Never thought I would again. But I'm closing my eyes and my lips are moving.

It seems way too long before I see the paramedics, raising sand in their rush to us. Four men gather round my father. I step back. And she's there. She's still there. Not moving, just staring, like she's watching a bad movie. And that's exactly what it feels like. A bad movie that I've stumbled into.

This is it, I think, this is how it ends. With one mad psycho on a beach.

35
NORMAL

I want to ring Simon Kelleher. I want to tell him, 'Never underestimate women.'

She punctured Dad's lung. Could have killed him. He's had a blood transfusion. There's a tube coming from his chest, draining blood and air. He's on painkillers. But he'll be OK. They're keeping him in for a week. Mike's coming out from Dublin. He'll find somewhere for us to stay till we can get home. Dad can't fly for weeks. And we can't go back to the beach house. Not with paparazzi everywhere. I don't know how the news got out. I guess it always does. Outside the room is security. Inside, nurses fuss over him. Calls are coming in from around the world. Even Uganda. Ed's sent flowers. The Stylist rang. I didn't mind.

I won't leave his bedside.

'This is my fault. If we hadn't come out here, this wouldn't have happened.'

'No. If I'd a normal job, this wouldn't have happened. When I saw her, there, on the beach, I couldn't believe I'd put you in such danger.'

'I wasn't in danger. It was you she stabbed. Remember?'

'She could have hurt you, Alex.'

'I'd have taken her,' I say, as though I'm some champion fighter. 'She got you in the back, Dad. And, anyway, she's in custody now, so stop apologising. You wouldn't be much of a rock star if you didn't have a stalker.'

'Which is why I'm quitting.' When he sees my face, he puts his hand up. 'There'll always be people out there, thinking they know you, thinking that somehow you are "connected".'

'You've been in the band twenty-five years. This happened once.'

'I should have taken her more seriously.'

'You got the barring order.'

'Wasn't worth the paper it was written on. So I'm out.'

'No. You can't let people like that stop you doing what you want to do.'

He looks at me. 'I've more than myself to think about.'

'Come on, Dad. I've Mike. We live in one of the safest places in the world. This was a once-off-thing. And it's over.' My phone rings. I kill it. 'Don't decide now. It's too soon. Leave it a few weeks.' He'll be over this then and missing his music. My phone goes again.

'You'd better get that,' he says.

Sighing, I answer it.

'I can't believe you're in San Diego!' Sarah says. 'Have you met David yet?'

'No, Sarah. And Dad's OK, by the way.'

'Oh, I know that. It was on Sky.' She starts into a stream of questions that I know will form tomorrow's news at school.

'Sarah, look, I gotta go, OK? I'm in the hospital, and I'm

not supposed to have the phone on. I'll call you when we get
out of here.'

'When'll that be?'

'In about a week.'

'Oh, right, OK.'

'Thanks for the call.' I hang up. Look at Dad. He's taken
a call from Ed.

My phone bleeps. I sigh. And feel like chucking it out the
window. But I check the message, because people are being
really kind.

I can't believe it. The text is from David! 'You OK?'

It's only two words, but that's all it takes. My heart starts
hammering. I get up automatically, and, for the first time
since Dad was admitted, I walk outside the room, past the
security guards and down the corridor. There are signs everywhere forbidding mobile phones. I can't leave the floor – not
with all the paparazzi around. So I duck into the public toi-
lets. I dial his number. His phone rings and rings. He just sent
a text, so he must have his phone. Doesn't he want to talk to
me, after all? I'm wondering if I should hang up, when he
answers.

'It's me,' I say.

'I know. You OK?'

'Yeah, yeah, fine. How are you?'

'So you're in San Diego?' His voice sounds flat.

'Eh. Yeah.'

There's a silence.

'I was going to call,' I say.

'No you weren't,' he says without emotion.

And because he's right, I feel guilty. 'Do you want to meet
for coffee?'

}|{

There's a long pause. Then, 'I don't think that's a good idea.'

'Oh . . .'

'Look, I gotta go,' he says. 'Glad you're OK.' He hangs up.

I stand, staring at my phone, not believing what just happened, not believing what I've done – hurt him so much I've turned him into me.

A week later, once Dad's been discharged, Mike drives me to David's school. Spending your time by a hospital bed makes you think. And what I've thought over the past few days is that I'm not leaving San Diego without apologising properly, without explaining face to face.

'Good girl,' Dad said when I told him. The last time I remember him saying those words to me, I was eight years old and hanging from monkey bars. I'll probably look as ridiculous now.

I sit on a low wall, surrounded by silence. Nothing moves apart from a giant US flag twitching in the breeze. I've been here twenty-two minutes (exactly) when I start to lose my nerve. He won't want me here. He made that clear. What was I thinking? He's got his new life now. Moved on. I said sorry in the letter. He read it. It made no difference. I should go. Just then, the doors burst open, and people spill out, talking and laughing. One guy shoves another. Just like home. I stand up, ready to go. And then he is there, coming out between two people, a guy and a girl. He's listening to what the girl's saying, hitching up the bag on his shoulder, same way he always did. And if I had any doubts before, I know now – I still love him. He laughs. And I see it. How well he fits in here. I have to go. But they're coming towards me now. If I move, he'll see me. If I don't, he might walk by. I sit down so I'm less conspicuous. I want to look away, but I can't. This is the last time I'll ever see him, and I want to see him for as long as I can.

He sees me. And stops. His eyes hold mine. I want to fast forward. Rewind. Anything but be stuck in this moment. His friends, who kept walking, realise he's not with them. They stop, look back. The girl follows his eyes to me, then looks back at him. And I know, right there, she likes him.

'Come on, Zac,' she says to the other friend.

Zac cops on. 'Tomorrow, dude.'

David looks at them. 'Sure.'

We stand looking at each other. I stand up. Then we're walking towards each other. And my heart feels like it's filling with too much blood, like it's going to burst.

'Why are you here?' he asks, coldly.

I knew this was going to happen. I knew it. But then I remind myself why I'm here. I remind myself why I'm doing this. 'I wanted to say sorry.'

'OK.' As in, you've said it now.

'I sent you a letter.'

'Got that.'

Oh God. So cold. 'I am sorry, David.'

He turns to watch his friends leave.

And then I say it, straight out. 'I love you.'

He squints at me. 'I'm not sure what I'm supposed to do with that.'

'You sound so cold.'

'What do you expect? I told you I loved you, and it meant nothing to you.'

'It meant everything.'

'Really? The way I remember it, you said you didn't love me.'

'I lied.'

He just looks at me. 'Why are you here?' he asks, flatly.

'To say sorry.'

'You already have.'

'I wanted to make sure that you're happy.'

'Happy!' He laughs.

'I don't know what to say. I've said sorry. I've said I love you.'

'Alex.' And only he can say my name like that. 'It's over. You ended it. And that's been hard enough, but to come here and say sorry means nothing . . . Unless you've changed your mind, unless you want what I want.' He looks me straight in the eye. 'Is that all you want, Alex, to make sure that I'm happy?'

I stand very still as his words sink in. He still wants me to wait, after everything I've said, everything I've done. He must still love me. He must still trust in us. I look into his eyes and know that if I say yes to his last question, that will be it: David McFadden will be gone for ever from my life. I look into his eyes and know that if there was ever a time for me to be honest with myself, it is now. I don't just want to apologise. I don't just want to make sure he's happy. I want something else. And I want it so badly it hurts. I'm just afraid. I close my eyes. And think of Mum, who trusted in Dad, right to the end. I think of Gran, who, after everything, still trusts in good things happening. I think of David, still ready to come back for me after everything I've done. Then I think of closing my eyes and jumping.

'No. It's not all I want.'
His eyes hold mine.
Then I say it. 'I want a second chance.'

Coming in autumn 2011

The second novel in the Butterfly Series . . .

AND FOR YOUR INFORMATION . . .

At my favourite cosmetics counter, I pick up an eye shadow. It's the colour of peacock feathers. When I move it under the light, it sparkles. I find a tester and try it out. It's amazing. It makes my eyes stand out. In a good way. Not like a frog's or those people you see with thyroid problems. I check the price. And put it back. I try to think of a way. If I went without smoothies for a week . . . But then you can't exactly sit with nothing in front of you while your friends suck away for hours.

'Sarah?'

I turn. Rachel is holding up two eyeshadows. They're practically the same colour.

'Which one?' she asks.

I hesitate.

'Oh, what the hell, I'll get them both.' She smiles, like she's totally mad. She goes to the counter – so easily, like money is air.

Alex is at a clothes rail. But she's barely touching the clothes, just gliding the hangers along without really looking. I know she's thinking of David.

I look back at the compact. Would they really miss one? I mean, how many just roll off the counter every day and get kicked under? Not that I'd take one. I'm not that kind of person. I run a finger over the colours. Longingly. Then I slip one into my palm. Just to see how easy it would be . . .

Very easy. All I'd have to do is put my hand in my pocket and let go.

I walk over to Rachel, the compact still in my hand. It's no big deal. I can put it back at any moment . . .

Only, I'm not putting it back. I'm slipping my hands into my pockets. Which is mad. Totally mad.

Oh my God. What if there are cameras? I try to look casual. Glance around. Oh God; they're everywhere. I try not to panic but my heart is pounding. I tell myself to just keep walking. Over to Rachel. Who's at the checkout now. I stand beside her. Fold my arms. She looks at me and smiles. I smile back. But I'm having a minor panic attack. Alex is coming over.

'Find anything?' Rachel asks her.

'Nah. I'm kind of tired. Must be jet lag.'

The checkout girl hands Rachel a bag. Oh my God. We are going. Moving. Towards the exit. My heart is going to explode. I'm waiting to be stopped, called. Caught. I can't believe I'm doing this.

'Was that totally extravagant?' Rachel asks me. We're walking through the door.

'What? Eh, no. No, it was fine.'

We're three steps from the shop. Five. Ten. Fifteen. I

Ж

remember to breathe. I glance at Rachel and Alex, chatting away like it's another ordinary day. They wouldn't believe me if I told them. Which makes me feel wild. And dangerous. And free. I didn't have to rely on anyone for this. I didn't need Mum's money. I didn't need to borrow from my friends. I did this myself. For once, I was in control. I lived on the edge. And flew.